STONE
of HELP

ROBIN HARDY

 NAVPRESS

BRINGING TRUTH TO LIFE
NavPress Publishing Group
P.O. Box 35001, Colorado Springs, Colorado 80935

The Navigators is an international Christian organization. Jesus Christ gave His followers the Great Commission to go and make disciples (Matthew 28:19). The aim of The Navigators is to help fulfill that commission by multiplying laborers for Christ in every nation.

NavPress is the publishing ministry of The Navigators. NavPress publications are tools to help Christians grow. Although publications alone cannot make disciples or change lives, they can help believers learn biblical discipleship, and apply what they learn to their lives and ministries.

© 1994 by Robin Hardy
All rights reserved. No part of this publication may be reproduced in any form without written permission from NavPress, P.O. Box 35001, Colorado Springs, CO 80935.
Library of Congress Catalog Card Number:
94-25938
ISBN 08910-98372

Cover illustration: Chuck Gillies
Interior maps: Dennis Hill

Unless otherwise identified, all Scripture quotations in this publication are taken from the *Revised Standard Version Bible* (RSV), copyright ©1946, 1952, 1971, by the Division of Christian Education of the National Council of the Churches of Christ in the USA, used by permission, all rights reserved.

Hardy, Robin, 1955-
    Stone of help / Robin Hardy.
        p. cm. — (Annals of Lystra series ; bk. 2)
    ISBN 0-89109-837-2
    I. Title. II. Series: Hardy, Robin, 1955- Annals of Lystra series ; bk. 2.
PS3558.A62387S8 1994
813'.54—dc20   94-25938
                                                      CIP

Printed in the United States of America

Other books by Robin Hardy

Chataine's Guardian
Liberation of Lystra
(also published as *High Lord of Lystra*)
Streiker's Bride
Streiker the Killdeer
Padre

*To Rita Bowden
who showed me by example
the beauty of walking with the Lord*

The Continent

The Sea

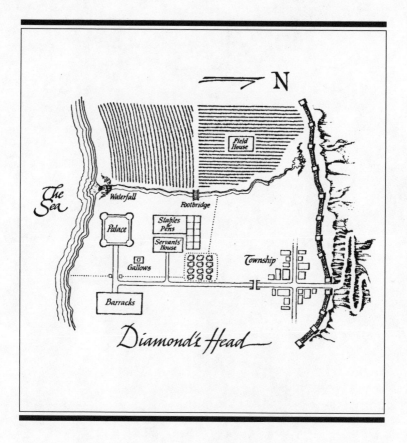

Come, Thou Fount of ev'ry blessing,
Tune my heart to sing Thy grace;
Streams of mercy, never ceasing,
Call for songs of loudest praise.
Teach me some melodious sonnet
Sung by flaming tongues above;
Praise the mount! I'm fixed upon it,
Mount of Thy redeeming love.

Here I raise mine Ebenezer;*
Hither by Thy help I'm come;
And I hope, by Thy good pleasure,
Safely to arrive at home.
Jesus sought me when a stranger,
Wand'ring from the fold of God;
He, to rescue me from danger,
Interposed His precious blood.

O to grace how great a debtor
Daily I'm constrained to be!
Let Thy grace, Lord, like a fetter,
Bind my wand'ring heart to Thee.
Prone to wander, Lord, I feel it,
Prone to leave the God I love;
Here's my heart, O take and seal it,
Seal it for Thy courts above.

—ROBERT ROBINSON, 1758

*1 Samuel 7:12

THE HISTORY

(From the *Annals of Lystra*)

. . . The events surrounding the end of the reign of Surcha-tain Karel of Lystra, being duly and truthfully chronicled in the aforementioned book,[1] may be summarized as follows: Karel, having discerned his daughter's life to be in peril, appointed a soldier from the standing army, a follower of the Way, to be guardian of the Chataine Deirdre. She, at that time, was ten years of age. The soldier, Roman of Westford, was then twenty-two. Albeit that his coat of arms has since been shown to bear the Bend Sinister,[2] Roman had gained respect for his abilities and leadership.

Thus did Roman perform ably in difficult circumstances as the Chataine's guardian until her eighteenth year, when she frustrated her father's intentions by choosing Roman as her husband. In his wrath the Surchatain sentenced the sol-dier to die, but Roman escaped the gallows to marry Deirdre and join Commander Galapos at Outpost One.

In the face of a dreaded invasion by Surchatain Tre-maine of Seleca, Galapos joined forces with Deirdre's uncle,

Surchatain Corneus of Seir. But as the price of that alliance, Corneus demanded that Deirdre be given to his son Jason. Thus Roman unwillingly sent his bride to Jason in Ooster, but Corneus betrayed Galapos in vile treachery and aligned himself with Tremaine. At Ooster, Deirdre discovered herself with child by Roman.

When the armies of Tremaine and Corneus surrounded the outpost to slay the defenders of Lystra, Roman prayed in desperation to his God. Following, by the power of God, the enemy was destroyed by plague. At Ooster, Jason learned of the battle's outcome and took his own life, having first told Deirdre that her husband was dead. Deirdre despaired, but was supernaturally defended until Roman and Galapos, the victors, found her at Ooster. Then did she learn that Karel was dead and that Galapos, the new Surchatain, was her true father.

Here begins the continuation of the story, it being two hours since Galapos and Roman have arrived at Ooster. . . .

---

1. *Chataine's Guardian.*
2. That is, he was of illegitimate birth.

I

Oh, sweet freedom! The Chataine Deirdre drank in clear sky and open air as Corneus's palace faded from her sight and mind. After months of confinement within stone walls, she saw the world as a greener, vaster place. And suddenly the wideness of the sky astounded her.

She sighed, stroking her mare's mane. In impulsive gratitude, she bent to hug Lady Grey's neck. "Wherever did you find her, Roman?" she asked, looking up to her right.

Her husband, riding so close to her that their horses frequently bumped, answered, "She was loose in the pasture, grazing. Waiting for us." He reached over for her hand, and she gave it to him. After four months of separation, she soaked in his familiar, beloved presence—tall and solid, black-haired and brown-skinned, riding habitually straight-backed even as he gazed at her.

She smiled, stroking his bristly face, and he pressed his lips to her fingers. He caressed as well the delicate face and golden hair that he had dreamed of every night those four months. Insatiable, he leaned on her saddle to kiss her, and she let go of the reins to hold his neck. But his mount, evidently not caring for intimacy, shied sideways out from under him, and he slid down rudely beneath Lady Grey's legs.

Deirdre choked back a laugh. "Are you hurt?" she demanded.

Commander Galapos, riding in front of them, turned around to shake his head, chuckling, "Can you never learn to control yourself around the Chataine, boy?" His large frame shifted so he could observe Roman remount smartly, then the Commander delivered a swift wink to Deirdre.

Smiling, she returned it. "Come ride beside us," she urged, holding out her hand to him. He obliged by dropping back to her left. "How long before we reach the outpost?"

"Hours, I fear, as you can't run." He cocked a bushy grey eyebrow at her unwieldy midriff. "We'd 'a' made better time with a carriage," he added.

"Oh, no," Deirdre said. "It always made me ill to ride in them before, so how could I possibly now? I'll be patient, and I won't complain," she promised earnestly.

At least the slow pace enabled her to ponder the stunning revelations of the past hour. Her father . . . her real father. . . . She looked over to Galapos. If she could have chosen anyone she wanted to be her father, it would have been he. "Galapos," she murmured. When he turned his bright blue eyes toward her, she saw in them the shape of her own. "How did you meet my mother?"

He unconsciously gave a little sigh. "After Commander Fortunado was killed, I was named Commander, and one of my first responsibilities was to accompany Karel on a diplomatic visit to Ooster. There, we met with Corneus to discuss mutual protection of trade routes. And there, at dinner the first evening, I met his lovely, intriguing sister, Regina. After dinner she drew me aside into the garden to ask me numberless questions about Lystra, Westford, the army, and myself. The more I told her, the more she wanted to know!" he said in exasperation.

"Her curiosity lives," Roman said drily, with a glance at Deirdre. But the look that he intended to be ironic was so full of love that she was not offended.

"Yes, well, as we talked, I saw—what?—interest, or desire, form in her eyes. At first I dismissed it as a girl's admiration for an older man. I could not allow myself to think otherwise, because it had been arranged long before that she would marry Karel. That night, though, I could hardly sleep for thinking of her." Galapos paused, dropping his eyes. Deirdre and Roman listened silently as the horses plodded on.

He coughed a bit, smoothing his bushy grey moustache. "Well, over the next few days, we seemed to chance upon each other every idle moment I had. Our little conversations began to run deeper . . . our walks in the garden, longer. I began to fear that Karel or Corneus would notice my undue attention toward her, but somehow I could not keep away from her. 'I'll be leaving soon,' I told myself. 'Enjoying her company while I'm here is harmless enough.' Madness! I ignored the certainty that she would be coming to Westford in a year as Surchataine.

"And so, our business in Ooster went on and on—we were there weeks longer than I had anticipated. Then came the night in the garden that Regina cried on my neck, saying she loved me, that she wanted only me! I should have leapt over the garden wall and run the length back to Westford. Instead, fool that I was, I kissed her to comfort her, and sent her to her chambers. Late that very evening, I awakened to see her standing over my bed." He stopped and coughed again. Roman glanced away.

"In truth," Galapos resumed determinedly, "the following morning I actually persuaded myself that her visit was a dream. But that same day Karel decided we would leave for Westford and, moreover, that Regina would immediately

17

become his wife. We had hardly set foot in the palace when he directed me to assume command from Outpost One. I was not granted leave to return for over a year. Not even when her funeral barge was cast to sea."

Deirdre listened in a mist of tears. After a silence, Galapos added, "As it was, Karel did her a great kindness to take her at once to Westford. For her untimely pregnancy to have become known would have meant terrible humiliation and debasement. But I will never know how he knew. Nor how a young, strong girl could die weeks following childbirth with the care she was given."

"She did not die from childbirth," sniffled Deirdre. "She fell down the stairs."

Roman and Galapos stared at her. "You are sure?" Galapos asked.

"Yes," she said. "Nanna had always told me she died in childbirth. But the night I ran away, she let the truth slip out. It shook her terribly."

"As it should have," muttered Galapos. "The official statement was that Regina died of stress from a hard birth. Why the lie . . . ?" He did not finish the thought, and none of them spoke what passed through their minds.

"And when did you come to the palace?" Deirdre asked Roman.

"In relation to all this, I'm not sure." He inhaled. "I never saw your mother."

"It was when I returned on leave that I picked up this urchin and made him my errand boy," Galapos answered gruffly, a smile returning. "You were just a baby, sweetheart—some months old." She nodded, and they rode further in silence. Paved with brick, Corneus's road was flat and easy riding. The summer sun was full but not burning, with the sweetness of a fat land stretching around them.

Galapos will be proclaimed Surchatain when we reach Westford, she considered. A thought complained, *I should have the title. I should rule.*

She shook her head in reply and both men glanced her way. *I cannot rule yet. I have no experience, no wisdom. They're right—he should be Surchatain.* She shifted her belly, sighing at the discomfort, then laughed out loud. "Roman," she gasped, laughing, "remember when you disguised me to look pregnant for our trip to Corona?"

He grinned. "Yes. We were traveling as husband and wife. If only I had known—!"

"If only you had known how absurd it is for a pregnant woman to gallop!" she cried. "Anyone who saw us riding that way must have thought we were mad!"

His eyebrows lowered. "That was something I didn't consider. My experience is limited in such matters."

Galapos chuckled, "You're in for a lesson or two, my boy."

"I shall be an attentive student," he promised, smiling.

She sighed again, musing on. What a remarkable deliverance they had experienced at the outpost. The villagers' disease! Who would have thought *that* would be the weapon to turn back Tremaine's army? Yet Roman and Galapos were living proof of God's intervention. And to think she had almost thrown her life away on account of a lie!

Then she recalled something Roman had mentioned. "Roman—" She stretched a hand to him, which he kissed again. He kissed any part of her that came within reach. "You said that when you prayed for deliverance from Tremaine, you prayed for me, also." He nodded. "What did you say?"

"I asked God to protect you, as I had failed you."

"Then it follows," she struggled, "that He would protect me from myself . . . ?"

He frowned. "No, Deirdre. We are free creatures. Free even to destroy ourselves, though that would grieve Him deeply."

"Not from myself, then, but from the consequences of

believing a lie . . . ?"

"I don't understand you," he said gently.

"I don't understand it either," she returned, perplexed. "All I know is, I should be dead now, but am alive. *You* should be dead, but you are alive! And Tremaine, Corneus, and all those who fought against you are dead. I don't understand any of it."

"When we return to Westford, I'll find Tychus's Scriptures and teach you something about the mercy of God toward those who believe Him," he said, that lesson vivid in his mind.

"I shall eavesdrop through the crack of the door," promised Galapos, and they laughed—Deirdre too, though she reddened to be reminded of her own habit of doing that. "Ho—look there," Galapos said, drawing back on the reins. Roman slid from his horse to the underbrush where Galapos pointed.

Deirdre strained to see. "What is it?"

"A Lystran uniform, I believe," Galapos said.

Roman emerged from the brush dragging a body. "That question is answered now," he said grimly. "It's the messenger I sent to Deirdre."

"Jason is responsible," she asserted. "He discovered the truth, but lied to me to drive me to despair. If I knew where he was now, I would—I would—"

"No need, my child. I'm sure Jason has suffered a greater vengeance than you could exact," Galapos said thoughtfully.

"Do you know where he is?" she asked.

"No, not precisely. But I'll wager his deception to you was a parting blow."

Deirdre nodded sagely as she watched Roman secure the body onto his horse, behind the saddle. She did not admit that she had not exactly understood Galapos's meaning.

Suddenly noting that Roman's mount was black, she exclaimed, "Roman, where is the Bay Hunter?"

"I don't know," he said wistfully. "I've surely lost him. I couldn't take him with me to the outpost—his disappearance after my 'hanging' would have aroused too many suspicions." He broke off to mount, then murmured, "I pray the Lord to find him a decent place of service and feed. He was a good horse . . ." he trailed off dismally. Deirdre was touched at his feelings for his lost horse, although she wondered at the propriety of bothering God about it.

At that moment a zinging arrow tore the air between Roman and Deirdre. Galapos exclaimed, "That came from the brush behind you! Run!"

"She can't run!" Roman shouted. "We have to stand and fight!"

"Oh, no! You'll not be sitting pigeons because of me!" And she planted her heels in Lady Grey's sides. The old mare sprang forward with remarkable agility, Roman and Galapos racing after her.

After her confinement, it felt good to gallop again, to feel the wind rush through her hair—for a minute. When they had reached a point of safety, Deirdre eased back on the mare's reins. Roman pulled up beside her, aggrieved. "Deirdre!"

She gave him a cocky smile, though feeling a little green. "I'm all right. You would be surprised at what I can do."

"Don't do that again," he said sternly.

"I won't, Roman. I promise." She patted his hand unsteadily while Galapos scanned the area around them.

"Must have been one loose from Corneus's army," he muttered. "Keep an eye out, my boy, at least until we're well into Lystra."

They rode on unmolested. Once they had passed the border, they gradually eased into their own silent considerations. Deirdre placed her hand on her abdomen and felt a determined little kick. She bowed her head from the weight of gratitude for the new life in her body and new hope in her future, for Roman and Galapos, who loved her. . . .

The men beside her let her weep quietly in peace.

❖

Much later, as the three came within sight of the outpost, a retinue galloped up to meet them. "Hail, Commander! You've recovered the Chataine!" a soldier in front called. He was one Deirdre had seen in front before—a natural leader with a fiery spirit and curly black hair and beard.

"Yes, Kam. She is well and whole, and then some. How goes it here?" Galapos asked.

Four soldiers pulled abreast of them and turned to escort them to the outpost. While Roman gave the others instructions about the body, Kam was answering, "Commander, we've salvaged many thousands of arms, equipment, and pieces of armor. Also, nearly two thousand horses, though many more escaped. We have far more horses and arms than we have men to use them. They're loading up the spare animals now to carry the spoils to Westford."

"Good," Galapos nodded, then demanded, "Kam—you are surely not using their water bags—?"

"No, Commander. All the pots we broke, and the skins we emptied on the ground and threw on the pyre."

"Well done," Galapos said, relieved. For everyone should have realized by then that the water Tremaine's army had been drinking is what led to their destruction.

Weary now, Deirdre looked toward a huge, hotly burning bonfire. So that was the peculiar smell. As they approached the northern face of the outpost, she stared at the massive battering ram jutting through the broken gates. The men working around it paused to salute or call greetings. Some even came forward to bow formally in welcome to Deirdre. She flushed, feeling how nice it was to be treated with honor again.

Kam was pointing out a problem to Galapos: "We've discovered that Tremaine's battering ram was built with a number of baffles and locks, to prevent its being taken apart on the sly. Our best machinists are looking at it now, but all they can say with surety is that figuring out how to disassemble and move it will require some time."

"Time I don't wish to take," said Galapos. "We'll leave it for now, and send a unit to work on it later. We must hie ourselves to Westford. Instruct the men to be ready to leave at dawn."

Roman dismounted and reached up to lift Deirdre down. "You must rest tonight for the return ride. . . . I wish there were a way to make it easier for you." He held her gently as she stretched, then leaned forward to kiss her, unconscious of the surrounding winks and grins. Embarrassed, she murmured a complaint he did not hear.

Kam, watching them, muttered to Galapos, "The Chataine . . . is she . . . ?"

"She will bear my first grandchild in the winter," Galapos stated proudly. Kam's eyebrows shot up in astonishment. "We'll celebrate upon our return to the city," Galapos added, almost as an order.

Deirdre stared in wonder at the shattered gates as Roman led her past them into the heart of the fortress. There, a kitchen squad had completed preparing a feast from the best of the outpost's supplies. A soldier clanged a noisy bell, bringing the men into the hall in a tidal rush.

As they plowed through the mess line, grabbing plates and mugs and bread, Galapos walked to the front where they could all see him and raised his hands. The soldiers stopped excitedly, some settling on the benches to eat.

Galapos said, "Before we eat, we are going to offer a prayer of thanks to God for the very fact of being here to eat." The men looked at him dumbfounded, and he barked, "On your feet!" They jumped up and stood at attention.

"Good," Galapos muttered, then, after an uncertain hesitation, inquired, "Roman, will you say it for us?"

Roman lowered his head and said, "Lord God Almighty, we thank You for Your mighty deliverance of us today. We thank You for giving life, and bread, and health. God, grant Your blessing on us all! Amen."

Some voices said, "Hear, hear!" and they crowded into the line again. Then the soldiers had for themselves a hearty, backslapping dinner, recalling to each other every incident of the battle and siege.

The head table, however, at which sat Galapos, Deirdre, and Roman, was quiet. Galapos watched the men as he ate, pondering the monstrous task that lay before him of rebuilding the province in the wake of Tremaine's invasion. He feared what they might find remaining of Westford upon their return. Those townspeople who had survived had certainly been stripped of their possessions and livelihoods. Or worse—Galapos had seen whole cities razed to the ground by Tremaine on a whim. And there were certainly soldiers on the loose who had defected from one army or the other, turning renegade and preying on the scattered villagers. How would he ever rebuild a stable population from the dispossessed?

From deep within him rose the conviction that he was unequal to the work before him. After all, he was only a soldier. His cunning had already failed him at the most critical point of their defense—he had misjudged Tremaine's strength and Corneus's loyalty. How could he then perform more ably in a harder task? He could not . . . he required a wisdom greater than his own. . . .

Roman ate without tasting or seeing the beef and lentils. *Why?* he marveled. Why had God been so good to him? To answer his prayer and spare his life and the lives of his men was enough, but—he felt Deirdre's presence beside him without looking to her—to reach into the depths of his heart

24

and grant him his most secret, most treasured dream . . . it was too extravagant. Too undeserved. He remembered his conviction after Deirdre's illness that God had both their lives in His hands, that He would resolve matters in His way. But he had never dreamed that God's way would entail such happiness, such fulfillment of desire. It was an uncalled-for kindness to grant a prayer Roman had never dared to pray.

And more. He raised his eyes to scan the room full of men newly released from the pit of death. To place him over such loyal, faithful companions who would not give him up to Tremaine even to save their own lives, and to give the rule of the province into the hand of brave Galapos, his father-in-law. . . . He looked to the Commander over Deirdre's golden head and saw Galapos eyeing him pensively in return.

Deirdre, for her part, was wondering how she would ever endure the ride returning to Westford.

Following the dinner, Roman led her up to his tiny room. Glancing about, she asked, "Roman, aren't you entitled to a larger room than this?"

He looked surprised. "There are no larger quarters than this, except for the Commander's, Deirdre."

"But how could the soldiers sleep in anything smaller?" asked the Chataine.

"I don't suppose they could, so theirs are much larger!" he laughed. She looked at him crossly, and he explained, "They sleep in halls of forty to fifty each. I, at least, have the privacy of my own room. It's the best I have to give you tonight, Deirdre. I know you're weary," he said anxiously. She looked dismally at the small, hard cot. It was ironic that the accommodations of freedom were so much less comfortable than Corneus's palace prison.

"Wait here," he said, and left.

She sat gingerly on the cot, rubbing her aching back. Momentarily the door opened and a cot walked in. Roman appeared behind it and set it beside the other cot. He piled blankets on the one next to the wall, as a makeshift mattress. "I hope this will do for the night," he mumbled.

"Yes, certainly," she acquiesced, lying down. "Thank you, Roman. You are always so kind."

He took her hands and pressed them to his face. "I still cannot believe God's kindness. I am full to overflowing . . . I could stand no more happiness." He leaned over her to rest on his elbow and kiss her. She responded, but winced at his beard. "Let me get water to shave," he said, drawing up. But a knock sounded on the door. Roman opened it to Galapos.

The Commander coughed. "I'm sorry to disturb you, my boy," he apologized, glancing at Deirdre. "I had a question for you."

Roman motioned him in, and they sat on the cot next to Deirdre's. "What is it, Galapos?"

"Roman . . ." he coughed again, seeming uncertain how to begin. "You know I have not spoken well of God in the past . . . it is not mannerly to call someone a delusion. Yet He has spared my life as well as yours. Would He help me now, as He has helped you?"

"You need only ask Him, Galapos," Roman smiled, leaning back.

"I do not know how, Roman," he said a little testily.

Roman inclined his head, sympathetic to his discomfort. Roman knew firsthand how difficult it was for a self-reliant man to relinquish control to anyone—even God. "First, Galapos, claim your redemption. You have heard Tychus tell of the Christ, haven't you?" Galapos nodded. "Well, then, will you acknowledge that Jesus Christ is the Son of God, able to save those who call on His name?"

"If it's His name you called on to bring our deliverance, then yes," Galapos said.

"And you, Deirdre?" Roman shifted toward her.

"I already have, Roman," she said quietly.

He turned back to Galapos. "Then confess this fact to God. Ask His forgiveness for your unbelief, and give yourself up to His power. Then He will give you whatever you need—and more," he said, glancing toward his wife.

Galapos nodded slowly. "That is a simple thing for me to do. Having done that, will I receive wisdom from Him to rule Lystra?"

Roman eased back on his elbow. "Ask Him. Fill His ear with your requests and complaints. Search His Word for the wisdom He has already made known. Then cover your head for the torrent of answer He will pour down upon you."

Galapos grinned, "You yourself look drenched, my boy."

"I am. I am covered with streams of mercy. Which reminds me—you both must be baptized straightway. Deirdre?" They turned again to see her sleeping sweetly.

Galapos stood. "We will, tomorrow. And we'll talk further." They clasped hands, and he left. Roman bent over Deirdre to kiss her on the forehead, then put out the candle and lay down on the cot beside hers, breathing in a yawn and out a sigh.

2

When Deirdre awoke in the morning Roman was gone. She did not even stir to look for a note, however. There was no reason she could see to rush getting up.

A little while later he came into the room, and smiled when she turned sleepy eyes toward him. "You must have rested well. I hardly felt you stir all night," he said, reaching over the cot to help her up.

"Yes, I did," she murmured.

He began to kiss her but stopped, suddenly turning serious. "Oh—now, Deirdre, the scouts have found Tremaine's personal carriage. It's a very good one, with springs and cushions, and I feel you should ride in it to Westford. We'll make much better time, and I'll drive it for you—"

"Yes, Roman," she acceded immediately.

He paused, caught off guard. "Oh—well, good. Come have breakfast, then—"

She was shaking her head. "No, nothing now but some water. You're all probably ready to leave."

"Yes," he said briskly. Stepping from the room, he summoned a soldier to bring whatever she requested. Then Roman strode away almost bouncing.

Soon she went out to meet him on the grounds. There she blinked at the procession that awaited her. She was blessed to have never in her life witnessed the terror of an approaching army; so to her, now, six hundred men and two thousand horses seemed like hordes.

Galapos greeted her with a kiss. "Chataine, you look refreshed this morning—and maybe a little rounder," he winked. She blushed and put a hand to her belly.

Roman broke away from a soldier to assist her into the open-topped carriage, then hopped up beside her. Pleasantly surprised, Deirdre glanced around the interior. It *was* a very satisfactory carriage, with gilded framing and embroidered seats. She decided she could probably endure riding in this for a while.

Galapos, on his charger before them, had raised his hand to give the signal to move when a mild hubbub reached his ears. A soldier came forward. "Commander, we saved this for you to wear on your return to Westford. It is rightfully yours now." He held up the magnificent golden robe that had been Tremaine's.

Galapos took it, grasping the fellow's shoulder. "Thank you, Lorean." Then he raised his voice. "I thank you all, but it is not rightfully mine. You know that it wasn't I who led you in this victory. This was God's work. So let's just hang this robe on the gates as a reminder of that, shall we?"

Shouting and whistling, the soldiers agreed, and as Galapos led them out of the broken gates, he tossed the golden mantle to hang on a standing post twenty feet off the ground. Roman and Deirdre followed in the carriage, and the soldiers cheered as they exited the outpost, each saluting the golden robe.

They spurred to a relaxed canter. Deirdre sat back in the

plush carriage, marveling at the comfort of it. "This is so easy!" she exclaimed to Roman. "I've never ridden in such a carriage. And there I was dreading this short ride!"

Roman smiled in satisfaction. "The Lord sees to all the details."

She smiled, too, taking in the green warmth of late summer. "This is wonderful." She looked over at him—his brown hands skillfully handling the reins, foot propped above the brake board, back straight, and face freshly shaven. "Nor have I ever seen you smile so much," she observed.

"I never knew I had so much to smile about. The years I spent warding you and wishing I was doing something else, something important—how little I realized the significance of what I did every day. I spent eight years courting you, and still fought alongside Galapos when he needed me most. I am reeling from these recent insights," he admitted, shaking his head.

In only a few hours they met up with the Passage north of Westford. From here, they needed simply to follow the river home. But Galapos suddenly called the procession to a halt. Roman drew up the carriage reins and called, "What is it, Galapos?"

"It is the river, Roman," he called back, trotting to the carriage side. Deirdre snickered, and Roman dropped his shoulders in mild exasperation. "It is water, Roman," Galapos continued thoughtfully. "So why shouldn't I be baptized here?"

Roman looked out over the lazy river. "You could, except we have no holy man here to baptize you."

"You are the holiest man I know," Galapos said evenly. "What prohibits you from baptizing me?"

"And me, Roman!" exclaimed Deirdre, sitting up.

Roman seemed taken aback. "But . . . I am not worthy . . . !"

"Then who on earth *is* worthy?" retorted Galapos. He

31

turned to the men mounted in ranks and shouted, "We're stopping here for a matter of importance. You've heard how the Lord delivered us when Roman called on the name of Jesus. Because of this, I have confessed belief in this Jesus, and Roman is going to baptize me—and the Chataine—here. Any of you who wish to confess likewise may do so." He dismounted.

Roman helped Deirdre from the carriage, and they walked to the water's edge. While Deirdre and Galapos shed some outer clothing, Roman took off his leather shortcoat, muttering, "Now how does this go?" (None of the soldiers presumed to come any closer until Deirdre was fully dressed.)

The three waded out into waist-deep water, where Roman faced Galapos and said, "As the resurrected Christ Jesus commanded us to baptize His followers in the name of the Father, Son, and Holy Spirit, so I baptize you. The apostle said, 'We are buried with Christ by baptism into death, so that as He was raised from the dead by the power of the Father, we also might walk in newness of life.'"

He lowered Galapos into the water and brought him up again. Then Roman turned to his wife. "And you, Deirdre, I baptize likewise." He carefully lowered and then lifted her. She sputtered a little, gathering her wet petticoats.

When Deirdre had returned to the carriage, Kam suddenly dismounted and stepped forward. "I wish to follow the Commander in baptism."

Roman asked him, "Do you believe Jesus Christ is the Son of God?"

"Yes, sir!" Kam said. Roman accepted him into the water and repeated the words he had said over Galapos, then dunked him. Meanwhile, several more soldiers waded out. Roman baptized each of them, then looked up to see a line forming. Briefly, he questioned each one before baptizing him.

After dipping the thirtieth or so, he paused to rest. Lifting his head, he uttered an exclamation at the size of the waiting line. "Galapos—come help me! I can't possibly baptize all of these men."

The Commander amiably splashed out to where he stood. "Getting feeble in middle age, my boy?" he jested before taking hold of the man standing before them. Roman nodded absently, watching the line grow.

Deirdre sat in the carriage, observing with amusement as they courageously struggled to baptize the growing tide of new converts. Roman would painstakingly lower each man backward into the water as if laying him out in a grave, but Galapos chose the easier method of gripping the front of the man's shirt, thrusting him under water and then yanking him up. Presently, Kam and another man were enlisted to help while Roman and Galapos rested. Deirdre scanned the river contentedly, combing through her long wet hair with her fingers. She nibbled on a bit of bread from the food pouch, then curled up on the soft cushions to nap.

Some time later in the golden afternoon, she was awakened by a bouncing motion. Roman, dripping and exhausted, had plopped onto the seat, panting. "Finished?" she yawned.

"I think we baptized the whole six hundred," he said between breaths. "I hope—they all realize what they have done."

"May we go home now?" she asked, sitting up and stretching.

"Yes . . . let me rest a moment, then we'll start again," he said, still winded.

"Oh, Roman—I can drive the carriage," she offered, taking up the reins.

"No, Deirdre—it's different from guiding a horse." He motioned to a soldier, who took the reins and sat in front of them to drive. At Galapos's command, the mostly sodden army moved forward.

Pushing into twilight, Deirdre grew excited to recognize

the lay of the land. Then, the shining towers of Westford came into view. "Home, home!" she sang.

Roman took her hand. "Deirdre, remember what we told you. Westford has fallen. What you see when we arrive may not look like home." She heard him, but did not believe him.

They crossed the ancient stone bridge just north of Westford, and all eyes peered anxiously toward the town. "The buildings stand," Roman remarked to Galapos.

"Aye." Wordlessly they trooped into the main thoroughfare. Galapos motioned for a halt, peering into the growing shadows. There was emptiness everywhere. No people, living or dead. No litter from war or violence. Abandoned shops, shutters banging in the wind. No animals, save some stray dogs yapping hungrily around the horses' legs. It was a riddle of emptiness.

Galapos, eyes scanning the town, gestured a soldier forward. "Search the shops for the slain or pillaged," he ordered. The soldier scrambled down from his horse and trotted to the nearest door. To a pair of men, Galapos instructed, "See what remains at the Village Branch." They spurred away.

Galapos hesitated then, showing reluctance. "Roman, let's leave the Chataine with Kam and inspect the palace—"

"You will not!" she declared hotly, determined not to be left behind. A glance from Roman recalled her to courtesy. "Galapos, please, let me come too. I can bear it."

"As you wish, Chataine," he said uneasily. The troops moved forward in tension to the palace gates, which stood ajar. Without waiting to be instructed, several soldiers dismounted and opened them wide. The army rode in.

The front courtyard was deserted and clean as the town—with one difference. "There are bloodstains here," Roman remarked, nodding toward the ground. "There has been fighting."

"But no bodies," Galapos mused.

A moment later the soldier he had sent into town hurried

up. "Commander—I went into every shop and store—they're all empty. But goods and tools are in place, for the most part. Nothing seems to be wrecked or stolen, but the folk are gone. . . ."

A light began to glimmer. For the first time in an hour, Galapos showed his sly smile. "They got wind of his coming and escaped. Well done!"

Roman lowered the one brow and arched the other. "If that's so, it doesn't explain why Tremaine would pass over the town untouched. Nor the empty grounds here."

"True, I don't know what happened here. But why should Tremaine bother with the town's spoil on his way to crush us? After we were done with, his men could pick it over at leisure. First things first, my boy." Dismounting as he spoke, Galapos then gave instructions for the care of the horses and the salvaged gear. Also, he sent a group of soldiers into the palace to scout it out.

Galapos and Roman remained outside and were examining the grounds in the deepening twilight when the soldiers sent to the Village Branch returned. "Commander," said one, "the village is deserted but untouched. There's no trace of fighting. We didn't see anyone until we were leaving, then Varan here spotted a boy watching us from behind a hut. When we saw him, he fled, and we lost him. It struck us odd that he didn't appear to be a villager. He was wearing a Lystran uniform."

"An errand boy?" Roman's voice rose in hope.

"Perhaps, though neither of us could recognize him." A pensive silence followed.

"What do you make of it, Galapos?" Roman asked.

The Commander stroked his moustache. "Nothing. He may be an isolated survivor who took a dead man's uniform."

"But then, who removed the dead or wounded from here? Tremaine's men wouldn't bother, would they?" demanded Roman.

"Certainly not," assured Galapos. "It is a puzzle."

While they mused over this, the scouts appeared from within the palace, bringing out torches. The leader saluted Galapos. "Commander, the palace is empty. We found blood-stains and damage in the great hall and the audience hall. There was a fierce fight here, to be sure. And the Surchatain's treasury has been forcibly opened and robbed. There's very little left—several hundred royals and some jewels."

"No bodies? Anywhere?" queried Galapos.

"No, Commander. There's been fighting, for certain, but there are no bodies."

"There must be survivors, Galapos," Roman declared with conviction. "What about the townspeople?"

Galapos shook his head forcefully. "Not them. If they were able to escape before Tremaine came through, they certainly would not return simply to bury the dead. It doesn't make sense. And Tremaine was always too thorough to leave any surviving soldiers or courtiers."

But then the men near the gates began shouting. Turning to look, Deirdre caught her breath and Galapos muttered, "Well, well!"

A line of Lystran soldiers and servants entered the gates led by a slim, grey-headed palace official and an errand boy. "I told you it was them; I told you!" the boy was declaring.

"Kevin! It is you! Thank God you're alive!" Roman cried, sprinting toward him. He grabbed the boy's shoulders and shook him in joy.

The official bowed to Galapos. "Commander Galapos, you cannot imagine our relief to see you and your troops return here. And Roman—how glad I am that the rumors proved true, that you are alive."

"I know you," Deirdre said abruptly, snapping out of thoughtful watching. "You're the secretary to the overseer—what is your name again?"

"I am your humble servant Basil, Chataine," he said,

bowing. Uncertain as to her title now, he merely added, "Welcome home, my lady."

There were renewed shouts and greetings as towns-people entered behind the servants, hailing the army as returning victors. Galapos glanced over them. "Basil, what happened here?"

"Commander, I'm not entirely certain, but I'll tell you what I know. About three weeks ago—I cannot remember the exact day—I was overseeing the wheat harvest when I heard a tumult from within the palace. A palace guard, one of the Cohort, came out into the courtyard and announced a new Surchatain was ruling Lystra—Sereth, or Serep, I could not hear the name well—another of the Cohort, though, I'm sure. At any rate, he was holding an open audience imme-diately to declare himself ruler, and those of us who valued our lives had best show up to swear allegiance to him. Well, Commander, this all smelled of a treacherous coup, and I wanted no part of it—"

"Where in heaven were the soldiers? The standing army?" Roman demanded.

Basil opened his mouth in surprise, then shut it in con-viction. "Then you did not know. The standing army was dis-solved by the Surchatain some time ago."

"What?" exclaimed Roman.

"Why?" grilled Galapos.

"Commander," declared Basil, "in truth, I don't know. The High Lord simply dismissed them as a unit—'costly and unnecessary,' was what the official decree said. He evidently believed the Cohort was all that was needed at Westford. I have since heard rumors that he doubted the soldiers' loy-alty. They could not believe it either—especially those owed back pay."

"What did the Counselor say to this?" wondered Roman.

"As I recall, he openly opposed it," Basil replied. "At any rate, most of the soldiers drifted away. A few stayed and attached themselves to some of the townspeople, to serve as protection. They are the ones with us now." He gestured to the fifteen or so soldiers, still in uniform, behind him.

"What then?" pressed Galapos.

"Well, as I said, I didn't care for rule by the Cohort. So I quietly gathered the servants under me, and we ran to the hillside caves to hide and watch. None of my people had seen any more than I had, and none of us knew what had happened, though someone said he'd heard the Surchatain had been murdered."

"Is Nanna with you?" Deirdre asked hopefully.

"No, Chataine, your nursemaid is not with us. I'm sorry," Basil said.

As he was saying this, Galapos was whispering to Roman, "The messenger who brought us news of the fall of Westford—is he among us now?"

"No," Roman answered. "He died shortly after delivering that message." Galapos nodded in remembrance.

At that point a mild commotion at the rear of the crowd was heard. The people parted, laughing, for a horse which nosed its way to the front. It was a bay.

"Roman—!" exclaimed Deirdre, as the horse trotted up to the palace steps.

"The Bay Hunter!" Roman cried. "How—?" The horse nuzzled its master, and Roman stroked its neck with some bewilderment.

A servant stepped up, grinning. "Sir, when the Secretary took us from the palace, I ran by the stables to release your horse. We couldn't take him with us to the caves, but I knew he'd be better off on his own than serving the Cohort. And I knew if you ever came back, he'd come back. You've always been good to me, so I thought, 'Say, someone should give a thought to the Captain's horse.'"

Heartened and amazed, Roman gazed at the fellow. "Thank you."

A grin passed over Galapos's face before he turned back to Basil. "Could you see anything from the caves?"

"From the precipice above, yes, Commander. Our lookout reported that the townspeople went into the palace for the audience and then came out again shortly. A number of them promptly packed up their families and drove out of town. And at nightfall, we could all see the windows of the great hall lighted as if for a fest. Kevin also spotted several of the Cohort leaving the grounds secretively, with bags packed on their animals."

"From the treasury," Roman whispered to Galapos.

"We posted a watch all through the night," continued Basil, "as we feared they would notice some missing and come hunt us down. But we had little to fear from them. For in the last watch, our lookout spotted a terrible army approaching on the road from the north—Tremaine's army. We sent men swiftly to gather up the remaining townspeople and bring them to the hills. Men went to the Village Branch also, to warn the villagers. The townspeople would not allow them with us in the caves, so the holy man among the villagers took them toward the coast. We did not go knocking on the palace doors. I assumed they too had lookouts. . . .

"Well, Tremaine attacked the palace before daybreak and swept aside the unit on guard, from what we could see. Then he simply walked in. When he and his soldiers came out again, they stopped at the Village Branch to draw water before going north.

"We waited until they were well gone, then went to the palace to look for survivors. There was none. We buried the dead and returned to hiding to this day. We had not hoped to see you come marching back, but the people refused to leave their land without fighting," Basil related.

Galapos pensively scanned the proud faces behind Basil. "Did you find the Surchatain among the dead?"

"No, Commander. We found the Counselor, however,"

Basil answered. Roman closed his eyes.

"Nanna?" Deirdre asked in a little girl's voice.

"No, Chataine, we did not find her body either."

The questions ran dry, and the crowd stilled. A mood of uncertainty began to spread upon them. By the light of the flickering, smoky torches, their eyes turned to the Commander in curiosity or apprehension. Galapos saw those eyes and perceived he must act immediately to gain their full trust.

Raising his voice to address the crowd at large, Galapos said, "I declare an open audience here and now to tell you the future of Lystra. Listen! I have accepted the title of Surchatain, to guide you into the future and hope. All I require of you is to return to your homes and shops and work with me to restore Lystra to soundness. Anyone who has suffered loss and needs a livelihood, I will give a portion of the Surchatain's fields to own and till for himself. Those who wish to resume service in the palace may do so, with the understanding that we cannot pay you, only feed and shelter you. We'll have no slaves here. Anyone who stays and serves must do it of his own choice."

He let them consider that a moment, then gestured to Basil. Startled, the secretary stepped forward. Galapos said, "Because of your actions, Basil, all these with you escaped Tremaine. Due to the prudence you showed, I appoint you as my Counselor, to benefit myself of your wisdom." Basil went directly to his knees in an attitude of humble acceptance, and the group behind him cheered.

Galapos lifted him and placed him ceremoniously on his right. He continued to the people: "I wish also to announce the coming birth of my grandchild in the winter to my daughter, Deirdre, and her husband, Roman." The claps and cheers attending this statement were muffled under startled whispers.

"And I have one last appointment to make. Roman—"

Galapos turned to his Second, who instinctively went down to his knees on the palace steps before the new Surchatain. "Roman, your actions at the outpost opened the door to our salvation from an unbeatable enemy. For that reason alone— not because I have loved you from childhood and trained you for war, not because of the pride I feel in your skill and stature, but because of your conduct as a good and faithful soldier on all fronts do I appoint you as Commander of my army." Roman closed his eyes and pressed his lips together in inexpressible thoughts.

Galapos added to the crowd: "Those of you who wish to hear how Tremaine was defeated, come now to the great hall, and we'll tell you." The murmuring crowd flowed into the palace behind their newly appointed leaders.

3

That evening, after relating the events at the outpost to the survivors of Westford, Galapos declared a feast for them all. Given a few royals apiece as wages, enough servants were found to serve the tables that night, though none had volunteered to remain longer. Galapos's offer of land was too appealing, and who would wish to stay a slave when the chains were unlocked?

Extra tables and chairs were found to seat all the guests in the banquet hall, and at once it was filled with laughing, chattering, good people, drinking in the refreshment of the hour. Galapos himself strolled through the hall, pausing to receive congratulations and heartfelt expressions of allegiance. He accepted it all graciously, warmly, yet with a reserve that commanded their utter respect.

Lord DuCange, the silversmith of Westford and a leader among the townspeople, placed himself in front of the new Surchatain to bow and say, "Surchatain Galapos, I speak for the town when I say we are united behind you. Now, I wish you to meet my son Lelan." Galapos glanced at the young man who bowed to him. "I had thought, Surchatain," continued the silversmith, "that he would make a fine addition to the Cohort."

Galapos gagged in surprise and coughed to clear his throat. Then he calmly replied, "Lord DuCange, we have no Cohort any longer, and after the recent events, I am astounded that you think of starting one up again. If the young man desires service, I will be happy to put him in the standing army."

DuCange darkened. "You should not judge the potential of the Cohort by the past members. With finer material to start with, it would be a finer unit."

Galapos darkened as well. "I have seen from experience that honor and advancement must go to the men who have proved themselves worthy in the lowest positions."

"No worthy man would serve as a slophand!" DuCange snapped.

Having stripped away the thin veneer of respect to expose the arrogance beneath, Galapos drew up his immense frame to address that as well. "You are speaking to one such man. Do you charge me with unworthiness?"

DuCange looked in sudden uneasiness at the shocked and scowling faces of soldiers standing near them and gulped, "Certainly not, Surchatain. Excuse us. Lelan—" Bowing, he and his son withdrew.

Galapos tightened his lips, knowing that there would be more and harder challenges to his authority in the near future. As he turned, another resident stopped him with a low bow: "Surchatain, may I introduce myself? I am Hylas. On behalf of Westford, allow me to express our utmost allegiance to you." Galapos opened his mouth, but Hylas had not finished his speech: "And how it thrilled me to hear you are a believer. I am also, and it has grieved me to see the chapel in the palace closed off. Will you allow me to put it to use, to teach others the way of God?"

"You're not a holy man," Galapos hedged, seeing that he wore the shiny breeches and long-tailed coat of a successful merchant.

"No, Surchatain, just a man earnest toward Him," Hylas admitted.

"Very well," agreed Galapos. "I've learned that not all holy men wear rough robes."

"Surchatain." Hylas bowed gratefully. "I shall begin immediate preparations." Galapos watched him hurry off, then turned toward where his daughter sat.

How right, Deirdre thought, watching Galapos advance by degrees to the head table. *It is so right for him to rule. He was born for this.* She glanced across the table to Roman, who also was watching Galapos, and her heart bounced a little, as it tended to do whenever she looked at him. *And he is all mine*, she thought, feeling a little greed satisfied in her.

He looked across to her and smiled just slightly. When Galapos gained the table they stood. As he sat, the people hastened to their chairs and sat. The hall grew still as they waited for the command to the servants to bring in the food.

But before Galapos could speak, Roman stood again and demanded, "Surchatain, may I speak?" Surprised by his formality, Galapos nodded. Roman picked up his goblet. "A toast in honor of our father and Surchatain. Galapos—may you rule long in peace and prosperity."

The guests stood to the last one. "Peace!" "Prosperity!" "And long life!" they echoed and drank.

"You are a well-mannered rogue, my boy," Galapos laughed. Roman, pleased, sat again. "Now let us attend to more important matters. Dinner!" Galapos commanded with a laugh, and dishes promptly began arriving at the table.

"Ah!" He inhaled from the platter set before him and declared, "I never thought to taste veal again—peppered just so!" and he sneezed violently. A laugh went around, and more dishes followed.

Deirdre smiled, considering how no one would dare to laugh at her father—the former Surchatain. Here, no one feared to laugh, as it carried no disrespect. Galapos understood their laughter sprang not from derision, but contentment. It was healthy and right.

Food continued to fill the table. Deirdre gathered a handful of plums from a generous platter, but turned up her nose at the chard. Roman observed, "It's a wonderful thing to have so much to eat that one can be picky." So she turned up her nose at him, too.

Roman averted his eyes. On his right, Kam coughed and turned to another soldier. After a hesitation, Galapos took Deirdre's hand and said gently, "Be freer with good graces tonight, Chataine. Save rudeness for more deserving souls."

She suddenly realized she had insulted Roman in front of the others with her haughty manner. Although burning with remorse, she could not bring herself to apologize to him openly. There was some part of her that still considered him her servant. Instead, she sat in silence the remainder of the noisy dinner, hoping that would show penance enough. Inwardly, she knew better. But she resisted the demands of her conscience until it soured within her.

The sulks were hers alone. The others around her were brimming with gladness—to be alive, to be free, to be eating and drinking—and they voiced it. Overhearing pieces of narrative as a soldier described Tremaine's siege to some townspeople, Deirdre complained to herself, *As if their lot was so bad—mine was worse. At least they could fight*.

She looked up then to see Roman studying her with concern, and blushed before she reasoned that he could not hear her thoughts.

Then someone exclaimed, "A song! Let's have a song in honor of the Surchatain and the Commander!" *But not in my honor*, observed a peevish voice within Deirdre. She tried to dismiss the thought as petty, but it lingered.

Kam immediately began a very silly verse, which other voices picked up gleefully. Apparently they all knew it.

> Let out a shout and be up and about;
> There's reason to sing today.
> Move from your chair and take to the air;
> There's reason to sing today!

> Ho wee oh,
> What do you have to say?
> Ho wee oh,
> Here's what I have to say:

> Lift up your feet and part with your seat;
> There's gladness afoot today.
> Free up your voice and let us rejoice—
> There's gladness afoot today.

> Ho wee oh,
> What do you have to say?
> Ho wee oh,
> Here's what I have to say:

> Give up your gloom and dance 'round the room
> It's laughter that rules the day;
> Perk up your ears and cast off your fears
> It's laughter that rules the day!

> Ho wee oh,
> What do you have to say?
> Ho wee oh,
> Now I have had my say.

This drivel went on at length, someone making up new verses continually, spurred on by laughter and cheers. Having placed herself above it, Deirdre soon grew weary of the joviality. She became irritated, then contemptuous, as the affair droned on.

Thinking she must be uncomfortable, Roman glanced at her from time to time as she sighed and shifted about. Immediately after Galapos's plate was removed, Roman stood and said, "Galapos, please excuse us. I fear Deirdre is exhausted from the day."

Galapos cocked his head and said, "Go put her to bed, by all means, but then come back here. I must speak with you tonight. Good night, Chataine." She nodded coolly to him in response.

Roman took her arm as they walked the old, familiar corridors to her chambers. "Deirdre, what's wrong?"

"Nothing," she said, and literally it was true. She had no reason to feel so aggravated and testy, but nonetheless she did, strongly.

"I know you're tired. . . ." He passed through her receiving room into her sleeping chamber. That old royalty within her bridled at the guardian's brash entrance into her inner chamber. She had to remind herself that he was her husband now. "Sleep now, and I'll join you later," he said quietly, stroking her back. She looked away and nodded.

Roman suddenly caught her arm and spun her to face him. She startled at the radiance of his normally stolid face. "Deirdre!" he exclaimed, as if to wake her. "Don't you realize what's happened? We're home! God has brought us home, together, whole and safe—and to rule Lystra, yet! Rejoice with me, Deirdre." It was a plea.

"Of course I'm happy, Roman," she insisted. "I'm only tired, as you said." She sat on the downy bed, looking toward the window.

His deflation was palpable. "I'll be back soon," he said and left.

Alone in the room, she looked around with a wave of sadness and nostalgia. The doll she had bought at the Fair sat beside her, waiting. She picked it up, smoothing its little crimson dress.

Yes, she was home, but it was strange to her now. Too many things had changed. And Nanna—where was Nanna? She pressed the doll to her cheek and let herself weep out her longing for her nursemaid, who had cared for her since infancy. How many times had she spoken badly to Nanna, lied, and been disobedient? How could Nanna have endured it? *Why* had she done it so faithfully?

In that moment, Deirdre wished more than anything to hold Nanna's neck once more, to ask forgiveness for the grief she had caused her long-suffering nursemaid. But opportunity to do that had been given liberally in the past. Now that door was shut and bolted.

❖

Roman walked the corridor on his way back to the banquet hall. The familiarity of these walls and the weariness of his body caused him to slip into a reverie. When he halted, he blinked to see that somehow he had taken a wrong turn and now stood before the door to the Counselor's chambers. Eudymon's chambers. Roman's . . . father. He stared at the door, motionless, while something deep within him began welling up, cracking. Scenes ran through his mind of his father's attempts to reconcile, to gain his favor, if not his love. And he saw himself aloof, stern, unbendingly proud.

He closed his eyes, shaking himself. Remorse was easy when there was nothing to be done about it. His past actions were etched in stone, never to be altered. For how does one reconcile with a dead man?

The thing inside him cracked full open, and he fell on Eudymon's door. "Father, forgive me," he moaned. "I behaved in ignorance and spite." He drew an unsteady breath and whispered, "God, have mercy on him. He is my father." He turned brokenly from the door to find his way to the banquet hall.

49

But Galapos met him in the corridor. "They are having such a romp in there, we'll leave them be and go elsewhere," he chuckled. Then he paused to assess Roman's face. "Are you well, my son?"

"Yes." Roman straightened.

"Then come." Galapos led to the Surchatain's chambers and put a hand to the door. He pushed it open and held out the candle. They stood scrutinizing the large, plush chamber from the doorway. It was clean and uncluttered, except for Karel's papers strewn atop the secretary—all his unfinished business.

Galapos shook his head, uttering a dry laugh. "I feel as if he is here still. Do we Christians believe in ghosts, Roman?"

"None that can harm you," he answered, gazing at empty space.

Galapos nodded. "That's good enough for me. Come sit, my boy." Galapos pointed to a straight-back, deeply padded chair as he sat in a like one near it. Roman sat heavily.

Galapos asked, "What's troubling you, Roman?"

He shook his head, not lifting his eyes. "I simply . . . never realized the importance of forgiveness."

"For yourself, or someone else?" probed Galapos.

"Those two are inseparable. That is what I'm discovering." There was a momentary silence as Roman passed a hand over his brow. The old bludgeon injury pained him afresh at times like this.

"You are referring to your father," Galapos observed.

Roman's eyes shot up. "You knew he was my father? How?"

"He told me," Galapos answered easily, settling back. "The night we plotted your rescue from the gallows."

Roman rubbed his brow. "You never told me you knew."

"It did not seem profitable to tell you."

Roman nodded inwardly, remembering his own harsh response when Deirdre had spoken of his father. "What else did he tell you?"

"That freeing you was more important to him than his own life," Galapos answered directly. "He knew we had little chance of keeping it a secret, with so many spectators around. And he knew that he would be the first to answer to Karel for it. None of that mattered—you had to be saved." Roman could not meet his gaze as he spoke. As Roman was silent, he added, "It must demand a lot of love to put another's life before your own."

Quietly, Roman said, "He did not fail me, in the end."

"No, he did not." Moments later, Galapos shifted. "Roman . . . the holy man, Tychus, who taught here at the palace . . . is he among the survivors here now?"

"No. I looked for him, but he is not here. There are many I looked for who are gone now."

"Aye. The price of war. . . . And his Scriptures, which you spoke of—can you find them? I wish to begin reading."

"Yes. But, now, Galapos? At this late hour?" Roman asked, drained.

A little twinkle showed itself in the Surchatain's eyes. "Like our precious Deirdre, I have a curiosity that will not rest until it finds answers. Please go get them."

Roman left, smiling and shaking his head.

He returned with a large volume bound in leather and gold. Galapos motioned for him to sit. "You're familiar with this book, Roman. You read to me."

"As you wish." Roman paused, then selected a starting point and read: "The beginning of the gospel of Jesus Christ, the Son of God. As it is written in Isaiah the prophet, 'Behold, I send my messenger before thy face, who shall prepare thy way; the voice of one crying in the wilderness: Prepare the way of the Lord, make his paths straight. . . .'" He read while Galapos settled back to listen.

Roman finished a page and stopped to look up inquiringly. Galapos lifted a finger for him to continue. So he read to Galapos of the life of Jesus: parables, miracles, healings. He read of confrontations and prophecies and teachings, and still Galapos sat listening. Then hoarsely he related to Galapos of the last Passover, the mocking trial and cruel execution, the Resurrection.

". . . So then the Lord Jesus, after he had spoken to them, was taken up into heaven, and sat down at the right hand of God. And they went forth and preached everywhere, while the Lord worked with them and confirmed the message by the signs that attended it. Amen." Finishing at last, Roman coughed and blearily focused on the Surchatain. Still Galapos sat, thinking. The diminishing candle flickered in the stillness.

Galapos said, "Go to bed now, Roman. We'll need to start early tomorrow."

Roman stood with creaking bones and bowed. As he exited and closed the door behind him, he saw Galapos still seated, still in thought.

In the lateness of the hour, he passed no one in the corridors but the solitary soldiers on watch. Roman entered Deirdre's receiving room and stopped at the door of the sleeping chamber, feeling suddenly a trespasser in this room that had so long been hers. He shook off the reservations and entered the dark room.

The heavy draperies were drawn back, allowing moonlight to illumine a swatch across the bed. Deirdre lay sleeping deeply, draped in a simple silk robe. Roman stood over the bed and looked down on her. In spite of his weariness, just the sight of her—beautiful, safe, resting—awakened to quick power in him those old yearnings for her.

He reached down to stroke her hair and shoulders, then bent to kiss her neck. She did not rouse. He gently turned her shoulders to face him and kissed her mouth. She struggled, still asleep, and pulled away from him. Hungry, he kissed her again. Though unconscious, she nonetheless clearly demanded, "Leave me alone!" He released her in frustration, throwing himself down on the bed.

4

A fortnight raced by as Galapos took control of the palace and slaved to make it function on sparse assets. First, he inventoried the palace possessions, soldiers, arms, and animals, to determine their needs and their resources. He appointed a palace overseer and staff from the soldiers, who struggled under Basil's tutoring to learn the most elementary requirements of maintaining a palace.

But Galapos soon found that the demands of his work were frequently superseded by the demands of the people to settle their quarrels and soothe their pride with appointments and honors. Therefore, once a day in the early morning hours, Galapos held an open audience to hear from them. He used the audience hall for this purpose, and sat on the throne to announce his judgments, but declined the purple mantle. He wished to establish his authority by what he did rather than what he wore on his shoulders.

In one such audience, Galapos sat on the throne with Roman standing to his right and summoned Kam before him. "Kam, you have been a faithful, hardworking soldier. You have served willingly wherever I have placed you and held nothing back. In recognition of your loyalty and service, I wish to appoint you as a captain of the army. Here is your charge: Do you swear to defend Lystra and the Surchatain with your life, to execute the orders of your Commander, and deal responsibly with the men under you?"

"I do, Surchatain." Kam's chest was puffed to bursting.

"Then you are so appointed. Commander Roman will assign you a unit," Galapos confirmed.

Kam bowed as Galapos rose, and Roman began to briefly instruct the new captain, "Your unit is the blue. You'll begin drilling tomorrow—"

A voice in the crowd flowing around them distracted him with the snide comment, "If he *really* wished to be honored, he'd be in the Cohort."

Roman and Kam both turned indignantly toward the voice, but whoever said it slipped back into the crowd. "Who said that?" Kam demanded, grabbing a startled merchant.

"Let it be," Roman muttered. "Now—"

"Did you see who said that?" Kam persisted, grabbing another.

"Captain!" Roman barked, and Kam looked over. "I gave you an order, Captain," Roman breathed angrily.

"Yes, sir!" Kam snapped to attention. For a brief, dangerous moment he had forgotten that Roman was no longer merely the Chataine's guardian.

"Go prepare your unit's gear to drill tomorrow," Roman instructed coldly—a menial task for a captain.

"Yes, sir." Kam saluted stiffly and went out.

Detaching himself from the hangers-on around the throne, Galapos gestured, "Roman, to the library."

They had just exited through the great doors when a flustered Basil called after them. "Surchatain, if you will, kindly step back into the hall. A dispute has arisen, and the parties ask you to hear them."

Galapos nodded grimly, making an about-face. All their disputes were of such importance that no less a person than the Surchatain could hear them. As Galapos reseated himself on the throne, Roman took a place near the edge of the spectators.

"I will hear first from the one who has a grievance," said Galapos.

"Surchatain." An elderly man approached the throne and bowed. "I'm a man of meager means, with only a modest plot of land as my subsistence. I've no family and can't afford to hire laborers. I alone must work my field. Now this man—" he pointed an accusing finger at a fellow nearby "—has four rowdy boys who are nothing but vandals and troublemakers. They've been raiding my field and stealing my grain. I ask that you execute them before they take all I have to eat!"

Galapos turned his eyes to the accused. "And what do you say?"

"Surchatain," he bowed, "it's true that my boys have been gleaning from his land. But he lets the grain stand so long it gets wasted! Now, I'm a potter, and you know how poor business has been. My family is starving! Will you hang my boys for bringing bread to their father's table?"

"Stolen bread!" exclaimed the first man.

"You would let it rot before allowing us to have it!" cried the second.

"Order!" demanded Galapos, then fumed, "Why do you prefer knocking heads to helping each other? You"—he pointed to the elderly plaintiff—"you've nothing to pay laborers, so your grain rots on the stalks? You will hire this man's sons as your laborers, and pay them as wages an eighth of what they reap for you. And you," he said, pointing to the defendant, "the harder your sons work, the more bread will be brought to your table. Moreover, if they work faithfully, and do more than is asked of them, perhaps this man may be moved to leave his field as an inheritance for them." He waited to see both parties eye each other suspiciously. "Then this audience is ended," Galapos declared.

He left the throne so that he and Roman could resume their walk to the library. On the way, Roman glanced toward the chapel as a pair of soldiers entered it. "The chapel draws much interest of a sudden," he remarked.

"Hylas is teaching the new converts there," Galapos answered, preoccupied.

"Hylas? I don't know him. Does he have Scriptures? He isn't using ours—I have them all the time," Roman said. Galapos did not respond, so Roman shrugged and left it at that.

They sat in the library with maps of all the Surchatain's land and began carefully piecing them together to discover the extent of the royal possessions. "Why hasn't this been done before?" Galapos grumbled.

"Who knows?" muttered Roman, poring over a mass of wriggly lines. "Perhaps because the Surchatain owns so much land, they found it easier to assume any particular piece belonged to him rather than not." He frowned, turning the map one-hundred-eighty degrees to look it over from a better angle.

"According to this, the Surchatain owns all the land east of Westford to the slate quarry," said Galapos.

"That can't be," Roman dissented. "Taine has a sizable plot just beyond the fuller's field."

Galapos squinted. "That must be what this blocked area is."

Roman leaned over to look. "No. That's the lake."

"No. That would put the lake due east of Westford."

"Where is the lake, then?" Roman shifted closer.

"There is no lake!" declared Galapos. He leaned on his elbow, exasperated, then raised a finger of authority and demanded, "Roman, banish the lake. It does not appear on the map."

"It must!" Roman insisted, taking it up. "My father drew up these maps himself. He would certainly make them accurate."

As Roman scrutinized the parchment, Galapos sat back and smiled slightly at him. "I hope," Galapos said, "that he is able to hear what you just said."

Roman raised his face, caught unawares. Then he said, "It occurs to me that the lake is only outlined on the map by the surrounding fields." He looked down again. "Here it is." And he placed the map in front of Galapos, pointing. Thus enlightened, they began to develop a reliable picture of the Surchatain's holdings.

Some time later, a knock sounded on the door and Kam appeared. "Surchatain, pardon the intrusion, but I've been hearing reports that you should be aware of. My unit's gear is ready, Commander," Kam said in a respectful aside to Roman, who nodded.

"Reports? Regarding what?" Galapos asked, pushing away the maps.

"We're hearing of renegade attacks on many villages and small townships—looting, killing, taking slaves. It's getting so that people are afraid to travel outside of Westford," Kam told them.

Galapos clenched a fist. "Are the renegades banded together or acting alone?"

"From what I hear, they're loners, or they go in twos and threes. I doubt they can cooperate enough to form a large band. There just seems to be more of them than ever before," Kam said.

"Do this, then," Galapos instructed. "Send two soldiers to every village that has been harassed. They're to stay three months, longer if they wish, before being relieved. They're to deal forcefully with any renegade attacks. If two men prove to be too few, send as many more as they request."

"Yes, Surchatain," Kam bowed and began to move away.

"Wait—Kam—" Galapos stopped him, concentrating. "There is more to be done. . . . I fear it will take a good portion of the men away from Westford, but—send a unit of twenty men each to Outposts Two, Three, and Four to clean up and salvage. Any unattached soldiers found are to be brought back to Westford. If they're unfit for the army, they'll farm. But they won't be running loose all over the countryside." Kam and Roman both nodded at this.

"Send a unit skilled in war machines to Outpost One, to disassemble that battering ram and get it back here. The gates also must be repaired . . . but that will have to wait. Also," Galapos continued, "send a unit to find the holy man and the villagers at the coast—what is his name?" he turned to Roman.

"Brother Avelon."

"To Brother Avelon," Galapos went on, "and communicate to them my offer of land for each family to own. And send to Avelon my invitation to live here in the palace—be certain he is told the full story of what happened at the outpost."

"Yes, Surchatain," Kam saluted vigorously, then paused.

"Yes?" Galapos asked, lifting a bushy brow.

"In order to carry out all these instructions . . ." Kam began uneasily, glancing at Roman.

"You're excused from drilling your unit," Roman said.

"Sir." Kam saluted and strode out.

Having been interrupted in their chore, Roman and Galapos sat back from the maps to rest. Galapos, yawning, rubbed his face, and Roman stared blankly out the window.

"I think," Galapos said abruptly, "that I should take a wife." That elicited an amused glance from Roman, at which Galapos protested, "I need *something* else to do besides work!"

"That will only add to your burden," Roman remarked before catching himself.

"Problems with Deirdre?" Galapos asked delicately.

Roman shrugged. "I don't know. She—she is different toward me. Cooler. I can't find out what I've done to put distance between us."

"You married her," Galapos observed wryly.

Roman winced. "I was afraid that was it. What shall I do, Galapos? How can I revive her love for me?"

"I don't know that there is anything you *can* do. Some people—children in particular—must learn by hard lessons to value the good they have."

A soldier entered with a knock. "Surchatain—Commander—the noon meal is ready." They stood in relief and made for the hall.

On the way, they met up with Deirdre. "Hello, Father—Roman. I haven't seen either of you all morning."

They fell to each side of her as Roman held her bulky waist and kissed her. "And I've missed you," he said. She smiled indulgently.

"Have you kept busy, Chataine?" asked Galapos.

"Oh, yes! I've begun furnishing the nursery. It's so much work—I'm fairly exhausted," she complained.

"When do the women say you're due?" Roman queried.

"Early winter, perhaps December," she said. "I wish the baby would come sooner."

"I also," Roman added so quickly that she glanced down her nose at him.

"All things in their season," Galapos said brightly as they entered the hall.

Basil and the other guests at the table stood until the three were seated. The wine was poured by a rugged-looking soldier who accidentally spilled a little on Deirdre. She glared at him with a reprimand on her lips, but Galapos said quietly, "Forbear, Deirdre." So with the look of a martyr she held her peace until the meat dish came before Galapos.

"Rabbit!" she moaned. "Stewed rabbit again! And they don't even know how to cook it right!"

"If you know how to prepare it better, perhaps you could help them in the kitchen," Roman said without sarcasm.

Deirdre's mouth dropped open, and she began, "Are you suggesting that *I*—"

"Counselor," Galapos demanded cheerfully, "have we anyone to entertain us today?"

"Surchatain—I'm not rightly sure," Basil said hesitantly. "Wait—yes, it seems there was a juggler here. Shall I send for him now, or at the evening meal?"

"Now seems appropriate," Galapos said. Basil gave the word to a nearby soldier. In a moment a young man with a painted jester's face appeared, bowed, and began juggling three, then four, then five colored balls in progressively faster circuits.

Watching him, Galapos sighed to Roman, "That is what I feel like I'm doing."

Deirdre muttered, "Perhaps we could have him serve the wine."

"Or prepare the rabbit," Roman added slyly.

"If he can do that right, he should be given charge of keeping accounts," Basil suggested. The juggler, hearing, bobbed the balls.

"Well, then, let's also have him drill the soldiers!" exclaimed a captain down from Basil.

"If he can discipline those rogues, what say we just give him the province to rule?" Galapos proposed. "Then we can all go to our homes and forget this great mess."

"Hear, hear!" lauded the soldier who had spilled the wine. The juggler ended his act abruptly, bowed, and fled the hall amid laughter.

"There goes a wise man," muttered Galapos. Roman nodded, stroking his brow.

A soldier approached Galapos to whisper, "Surchatain, one of the townspeople has an urgent grievance and asks—" but he was interrupted by a merchant striding into the hall.

Galapos lowered his fork in surprise as the merchant demanded, "Surchatain, you must do something about the problem of these peasants!"

"Can't your grievance wait until tomorrow morning's audience, man? And would you make demands on me?" Galapos returned scathingly.

The merchant bit his lip and forced a slight bow. "Pardon, Surchatain, but it is a severe problem. These peasants are hounding my shop—"

"What is your business?" asked Galapos.

"Why, I'm Lewyn, the butcher."

"And how do the peasants wrong you? Are they stealing from you?" Galapos asked.

"No, not precisely, Surchatain."

"Then how, precisely, Lewyn?"

The butcher composed himself in the extremity of his complaint. "Surchatain, they pester me endlessly for the hoofs and heads of the animals I butcher, but they cannot pay for them, and—"

"What do you do with the waste parts?" Galapos asked, picking up his fork again. Deirdre suddenly lost her appetite and pushed away from the table petulantly.

"I feed them to my dogs," Lewyn answered.

"The hoofs? And heads?" Galapos asked skeptically.

"Well, no . . . those are burned. For fuel," Lewyn added defensively.

"I suggest," Galapos said in steely tones, "that you feed your dogs, but give the peasants any waste. I will send a soldier with you to see they wait quietly for what you have to give." He waved to the sentry nearby. "You may burn useless brush for fuel, Lewyn. You are dismissed."

Dissatisfied, Lewyn stood his ground until the sentry firmly nudged him out. Roman muttered, "He bears watching."

"That, my boy, is why I sent Cole with him," winked Galapos. "Where is that juggler now, anyway?" he wondered.

❖

The weeks sped by as the remnant at the palace stayed with the task of rebuilding Lystra. On one vexing day, Basil came to report to Galapos in his chambers: "Surchatain, we're faced with a rather immediate problem. We have all but exhausted the treasury. Already we owe the soldiers pay, and have not enough to buy meat and beverage for them through another week."

"You mean we can't even feed our men?" Galapos asked, exasperated.

Basil was hedging around a reply when Roman entered the chambers. Galapos turned on him. "What is the situation with the soldiers?"

Roman braced his jaw. "We're getting by. I suppose the Counselor has told you we can't actually *pay* them . . . even so, our numbers are dangerously low. We must have more men. There are barely enough to maintain the horses and arms, with their added responsibilities."

"Added responsibilities?" Galapos's thick eyebrows arched.

"Ah, yes." Roman shuffled uneasily. "They're working in the fields with the few servants who remain. And I have sent teams out hunting game."

Galapos muttered, "I see it must be done, if they want to eat. How do they feel about it?"

Roman shrugged, "They see the necessity for it also. They are intensely loyal, being so few. But overburdened and not paid a piece."

"So," Galapos summed, "our basic problem here is that we need money and men, and much of both." With confirming nods, Roman and Basil stood looking to him for answers.

He gazed out the window in thought a moment, then shook his head. "I'm empty-handed, men. Perhaps God will take time out to grant a prayer or two on this matter. And Counselor, be certain to inform all those wanting land that their crops will be taxed. We'll begin dividing up the land as soon as possible. I'll need both of you to help me. Counselor, please gather the list of names and maps and bring them here."

"Surchatain." Basil bowed and departed.

Roman sat with a sour look on his face. "My boy?" Galapos questioned, surprised that he would balk at helping.

"More parchment, Galapos?" Roman pleaded. "I am weary already with all the records and payments due."

"You should delegate that work."

"I have, to Basil. But he is only now learning the soldiers' names and how to keep the records. Teaching him all he has to know takes as much time as doing it myself," Roman complained.

"That's the advantage to delegation within the army," Galapos observed carefully. "You need to appoint a Second."

Roman did not answer at once. "I don't know whom to select."

Wrinkling his brow, Galapos offered, "If you need a recommendation, I believe Kam would be well suited to that position."

Roman dropped his eyes to the padded arm of the chair and fingered the fine upholstery, then said, "No. Not Kam." Galapos looked surprised, but held his peace.

"So." Roman straightened. "Do you wish to see the wealth of arms our men have gathered from the outposts?"

"Certainly," Galapos agreed. "In the time that it takes Basil to fetch all that parchment, we could inventory the whole armory."

Roman quickly advised him, "There was not space enough in the armory for it all, so we've filled several store-rooms near the kitchen with them. I thought to show you those rooms first."

"Very well," said Galapos, and they headed downstairs.

Passing the chapel doors, they also passed a soldier exiting who dreamily sighed and ran his hand through his hair. Not even seeing the two, he strolled leisurely away. Galapos and Roman stopped on the same stride, frowning. "I smell perfume," said Roman.

"I saw red tapestries," said Galapos. They turned to each other with puzzled frowns, then ran to throw open the chapel doors.

There they stood gaping at a room filled with love couches and lewd tapestries. A barely dressed woman leapt off a couch and escaped through a rear door.

Roman stood speechless. Galapos shut his eyes and bellowed, "Hylas!"

He appeared at the rear door and came up to them bowing and smiling. "Yes, Surchatain?"

Roman laughed in disbelief. Galapos turned a deep shade of red and growled, "What are you doing here, Hylas?"

"Why, teaching the love of God, Surchatain."

"The love of God! You've turned this prayer room into a bawdy house!"

"Precisely so, my lord." Hylas was still bowing and smiling.

Galapos gritted his teeth. "Explain yourself quickly, while you can still talk."

"Why, Surchatain, I'm merely demonstrating to the men that God forgives all their sins. How can they know His forgiveness until they know they have sinned?"

"You are a fool!" Galapos sputtered. "They all have sins aplenty, without your adding to them. These men have been baptized! They're to follow the old ways no longer. Now get yourself and your blasted teachings out of here!"

Hylas drew up in righteous coolness. "It pains me to see that your views on God's love are so narrow and intolerant. I had thought the religious persecution under Karel had ended. I see I was wrong."

"You're perverting the meaning of the Scriptures," Roman said earnestly. "Yes, they say God forgives completely, but they also say we are to put aside immorality."

"And so the men do. Once they have tasted the bitterness of sin, they can experience the freshness and cleansing that come with repentance. And they do it as often as they like," Hylas said happily.

"No," grimaced Roman. "You're leading them into a life of presumption. The whole point is that they're to *try* to live rightly, and depend on God to make them stand. The point is lost if they don't choose rightness, pursue it and desire it more than any beautiful woman."

Hylas studied Roman with a mixture of condescension and incomprehension. "You have a strange manner of speech."

Galapos uttered, "Then understand this, Hylas: You are banished from Lystra. Practice what you will, but not in my palace!" Seething, he turned his back.

At that moment a soldier appeared at the door. Seeing the Surchatain and the Commander, he turned to run. But Galapos collared him. "Your arrival is timely, fellow. You may haul out all these furnishings and dump them outside the gates. And spread the word that the gospel of Hylas is finished. Go!" The soldier went in to begin yanking down tapestries over Hylas's anguished protests.

Galapos strode to the storerooms. Roman caught up with him after pausing to grab a lamp from the chapel. He opened a storeroom door and set the lamp on a table. Surveying rows upon rows of chest plates, helmets, swords and shields, Galapos muttered, "If we had the men to wear all this gear, we would be formidable. Am I dreaming, to see armor stored where grain had been?"

"The grain will be supplied in time," Roman assured him. "But we never could have hoped to buy so many arms over the next hundred years. With a disciplined army, we could withstand anything."

"A disciplined army!" Galapos slumped his shoulders. "What am I to do, Roman? These men are like children, ready to follow anyone with a good song. How shall I hold their attention?"

"You really needn't worry, Galapos. You're the only one who *can* lead them. And I'll be here, for you to lean on when you grow weary." He smiled steadily at Galapos in his wry way.

Galapos returned his gaze. "I do need you, Roman. I need you to help me prepare those blasted maps. Are you willing?"

Roman's eyes flicked downward at the gentle chastening, but immediately met the other's again. "I am now." So they left the soldiers' toys to return to parchment and lists.

5

The following morning when Deirdre awoke, Roman was not there. She was not in the least surprised. He was an habitual early riser, and she had never yet awakened in the morning to find him still beside her.

Yawning, she rolled out of bed and stretched. She put a hand to her belly, feeling that she had grown larger overnight. She scrutinized her reflection in the looking glass, then pursed her lips and turned away, remembering a time when she had been proud of her nymphlike shape.

She dressed and wrapped her hair in strands of pearls, then descended the stone stairs in time to hear Roman below giving curt instructions to a soldier. He turned to her with a sigh and a smile just as she gained the floor. Lazily, she twined her arms around his neck to kiss him.

"I hope you got some sleep," he murmured. "You seemed restless last night."

"I can't seem to lie down comfortably," she admitted. "I feel like a cow." That drew such a sudden laugh from him that she widened her eyes and inquired, "Do I look like a cow?"

"In no way," he assured her, then coughed. "Only vaguely." Her eyes widened further, and he hastened to add, "But no cow so beautiful ever existed!"

She was speechless, floundering for a retort, when Galapos entered roaring, "Oh no! Is he talking of beauty? Such arrogance! We will earnestly pray that this child favors you, Chataine!" Roman grinned, and she was satisfied.

Galapos took her arm, and the three entered the dining hall, where Galapos instructed a soldier who stood as sentry to bring her breakfast. "Only rolls with honey and milk, Father," she said. "I don't feel like eating much this morning." Galapos nodded at the soldier, who bowed and moved off.

As they sat at the table to wait, Roman's eyes rested pensively on Deirdre's belly. "When do the women say you're due, Chataine?"

She sighed at the question he asked almost daily. "In a month, perhaps. Hopefully before the winter storms."

He nodded, eyes on the future. "He will be a great warrior," he murmured.

"She certainly could be," she returned testily.

He blinked. "Of course a daughter would be welcome here," he said easily, adding, "I know what power a woman can hold." Galapos smiled at the table, and Deirdre sensed something had gone over her head.

The soldier reentered the hall and set a goblet and pitcher of milk before Deirdre. "Surchatain," he said apologetically, "honey we have, but there are no rolls, and no one here knows how to make them. We have brown bread, though."

Deirdre screwed up her face in disgust. "Brown bread! No! Can't you get some rolls from the baker?" she pleaded with her soft-hearted father.

He creased his forehead and drew a few coins from the purse at his belt. "Get what you can with this," he told the soldier.

Deirdre, meanwhile, took a swallow of the milk and gagged. "It's soured!"

The soldier shrugged, and Galapos patiently ordered, "And have someone milk a fresh bucket."

Deirdre shoved away the pitcher, muttering, "I will surely starve before this baby comes."

Roman, still thinking, asked Galapos, "How old must he be to handle a bow?"

Deirdre glared at Roman, but Galapos winked at her and replied, "Why, I don't know. How old was Deirdre when you taught her?"

Roman, catching his error, confessed, "I don't remember. But she learned well." As they waited on Deirdre's breakfast, he remarked, "I haven't seen Brother Avelon. Has he come from the coast?"

"No, as a matter of fact," Galapos answered. "He sent back word thanking me for my offer, but saying many of the villagers have prospered there learning the fishing trade. He says his service is there, with them."

"Then the villagers are not coming to take the land you offered?" Roman asked.

"Oh, some will, for certain. And the word spread so that people are coming from villages around Westford. We may not have enough land for them all—by the by, Basil has compiled everything so that we can begin the actual mapping today."

At this time the soldier brought in fresh rolls and milk for Deirdre. She continued to listen vaguely to their conversation while she ate.

"What word from the villages? Are they still suffering attacks?" Roman asked.

"Not like they were. We had early reports of confrontations in almost all of the villages—"

"I recall them," Roman nodded.

"Well, when word got around the renegade camps that those little matrons and children had a few mean men with swords among them, most of the outlaws had no stomach for a second encounter. At Dansington, though, we had to send in extra men to clean it up," Galapos said, wiping crumbs from the table with a knife blade.

"What was there?"

"A newly hatched slave market," Galapos said, ramming the knife point into the table.

Roman gaped. "I'd heard no word of this. As Commander, shouldn't I have led the men in this attack? Or at least dispatched them myself?"

Galapos hesitated, open-mouthed. "Ah . . . yes, Roman, you should have. I'm sorry—I seem to still be acting as Commander. From now on these reports will go directly to you. And as Commander, you shall deal with them as your judgment dictates. I have plenty else to keep me occupied."

"Thank you," Roman acknowledged grumpily. Then, "But what of this slave market?"

"It was headed up by a renegade from Tremaine's army," replied Galapos. "We shut them down quick, but I fear there are more."

"That's what we need that battering ram for, to plow them under," Roman growled. "I haven't seen it yet, either."

Galapos stretched in his chair. "The unit we sent hasn't had any success taking it apart—they swear they've never seen a machine like it. We still have a squad at work on it, but for now, it sits."

By this time Deirdre had eaten her breakfast and motioned for the soldier to take away the dishes. Galapos stood. "We have a moment to spare now—Roman, come to my chambers. I have questions about the passage I read last night."

"Passage?" Deirdre asked curiously.

"Scripture, my love," Roman answered, extending an arm around her. "And you need to come too. You're a believer now, and you should hear what your Lord has to say to you."

She made a face. "Oh, Roman, you know I was never good at studies."

"Please, Deirdre, come. You've no idea how important this is," he pleaded.

She remembered her tutor saying the same thing, and she had already decided he had overstated the case. She balked, "Roman, I had so wanted to see the lake this morning. We haven't been there since we returned, and if I don't go soon, it may be next spring before I see it again. Please—may we go there now? For just a moment?"

Roman cast a questioning look to Galapos. The Surchatain smiled tightly. "You may take her to the lake, and Basil and I will begin the maps. But Deirdre—you will study with us later. You are no longer your own. You're God's now, and He will see that you're instructed in the faith. Be a willing student, Chataine. It's so much easier that way."

Deirdre bowed her head and murmured, "Yes, Father," content that she had her way.

She wanted to ride, so Roman reluctantly saddled Lady Grey and the Bay Hunter, and they rode slowly out to their old haunt by the lake. He would not let her even dismount by herself, but lifted her down from the saddle. They walked, his arm around her shoulders, to the water's edge. With autumn in progress, the lilies were gone, but the place was aflame with the beauty of reds and golds.

They sat beneath the willows. He eased her back on the grass, then kissed her. For a time there were no words as Roman caressed her with his lips. He touched her swollen belly very lightly, as if he was afraid of hurting her. Lying beside her, he contentedly buried his face in her hair.

Deirdre suddenly laughed, "I can see us in twenty years,

still coming to this same place!"

He smiled. "By then we'll have worn a path from the palace to here."

"Anyone will know where to find us."

"Yes. They'll need only follow the trail of children." His look was unmistakable.

She gave a little mock cry of offense and struggled up to a sit. He laughed outright, hugging her tightly to him. "Roman, I almost forgot! The Fair starts this week! Oh, there are so many things I need for the nursery!"

His face sobered. "I'm sorry, Deirdre—I can't go this week. Reapportioning the Surchatain's land will take days."

"Oh," she frowned. "Well, I'll just take—"

He was shaking his head. "No, Deirdre. You must not go without me."

"Roman!"

"I promise we'll go before the Fair is over."

"But the best things will be gone if we don't get there early!" she protested.

"There will still be good things left. I'm sorry, Chataine. It can't be helped." He stroked her hair while she sat pouting.

At that moment a soldier appeared: "Excuse me. Commander?" Roman turned. "The Surchatain requests your aid now in preparing the reapportionment maps."

"I'm coming." Roman stood and bent for Deirdre. "We have to go now."

She felt a slight irritation on top of acute disappointment. Would he be forever acting like her guardian? "Roman, I want to stay here just a while longer," she said. He hesitated, then motioned to the soldier, but she stopped him with a wave. "Alone! Roman, there's no danger here! I'll return to the palace in a moment. I promise."

He knelt beside her and took her unwilling hand. "Deirdre, I know you're angry. I understand why. But don't stay here by yourself to—"

"In heaven's name, I only want to enjoy the lake! Now leave me alone!" She thrust her back to him spitefully.

In the sting of her words, he quietly surrendered. "Very well. I'll be waiting for you." He left with the soldier.

Immediately Deirdre felt remorse, and almost called after him, but a little reserve of pride inside caused her to stay silent. She would leave in a few minutes, just as she said.

She began listlessly picking blades of grass and tearing them up. It seemed, as she scanned the lake, that most of the sparkle had gone from the water. Clouds were beginning to gather and darken behind the trees on the other side.

Suddenly, she focused across the narrow end of the lake. There was a figure on the far shore. It appeared to be—no, that was impossible!

Deirdre's heart began thumping as she grabbed Lady Grey. She rode as hard as she dared to the other side of the lake. When she reached the spot where she judged the person had stood, she dismounted and anxiously looked all about. But no one was there.

Hanging her head in disappointment, she turned back to Lady Grey and then saw that person standing behind the horse. "Nanna—is that you?" she gasped.

"Darling!" Nanna cried, and they rushed into each other's arms. The nursemaid observed, "So it is as she said. You will deliver soon."

Deirdre hardly heard her. "Nanna, you must come right back to the palace with me! I need you more than ever now!"

But the nursemaid recoiled. "No! I—I can't do that, dear. But you must come with me. I have a friend who will help you."

Deirdre gazed at her in bewilderment, then concern. Nanna looked different—more than just from the passing of months. There was an alien look in her eyes. "Who?" Deirdre asked, watching her.

The nursemaid patted her hand and said confidentially, "She told me I would find you here, you know. You must come with me now."

"Who told you?" Deirdre raised her voice in vague alarm as Nanna moved off into the forest. Deirdre hesitated as a picture of Roman's wary face flashed through her mind in a warning. Nonetheless, concern for Nanna's strange behavior impelled her to follow. "Wait, Nanna!" Deirdre caught up with her, then awkwardly climbed up on the mare and helped Nanna up behind her.

They rode in the direction Nanna pointed. "Why were you limping so?" Deirdre asked.

"A bad fall, dear. Nothing to worry about—my old bones just didn't knit together right," Nanna said lightly.

"Where were you when Tremaine came through, Nanna?"

"With a friend who hid me. You'll meet her soon." To other questions, Nanna merely smiled or patted her arm.

Minute trailed long minute as they rode farther and farther from the palace. Deirdre began to feel anxious to return to Roman. The forest got darker, her back hurt, and Nanna's behavior was most disquieting. "Nanna, please, I mustn't get so far from home. Please come back with me. There's nothing to fear now. Galapos is the new ruler, and—"

"Hush, hush, dear. I know all that."

"Then why won't you go back with me?" Deirdre cried in a spasm.

"It's not possible, Chataine. I can never go back." Nanna would say no more.

"But I must," Deirdre declared, abruptly reining the horse around. "I'm returning now. I wish you would come with me, but—"

"Here." Nanna pointed to their right. "We can stop here. There is shelter."

Deirdre peered. In the side of a low hill she saw a black hole almost entirely obscured by rocks and brush.

Nanna slipped off the horse and limped to the opening. Deirdre also dismounted; as she did, she felt a twinge in her abdomen that spread to her back. "Nanna—" she pleaded, and the woman waved Deirdre to the cave.

"You can rest in here, Chataine." Hesitantly, Deirdre stepped into the hole. The cave was not more than thirty feet deep, and the walls were lined with sconces. It did not seem to be a natural cavern, somehow; Deirdre wondered how it had been carved from the rock.

As she gazed inside, the urgency she felt to return to the palace pressed her more strongly. Then immediately she felt nauseated and weak-kneed. A sudden sharp twinge and her water broke. Deirdre lowered herself to a bed of blankets on the dirt floor, realizing her labor had come early.

"Nanna, please, please ride to the palace and summon Roman," she moaned.

"I will bring help," Nanna assured her, then disappeared back out the hole.

❖

In the hours that Nanna was gone, Deirdre waited and prayed, feeling the pains come stronger and stronger. There was no sound except for growls of intermittent thunder outside. At intervals, she talked to herself and God. "Fool! What a fool, to insist on staying at the lake alone. Roman will be so vexed when he sees all the trouble I've gotten myself into. . . . Oh, I'll be so glad to see him come charging in here, angry or not. . . . He'll be furious with Nanna for bringing me here. . . . Lord, what's happened to her? Why is she so strange?"

At last, when the pains were causing her to gasp and cry out, she heard a rustle. Looking down past her feet to the mouth of the cave, she saw Nanna enter, then step aside.

"Oh, thank goodness!" Tears of relief came to Deirdre's

eyes before she saw that the other person to enter was not
Roman at all, but a beautiful woman with blue-black hair.
Deirdre recognized her at once as the witch, Varela, who
had once cursed Roman. She carried small blankets, a basin,
and a knife. Smiling with satisfaction, she approached the
Chataine.

Deirdre screamed in helplessness, "Don't touch me!
Oh—Lord Jesus!" and another pain squeezed her with new
intensity.

The sorceress came no closer. Deirdre was unable to
notice that she was trying to approach, but could not. Varela
pushed forward all around, only to be invisibly repelled at
every attempt.

Finally, she spun away in frustration and shoved the arti-
cles at Nanna. "You deliver her, and bring me the child. I will
send Bernal to rid me of her." Nanna nodded and gingerly
knelt beside the prostrate girl.

Outside, the autumn storm had begun, deluging the forest and seeping into the mouth of the cave.

6

"That completes the first map," Galapos grunted and straightened his shoulders. "Eighteen families will each have a field in that area. Now here—" He began to outline another region, but Roman was staring distractedly out the window.

"She should have returned by now," he muttered.

"Are you sure she hasn't? She probably went straight back up to the nursery," Galapos said, hunched over the desk again.

Roman leaned down out of the window. "Marc! Has the Chataine returned?"

The soldier below looked up, cupping his hand around his ear. After Roman repeated the question he shouted up, "No, Commander!" Roman leaned back, drumming his fingers in aggravation on the windowsill.

"Would you like to go after her?" Galapos asked, raising up.

"No," Roman said firmly. "I'm sure she intends to worry me."

Galapos pursed his lips and sat waiting. Roman looked at him once or twice, then mumbled, "I will return directly," and hurried out.

He muttered to himself on the way to the stables, "This is ridiculous. I must be firm with her this time." Then he noted the grey and gathering clouds.

Roman saddled the Bay Hunter with unconscious speed and galloped to their spot by the lake. She was gone. Glancing again at the darkening skies, he calmly searched the grass and dirt until he found her mare's hoof prints.

He followed them around the lake, then his brows knitted as he saw another set of footprints. Then Deirdre's prints, here. Twenty paces farther, both human prints disappeared and the mare's sank deeper in the soft earth. Deirdre had taken on a rider, and the trail led directly away from the palace.

As Roman followed the prints at a trot, great raindrops began falling, one by one, making large dark circles on the earth. Although his apprehension swelled, he grimly kept his eyes away from the black skies and concentrated on the tracks.

Soon, with a flash, the rain came in furies. Squinting against the blinding wall of water, he doggedly followed the blurring prints. In moments they were gone—washed away.

Still he rode in the direction they had led, calling, "Deirdre! Deirdre!" His voice died in the crashing of the rain, which pounded down like a hammer on the ground. "Deirdre!" He could not see two paces ahead, but he urged his skittish horse on, angrily, fearfully calling her name.

The bay stumbled into a narrow ravine, and Roman was almost pitched from his seat. He dismounted to pull and prod the edgy horse back onto somewhat solid ground, then stopped to get his breath while rivers ran down his hair and face. It was useless to search like this. He needed help. What if she . . . ? He refused to think further, but remounted the snorting bay to head back to the palace.

He was shaking when he finally rode through the gates. But he did not take time to change before rushing to the Surchatain's chambers. "Galapos! She's gone! She took on a rider at the lake and rode away from the palace—I lost the tracks in the rain. We must gather a unit to search for her," he finished, panting. Puddles gathered at his feet, absorbed by the woven rug.

Galapos and Basil stared at him and each other. Galapos glanced out the window. All that was visible outside was a blanket of white rain. "You say you lost her trail . . . and she was not alone," he murmured. Roman nodded, wiping water from his face with a soaked sleeve.

"Then we must assume she has found shelter elsewhere for now," Galapos said carefully. Basil nodded.

Roman stiffened. "We must search for her. Now."

"We can't, my son. We haven't a prayer of finding her in this torrent—and night comes early these days. We've no choice but to wait until morning to search. But then I will call together every available man—"

"Morning could be too late! Have you forgotten she's near her time?" Roman cried.

"No, I haven't forgotten! I'm not yet feeble-minded, Roman!" Galapos said with a trace of sarcasm. "Look outside! What do you see? Are you such a superb hunter that you can track her in the storm and the darkness?" He cut himself short, and there was a heavy silence.

"No." Roman's voice cracked.

"We must leave her in God's hands tonight," Galapos said gently. "We'll set out to search at dawn."

❖

Dinner that night was a useless affair. Roman did not even appear at the table, nor did Galapos send for him. The crackling tension in the atmosphere outside came through the stone walls and filled every corner. Hushed soldiers discreetly avoided their Commander. He strode past them through corridors on minute errands to distant storerooms, where, upon arriving, he could not remember what he had come for.

When he wearied of that, he retired to the chambers he shared with Deirdre. Unable to look for long at her things, he opened the shutters to let the rain sprinkle in. The prayers he sent up did not even seem to penetrate the dark clouds, so he paced and watched the rain.

Strange, how the fury of the storm was so calming— almost hypnotic to an observer in the safety of a stone palace. There seemed to be a voice whispering that the God who created storms could also control them. See how the fierce wind flung each drop in rhythm with myriads more, creating a wild, cascading dance. But . . . was she watching from as secure a shelter?

He spent the night at the window, hypnotized by the rain.

❖

With sunrise came the birth of a new earth, fresh and wet and cleansed by the torrents. The sky had cleared, but droplets still hung from leaves and grass, shimmering in the early golden light.

Roman and Galapos nodded to each other with heavy eyes as they gathered a score of men in the courtyard. They rode to the far side of the lake, as far as Roman had been able to follow the prints. From there, they separated into groups of five. Cutting through the forest, searching and calling, they spread out again and again until each man searched alone.

As Roman rode deeper into the hill country, fear for Deirdre chewed at his frayed nerves. There were wild animals in this area—large cats and wolves. Dogged by thoughts of disaster, he instinctively prayed.

Then he heard a rustle in a nearby grove. Suddenly aware that he had been riding silently for some minutes, he slid from his horse and ran forward, wishing fervently to find her there.

But on the edge of the grove he came face to face with Nanna, carrying something all wrapped up. They stared at each other in dumb astonishment for seconds, then Nanna's burden squirmed and fussed. The realization of what she carried stopped his heart.

He clenched his fists. "Give me that child."

Nanna's face drained to a deathly white, but she vowed, "No. Never."

Finesse never entered his mind. He reached out to seize her, but she screamed and dropped the bundle. Roman fell to his knees and deftly caught the baby while Nanna fled into the woods. He gave a piercing whistle, and soon his fellow searchers came at a run on horseback.

"Deirdre's nursemaid!" Roman gasped. "She escaped—there—after her! Go!" They galloped heatedly in the direction he pointed.

Then cautiously, breathlessly, he pulled back the little blanket to look down on his child. The baby was so tiny and red, with thick dark hair and eyes shut fast. It was a boy. Roman, still on his knees, rocked his son and wept. Where was Deirdre?

Behind him, Galapos quietly gave orders for the baby to be taken to the palace. Roman held him stubbornly at first, then gave him up into the arms of the gentlest soldier with them, who rode away with him at a walk.

Galapos put his hand on Roman's shoulder and opened his mouth to say something, but was interrupted by the silent return of the soldiers who had ridden in pursuit of Nanna. "Well?" demanded Galapos. "You couldn't have lost her!"

Reluctantly, a man in front said, "No, Surchatain. We did not lose her. We found her . . . body."

"Her *body*?" Roman sank back to his knees in dismay.

"Yes, Commander. She was mauled to death—torn to pieces not a hundred yards from here."

"How could that be?" Roman choked. "I never heard a sound." The soldiers stood in uneasy silence.

Galapos pulled Roman to his feet, ordering, "We'll start a new search from this point. Men, gather here and fan outward toward the hills. The Chataine must be around close by. Watch particularly for hidden shelters and unnatural brush. And don't waste your wind calling—she's probably unable to hear us, or unable to come if she can hear. But we'll find her. Roman?"

The Commander nodded and straightened his belt. The men moved out precisely as instructed.

Twenty feet from where they had stood was the opening of the cave in which Deirdre soundly slept.

✛

Presently, a man entered the cave stealthily and knelt beside the sleeping girl. He shook her. She awoke—somewhat—with a groan. Disoriented, she glanced from sconces to ceiling to the man's face, trying to find herself.

"Can you walk?" he whispered, tying her hands. Seeing the pearls in her hair, he studiously unwound them and stuffed them into his shirt.

She startled and twisted around. "My baby—where is the baby?"

"You be quiet, or I'll have to gag you," he warned. Deirdre gazed at him. Lifting her, he grunted, "Soldiers everywhere . . . almost got caught. . . ." He carried her out of the cave and through the forest cautiously, pausing often to glance around and listen.

He seemed so tentative, she quickly collected her resources to demand, "Where are you taking me? To that witch? Does she have my baby?"

He hissed, "Shh!" She recoiled at his breath but let him carry her quietly, feeling too weak to struggle. She glanced down at his frayed breeches contemptuously. It would be quite satisfactory to see what Roman did to him when he caught him—as surely he would.

Soon, they came upon a muddy road where he placed her in a waiting cart. He tied her hands to an iron ring, then climbed up in front and clucked to the bony horse, slapping the reins.

The cart lurched forward, and Deirdre screamed, "Where are you taking me?" He turned abruptly and made as if to slap her. Cringing back, she tried a new tack: "My father is the Surchatain. He'll reward you well for my safe return to the palace!"

He glanced back at her in amusement, slapping the horse to pull out of the mud. Silenced by his manner and the noise of the cart, she rode warily, biding her time, until finally he slowed. Then she insisted, "State your price. He'll pay it!"

"Beg pardon, lady," he said sarcastically, "but I'm about to be paid." She then saw a dark figure on horseback waiting in the shadows of the trees ahead. A renegade soldier.

Deirdre's captor halted the cart in the road twenty paces off, but the renegade only lifted his chin. After some uncertainty, the driver prompted his skinny horse to the shelter of the trees.

The renegade then got down from his horse and walked over to scrutinize Deirdre. She shrank back at the smell of him—*are Roman and Galapos the only men who ever bother to bathe?*

He grunted, "Twenty royals and five pieces."

Her driver huffed, "That's a crock! I could get thirty royals for her from the first man I met in Corona!"

"Twenty and fifteen," offered the renegade.

"Twenty and forty," countered the driver.

"Twenty and twenty. That's all I'll put out for such risky business," the renegade grunted.

"Twenty and twenty, then," sighed the driver. He waited with the look of a man who had been cheated out of a fortune while the other counted out the purchase price into his palm.

Then the driver loosened Deirdre's hands from the iron ring and turned her over to the soldier, who retied her hands with a length of rope to his saddle. He mounted wordlessly and kicked his horse, leaving Deirdre to stumble along in shock behind him.

"Please, please," she began, "I've just had a baby . . . please at least let me ride." He did not so much as shift to look back at her.

As Deirdre half walked, half trotted behind her new captor, blackness kept crossing her vision and her knees kept giving way. Feeling that sickly cold twinge that precedes a faint, she fought to retain consciousness lest she be dragged.

Dimly remembering how Roman was delivered from Tremaine through prayer, she prayed urgently for deliverance herself: *God, help me!* Gradually, her sight cleared and she walked steadily, watching intently for some sign of a rescue in answer to her prayer.

She walked for hours staring at the flanks of that horse. "I'm thirsty," she said at length. The renegade did not slow. "I'm thirsty!" she shouted desperately. "How much will you get for me if you walk me to death?"

He cast a backward glance at her and grudgingly stopped. Then he extended a small flask toward her. She grabbed it and uncorked it, swilling the cheap wine. He jerked it away before she could drink it all.

While he allowed her to rest, she calmly considered what to do. Sitting straight in the saddle, he had the look of a fallen officer—one who had honor, at one time, before something or someone had taken it away. Perhaps she could appeal to that lost honor. "Do you know who I am?" she ventured. "I am the daughter of Surchatain Galapos."

"So?" he growled.

He seemed not to doubt her; it simply meant nothing to him. She floundered, "Well—if you return me at once—"

"Return you?" he laughed, rasping. "So he can flay me alive? Nit!" He kicked in his heels, jerking her forward for another march.

She began walking with thoughts of escape—getting the rope off, running into the surrounding forest to hide—but for all she twisted her hands, the rope would not come loose. She worked her wrists until the rope burned her, but it still held fast. The other end was unreachable, tied to his saddle. Perhaps she could get help from some brave soul they met— she kept her face up for the longest time, watching, but this was a poor, narrow road that was seldom traveled. They met up with no one, and she could think of no other way to escape.

As she walked, thinking became so hard that she gradually gave it up. Roman and Galapos became shades of an age long past. The tiny baby boy she had glimpsed was a dream. There was no reality now but the sweaty horse before her, the rutted road beneath her, and the sun climbing to its height in the sky. She lost her slippers but stumbled on blankly, kicking her skirts out from between her legs. She did not know how she continued to move one foot in front of the other, ignoring her hunger and pain.

Hours had lapsed when Deirdre raised her head briefly to see a signpost, which announced they were nearing Bresen. Bresen . . . a trade city in Goerge. When had they crossed the border? Many of the fine woolens she had bought at the Fair had come from Bresen.

Her attention revived as they began to pass huts and cultivated fields. Surely someone would see her and help her! Her heart jumped when she spotted a peasant farmer driving an empty cart toward them. As he drew closer, she stared at him with intense, pleading eyes, but he ran his cart off the road rather than crowd the soldier, and never looked up at either him or her.

As they passed more people, Deirdre began to notice a pattern in their discreet avoidance of the soldier. They made way for him on the road, running their own animals off the shoulder if necessary, but they never risked looking at him directly. And they gave her no more notice than if she were a natural appendage of the horse.

Soon, soldier and captive entered the entrails of the city. To Deirdre, it looked no different from Corona—dirty and crowded. Abruptly, the renegade turned off the road to a large tent. He untied the rope from his saddle and led her inside.

The stale, rank air within the tent made her stomach churn. Or was it the sight that sickened her?—rows of people chained to posts while buyers strolled up and down the aisles, surveying the merchandise.

A trader was saying to the soldier, "She looks pale. You sure she's healthy?"

"Sure, sure. She just birthed," he grunted.

"You say? You have the baby?" the merchant asked eagerly.

"No, but she's good for more."

The merchant looked her over closer while she glared at him. "Good hair," he muttered, then forced open her mouth to look at her teeth. "Yeah, good teeth. So what do you want for her?" he asked. Deirdre drew back, stinging with humiliation.

"Forty royals," stated the renegade, adding, "I paid thirty-five for her."

"I wouldn't give forty royals for my own mother!" spat the merchant. "Give you thirty-seven and twenty pieces."

"Thirty-eight and twenty."

"Thirty-eight. That's all I'll offer," declared the merchant.

"Taken." So the trader counted out the money to the soldier and untied the rope from Deirdre's hands. She sighed, touching her chafed wrists. But immediately he put chains on her wrists and fastened them to a post near the front.

"Please," she grabbed at him as he turned away. "I'm so hungry—I haven't eaten all day. And thirsty—!"

He grunted and left, but returned shortly with a plate of corn meal mush and a cup of warm water. "Where is the spoon?" she asked.

He contorted his face in derisive mirth, then spotted a potential buyer too freely handling nearby merchandise. "Hey, you! Hands off!"

Deirdre was left to eat the mush with her dirty fingers. She choked it down as best she could, pausing to dig out a dead beetle. But when some mush remained that she could not pick up with her fingers, she was reduced to licking the metal pan. Tears ran down her face into the pan.

When the trader returned for the pan, she pleaded, "I need to bathe."

"Look, girl, who do you think you are? The Surchataine?" he asked impatiently. Then he assumed a tone of mock obeisance. "Forgive me, lady, but we have no bath house. We can strip you and splash you down with buckets, if it pleases you."

"No!" she cringed, holding on to the post.

"Then bottle up your whining!" he roared in her face.

Deirdre gritted her teeth to stanch the tears. As the chains allowed her just to sit, she did, looking timidly around. All she could see were slaves, chained to posts as she was. They were mostly young peasants, men and women, but there were some children, too—at the sight of them, Deirdre felt a sharp pang. "Lord, how can you allow this?" she moaned. "If you won't save me, save the children, at least!"

Beaten down with exhaustion and despair, she held her

head and wept. One or two blank faces turned her way, but they turned away again. They had too much pain of their own to concern themselves with her sorrow.

Soon she became aware that someone was staring at her. She raised her face to look into the greedy eyes of an oily faced man. "Give you sixty for that one!" he offered the trader. Deirdre eyed him in disgust. It was apparent from the ragged state of his clothes that he did not have six royals to his name, much less sixty.

"Go away," motioned the trader impatiently.

"Say, who is she?" pressed the oily man. "Look at her clothes!" He gestured at her embroidered velvets. "Is she royalty?"

"Of course," the trader replied with a haughty sneer. "We have nothing but the best here."

"Give you sixty-five!" The would-be buyer reached out for her, and Deirdre fell away from him, straining the chain.

"Get out!" The trader drew out a short leather crop and whipped the man's hands fiercely. With a yelp, he backed stumbling from the tent.

Deirdre sat on the dirt floor with her eyes squeezed shut, shaking. That buyer could not afford her, but the next one might, and who could say what kind of person he would be?

In a moment she stilled, as someone else had stepped in front of her. She kept her eyes shut tight for fear of what she might see. Her curiosity proved dauntless, however, and warily she opened her eyes.

Before her stood a neat, clean-shaven palace official who carried the insignia of the late Surchatain of Goerge, Savin. This buyer was a rather handsome man with a princely bearing. "How much?" he asked the merchant.

"As you can see, this is no mere peasant we have here," the trader began. "It is rumored that she is a niece of the deceased Tremaine—"

"How much?" interrupted the official.

"One hundred royals."

"I will give you eighty."

"I can't possibly sell her for less than ninety," swore the merchant. "The babe she just birthed sold for fifty-five!"

"Eighty-five."

"Eighty-seven, and she goes with you." The merchant was paid out of a palace purse, and Deirdre changed hands again. The official led her out at arm's length to the back door of an inn, where he called the matron and gave her a few coins.

"Have her washed up and fed," he instructed, "and lodge her overnight—where, I don't care. But we leave tomorrow morning, and if she's not here, *you* will go in her place."

"No need for concern, Lord Troyce," the matron assured him hastily. "She'll be ready for you. Come here, dearie—" She closed a fat hand around Deirdre's upper arm. "Let me get you cared for."

The official departed as the matron steered Deirdre toward a back room. There, a washbasin sat filled and waiting. Deirdre gratefully undressed and bathed herself while the matron stood by, scraping dried mud and dirt from Deirdre's clothes. She held up the velvets in reserved admiration, glancing curiously at the girl washing blood from her legs.

Deirdre dried herself and began dressing as the matron stood by. Sensing something tender in her, Deirdre appealed one last time for aid: "Please, help me . . . do you know who I am?"

"It doesn't hardly matter, dearie. Whoever you *were*, now you belong to the Surchataine."

"Who?" asked Deirdre, and the matron looked at her as if she were an idiot.

"Surchataine Sheva, Savin's wife. You're to be a serving maid in her court," she said. Finding Deirdre's underskirt hopelessly soiled, the matron tossed it aside before handing her the velvet skirt.

"But Galapos rules all this territory! He defeated Savin

89

at the outpost!" Deirdre exclaimed.

"Savin is dead, true, but Galapos does not rule here. Sheva rules, and everyone serves her—if not by choice, then in chains." The matron spoke the last phrase in a whisper.

"Listen," Deirdre whispered urgently, "Galapos is my father! If you'll allow me to return to him, he'll send an army to free you from this tyrant!"

The woman laughed incredulously. "Should I stake my life on what you say? Even if you're saying the truth, and Galapos is your father, why hasn't he already sent an army to depose Sheva? Does he even have an army?"

Deirdre, confounded, did not answer, and the matron bristled, "You speak nonsense, girl. Now be quiet and come with me." She led Deirdre to the kitchen, where she gave her a bowl of soup and bread.

While Deirdre ate, the matron eyed her silently. Then she gave Deirdre a blanket and led her out to the stables. "You'll sleep here until Lord Troyce returns for you," she said gruffly. She set down her candle on a sawhorse to fasten Deirdre's slender neck into a chain hanging from an iron ring on the wall. Utterly despondent, Deirdre lowered herself to the musty straw. A horse in a nearby stall snorted mildly at the intrusion.

The matron paused. "You say you're Galapos's daughter."

"Yes, yes, I am!" cried Deirdre, at which the matron motioned vigorously for her to lower her voice. Deirdre continued in a fervent whisper: "I am Chataine Deirdre—my husband is the Commander of his army—I was kidnaped after the birth of my baby—" she began to sob.

The woman watched her, then said slowly, "There is only one thing I can do for you. If Galapos comes here looking for you, I will tell him where you are—he's been this way before and I know him. That is all I can do." Without waiting for a response, she took her candle and left Deirdre to face the night in a corner of the stables alone.

7

The matron roused Deirdre while it was still grey out-side. "Lord Troyce is here to take you to Diamond's Head." Deirdre raised herself groaning as the matron unlocked her chains. "I will do what I told you," she whispered, but Deirdre did not hear. Her whole body ached with stiffness, which was pain enough, but a new sensation commanded her attention. Her body, having successfully delivered the baby it had sheltered, had now made provision for his feeding. Her milk had come in. Her breasts were swollen hard and painful to the touch.

Deirdre was led out to a flat cart and chained to a ring in the floor with a few other passengers. Beyond them, Lord Troyce was giving instructions for the loading of goods on another cart. Deirdre glimpsed bolts of purple and silk, piles of furs, and locked wooden boxes. In a wave of envy, she noted that Sheva had money to buy the things she herself would like. Then Deirdre sighed at the absurdity of lusting after jewels while she was locked in chains.

At length, the loading was completed and a caravan consisting of the lord's carriage and the two carts left the courtyard of the inn. Escorted by a handful of soldiers, the caravan began its journey to Diamond's Head, capital of Goerge. Deirdre had never been there, but had heard others speak of it.

The palace was built on granite bluffs overlooking the Sea, and the natural defense of sheer rock cliffs made it secure from all sides. When Galapos had returned to Westford from Outpost One just this past spring, he had mentioned the disturbing possibility that Tremaine would move his headquarters from Corona to Diamond's Head. "And if that snake lodges down in that rock," he had said, "it would take fire from heaven to smoke him out."

Deirdre was grateful to be riding now instead of walking, but the pain—! She bit her lip and massaged her hard breasts. Then, self-consciously, she glanced at the other passengers, slaves like herself. One was a young peasant girl who hid her face down in her arms the length of the trip, and the other was a large, brown, muscular man, obviously destined for the Surchataine's fields. When he bared his teeth at Deirdre in a grin she quickly turned her face away, unnerved to find that he reminded her in some way of Roman.

Idly, she thought of the condemned prisoner hanged in Roman's stead—when?—years before? That man had so closely resembled Roman that on the night he killed a kitchen maid, she had been certain it was Roman she had seen. The same brown skin and straight black hair . . . the same husky build. . . . Lulled by the motion of the cart, Deirdre let her thoughts trail off into disjointed half dreams.

She glimpsed a flock of black birds flapping away from the cart, but before they reached the blue summit of sky they dipped and scolded her: "Nit! Ha, ha, ha, ha, ha!" She roused with a jerk and waved them away.

Then she was staring at the sweaty flanks of the renegade's horse. Its tail endlessly twitched, brushing away flies, which settled on her face instead. Deirdre startled up to wipe drops of perspiration from her face. She tugged at her bodice with a moan and lay down again. Unmeasured minutes later, she was jarred full awake by the cart lurching to a stop.

Lord Troyce had signaled a rest to eat, but the three slaves were not permitted to leave the cart. Rather, they were given plates of mash to eat where they sat. Deirdre devoured hers, as did the man slave, but the girl refused to eat. When the man observed that, he amiably reached over and helped himself from her plate. Deirdre glared at him, and he grinned back at her. Again that resemblance—angrily, she gave him her best haughty snub.

The jerking of the cart as they started again reminded her acutely of her swollen breasts. How she wished to be home, safe and comfortable, with her baby! The thought of the little one she might never know was so painful that she closed her mind to it immediately. If she allowed herself to think of him, to wonder what had befallen him, she would lose her sanity altogether.

Why, God, why? Why have you done this to me? Other thoughts joined in quickly: *I trusted Him, and look what happened. . . . I may never see Roman or Galapos or the baby again. . . . If I had known this was going to happen, I would never have believed in Him. . . . Roman was wrong*— at that, a cold chill swept over her. What was she thinking? During her imprisonment at Ooster, she herself had seen the bright presence that had restored her at the breaking point. Wasn't that from God? And surely God knew of her trouble now.

Perhaps yesterday when she had prayed, she had not had faith enough, had not really believed He would help her. So now she prayed intently, *God, I am hurting so. Please, please, God, rescue me!* Then she watched for the presence to appear again. In such terrible trouble as this, surely it would come!

Barely breathing, she looked over the horses to the road ahead. That was the most likely place it would appear, so the whole caravan would see it and stop. She waited.

The soldiers ahead talked among themselves. The horses jangled their bits. The cart wheels went round and round. Deirdre waited until she could stand it no longer. *Where are you, God?* she screamed inside.

Deirdre passed hour after hour riding in that wretched cart in utter misery. No help was given her. Her pain increased, and the jolting of the cart never ceased. Endlessly, they rounded curves and climbed hills. Dusty, dirty, stinking cart—she put her head down, only wanting to die.

Suddenly the road began to ascend. They climbed for some time, until the only possible route upward was a winding road that snaked up the face of the mount. After each sharp curve in the road, Deirdre could look down twenty feet to the section they had just been on. They passed a sentry station positioned at the gates of a great stone wall, then the road leveled into a paved street. They had topped the cliffs.

The caravan passed buildings and shops and houses that comprised the township of Diamond's Head. Then the palace complex of Surchataine Sheva stood majestically before them, gleaming golden in the light of the late sun. By the time the caravan had reached the front gates, the palace had turned deep red.

Lord Troyce dispatched the soldiers to unload the merchandise. Deirdre was separated from the other two slaves and taken to a dank little room in the back of what appeared to be the servants' house. Beyond caring about anything, she slumped to the floor, leaning against a wall. She only slightly noted an official talking with the soldier who had brought her in.

The official entered the room and lifted his torch toward her. She did not raise her head. Then, surprisingly, he angled the torch and spoke to the corner of her room: "Old Josef, look here." Startled, Deirdre glared toward the torch-lit corner.

A withered, white-haired slave roused out of a little pile of straw, blinking his eyes. He sat up suddenly and stared at her. Exclaiming, "Praise God!" he scrambled up and hurried from the room as fast as his crooked feet would allow. The official stood aside to let him pass.

Deirdre gazed at the official in dumb amazement. He was a thick-chested, ruddy man with a curly red beard. When his eyes met hers, she saw lines of compassion on his weathered face. "There's a babe here," he began sheepishly, "born some days ago to a slave girl who died. . . . He can't seem to take goat's milk, and there has been no one willing to nurse him. . . ." At those words Old Josef hobbled in with a ragged bundle. He held out a dirty, feebly crying newborn to her.

At the sound of his cry, Deirdre felt a sharp twinge in her breasts, and milk began to soak through her bodice. She took the baby and opened her blouse without a second thought as to the men standing by. Cradling the baby in inexperienced arms, she tried to guide the nipple into his mouth, but the moment she touched his face he began rooting so frantically that he kept overshooting it.

The old man said softly, "Hold still at his cheek and let him find you." The babe latched on and began sucking mightily. Deirdre sighed, feeling rapid relief. Old Josef stepped back with a radiant smile. The official nodded and left.

Josef, beaming, stretched his hands toward heaven and said, "Lord God, how excellent is your name in all the earth! You hear the humble and defend the orphans—excellent, excellent, Lord! How I rejoice in your splendor and revel in your freedom! How I glory in your riches and treasures! Power, wisdom, and honor, forever, forever, Lord!"

Deirdre gaped at the exultant old man and thought, *They have put me in here with a madman*. Suddenly he looked directly at her. She quickly lowered her eyes to the nursing infant.

He said serenely, "I have prayed for a nursemaid that the baby might not die. You are the answer to my prayer."

She felt sharp tears. "Then God answered your prayer by taking away my own baby!"

"Your child is dead?"

"Well—probably. I don't know. I don't know what has become of him!" she said, anguished.

"Then I will inquire." He carefully knelt and closed his eyes in silent, earnest prayer. Deirdre watched skeptically. In a few minutes he straightened and said, "Your baby is healthy and in good care."

"How do you know that?"

"The Lord showed me your child in the arms of a black-haired warrior. Behind him stood a great ruler," Josef replied.

Deirdre shut her mouth to keep her heart inside. The baby she was holding began suddenly to cry. Without thinking, she turned him to the other breast and he set to as before.

She watched him as she thought breathlessly of her child. He was safe—safe with Roman! She could endure anything now, knowing that.

Subdued, she looked up at Old Josef. He cocked his head at her, smiling slightly. Then he came up close and knelt on bony knees in front of her. "Child," he said softly, "I'm going to tell you something, and I want you to remember it always." He paused and she waited. "God is good," he said. "*God is good*."

At once she saw how foolish she had been to think God was torturing her like some petty despot wielding power for fun. But she fought the insight. "Then why does He let me suffer like this?" she demanded with tears.

"I don't know what has happened to you or why. But He has said, 'Behold, I have refined you, I have tried you in the furnace of affliction.' I, too, have suffered in my lifetime, child, and I know it has all been done for good."

She chewed her lip, not really understanding him. Bitterly, she rejoined, "It is not good. It's mean and cruel."

"And His servant has said of Him, 'With the faithful you show yourself faithful; with the blameless you show yourself blameless; with the pure you show yourself pure; and with the perverted you show yourself perverse. For you deliver the humble people, but the haughty eyes you bring down.'" His faded eyes were glistening with just a touch of humorous reproval.

"How do you know so much about God?" she demanded, stinging.

"I have been walking with Him for years now, and He has shown me many things. But the first thing I had to learn was that He is good and rewards those who seek Him," Josef said, laying a gnarled hand of affection on the baby's head.

"I know a man," she said, thinking of Roman, "who has followed God since he was a child, and for a long time it brought him nothing but trouble." She recalled vividly Roman taking the kidnaper's bludgeon . . . being beaten on the post . . . suffering humiliation and the sentence of death at the hands of Karel.

"I know nothing of this," he said, "but I will ask the Lord to give you insight regarding it."

What she wanted, however, was something else: "I'm so thirsty—" she began, but before she had finished speaking, the ruddy official entered with plates of meaty stew and cups of cold water. Then he knelt before the old man and fastened irons on his ankles. The length of the chains permitted him to cross the cell, but not leave it. Deirdre gazed at the official pleadingly when he turned toward her.

"I am sorry," he said sincerely, locking chains on her

ankles. "I must do this." She mutely accepted them. What was one more insult after what she had endured?

She and Josef ate and drank while the infant slept close by, then the old man made a neat bed of straw for her. She lay down on it with the baby tucked beside her and the chains kicked out of her way. Old Josef covered her with the thin blanket he had been using.

As sleep crept upon her, Roman entered her thoughts and she saw him once again gripping the cold chains of the whipping post, silently taking blow after blow. Suddenly she saw something else as if superimposed over the memory— the love, the love in him that poured itself out for her more readily than the blood from his wounds.

She sat up, gasping. It was a demonstration of love— every blow he took, every insult he endured was drawn from a boundless well of sacrificial love.

Tears rolled down her face as she saw the cheapness of her own affection in contrast. There was no love without sacrifice, without self-giving. And he had been willing to give up his life for her.

She lay down again, weeping for him now, and Josef knew insight had been given her.

8

"Here, Commander." Kam tossed the brush aside from the cavern mouth so he and Roman could step inside. They studied the interior grimly. "She was here, for certain," continued the captain, picking up a blanket.

Roman was examining the dirt floor. "Too many prints . . . but look at these—a man's. . . ." He halted abruptly and knelt to touch the earth. "They are deeper here, leaving, than those entering. It appears she was carried out."

The two men stepped outside the cave again, intently searching the ground, but whatever prints there once were had been obliterated, in part by the search party. Roman stopped at a dead end. He scanned the ground around in all directions. Kam stood silently, stroking his beard and eyeing Roman.

"Commander," he said hesitantly, "I see nothing more that can be done—"

Roman turned on him with a vengeance. "We'll send scouts to every city and village and hut on the Continent to

99

find her."

"Certainly, Commander. But . . . we have so few men to begin with . . . it may require some time—"

"Then dispatch them immediately!" Roman barked.

"Yes, Commander!" Kam saluted and hurried to his horse. He rode back to the palace with all due speed, yet shaking his head over the futility of further search.

Roman mounted and rode aimlessly through the forest, looking everywhere but seeing nothing. For the first time in his life, he was tasting the bitter draught of real, undeniable defeat. To lose her, of all, whom he loved more than his own life. Why had God given him this treasure only to take her away from him again?

The irony of it was terrible. How many times before had he rescued her? How many times had God strengthened his hand to protect her? Here was the perplexity that gnawed at him: Why had God deserted him now? And what evil had He allowed to befall her?

Roman stopped dead at a crossroads—not in the forest, but in his mind. It was a choice presented without words or images: Would he pray to God or accuse Him? Did he believe God was Master in even this or not? Would he admit his despair or maintain his facade of self-sufficiency?

Seconds passed as he was frozen in thought. Suddenly he realized there was a clearing ahead. He pushed the silent choice aside and rode blankly toward the gap in the forest. A small hut stood there. Tied to a stake in the ground near it was Deirdre's mare. How had they possibly missed this hut in their search?

He slowly got down from his horse, recalling in a flash this hut and who lived there. Then he set his jaw and strode to the door. Ignoring niceties, he thrust it open. Inside, the sorceress Varela sat at a crude table crushing herbs.

"Where is she?" he demanded.

"Gone. And you will never find her without my help,"

she replied, not looking up.

Roman drew his sword in a fit of anger. "I am here now, witch, and you will tell me where she is."

"Will you slay me, O warrior?" she chuckled sarcastically. "Nonetheless, I will tell you that, and more. Your wife has been taken to Corona. She has gone to join the Surchatain of Lystra, who will soon regain his rightful throne."

"Surchatain of Lystra . . . ?" muttered Roman.

"Karel, the true Surchatain. He is not dead, as you assume. Oh no! He is planning his revenge. It is a certainty that Galapos will die within the year, and the rightful Surchatain will reign," she predicted.

A chill ran down Roman's spine. He turned away in agitation, then hesitated. "Tell me she went willingly to join him, and I'll know you're full of lies."

Varela smiled. "She did not go willingly, but she will gladly stay to receive a husband of *legitimate* royalty," she replied, unerringly hitting the most vulnerable spot.

Roman stared as the urge to kill her surged up in him. Appalled at himself, he withdrew backwards from her hut. Mounting, he noted with dry satisfaction that Lady Grey had freed herself from the post and run off.

Roman rode back toward the palace slowly at first. Then, setting his mind, he urged the Bay Hunter on to such a pace that, upon arriving, the horse was in a lather. He shouted orders into the kitchen for provisions and was rushing to gather gear when he collided with the Surchatain.

"Whoa, son!" Galapos exclaimed, holding his shoulders. Seeing his dark face, he asked, "Where are you going?"

"To Corona," Roman answered, winded. "To get Deirdre."

"Wait, now, just wait." Galapos seriously turned him aside. "That is lawless and dangerous country now, son. The renegades have made a hell of the place. What makes you think she's in Corona?"

"She's there," insisted Roman, "and Karel is also. He's

plotting your overthrow, Galapos!"

The Surchatain's mouth dropped open, and his eyebrows gathered in a scowl. "What—? Roman, at the outpost, Tremaine himself announced that Karel was dead, remember? Do you think he would have made a mistake about that? Don't you know he would make sure of it? Think, son!"

Roman set his face stubbornly and would not answer. Galapos asked quietly, "Who told you Deirdre was in Corona?" Again Roman was silent, and Galapos added, even more gently, "I think you have been ill advised, my son."

Roman loosened. "Perhaps. But I must go, on the outside chance that she *is* there. . . . I must find out. . . ."

Galapos studied his face, then released him in resignation. "I see that you must, and I'm sorry. God go with you, son."

Roman lowered his eyes and turned away.

Before departing, he stopped in the half-finished nursery. The nursemaid, Gusta, had just laid his son down to sleep. Roman caressed the tiny head and whispered, "I must leave you now, son, but I will return and bring your mother with me." He leaned over and kissed the fine black hair. "Farewell."

On his way out the double doors, he was stopped by Basil. "The Surchatain tells me you believe Deirdre is in Corona."

"She may be. I'm going to find out," Roman said crisply.

"Then you'll need this." Basil handed him a sturdy pouch. "It's the last hundred royals from the treasury, which I held back for a crisis. Spend it carefully, Roman—and good journey."

"Counselor . . . thank you," said Roman, touched. Looking at Basil, the thought occurred to him, *Is it worth it?* He left with downcast eyes.

Galapos stood watching from the window in the northern tower as Roman rode out of the gates alone. He closed his eyes as if deep in thought, but now and then a whispered plea escaped.

Kam entered the room quietly. "Surchatain," Kam began, "the Chataine's horse has just trotted up to the rear gate unridden. We've no idea where she came from." Galapos merely nodded. Kam continued, "How many men shall I send out to search for her?"

Galapos shifted. "How many would *you* say, Kam?"

He cleared his throat. "Well, Surchatain, I would send a hundred . . . if I thought there was any chance of them finding her."

Galapos nodded. "Send two to the east, two to the west, and two following Roman to Corona. Dress them as peasants and have them conceal their weapons under their clothing. They're to alarm no one, nor is Roman to know he's being followed, except if his life is in peril."

"Yes, Surchatain." Kam bowed and left to carry out the orders.

Galapos stood still watching the point on the earth where the forest had swallowed Roman. His eyes were distant and sad. Shaking his head, he murmured, "I don't know why, but I am certain I will not see him on this earth again."

❖

Deirdre came to groggily at the baby's first cry and put him to her breast. Hungry again! It seemed she had fed him at every hour during the night. She yawned and turned her head. Just enough morning light filtered through a shuttered window for her to see that Old Josef was gone.

Shivering, she pulled the lightweight blanket over her and the baby. The air was chilly—winter would soon be coming. How could she spend the winter in this nasty little cell? She would die of cold. Deirdre sniffled, wiping her nose. *I'm already becoming ill*, she fretted. She grimaced, remembering her miserable experience with the villagers' disease.

The door creaked open, and Old Josef hobbled in. "Ah, good! You're awake." He set a warm bowl of mush and a cup of milk before her. "Sevter got the milk from the kitchen," he chuckled. "He knew you would need it."

"Thank you." She gratefully drank it down. "I *was* thirsty—I seem to be thirsty all the time . . . Sevter?"

"The official who was here last night. He is palace overseer, in charge of the domestic slaves."

"Domestic slaves?" *Is that what I am?* she thought in horror.

"Those who work in the palace and stables. We're fortunate God has placed him over us. He is a just and kind man," Josef said, settling down to the straw. His ankles were cruelly bent and knotted, and he unconsciously stroked them as he sat.

"If he's so kind, why doesn't he release us?" she asked bitterly. She stuck her fingers into the mush over the orphan.

"Why, child, Sheva would execute him for such folly, and put who knows what in his place. And you and I, when we were caught, would be flogged and put out to work in the fields." He picked up a skimpy pan of mush to eat as he talked. "You would not survive a day's work in the fields. The official over the field slaves is a blood-loving beast. His name is Caranoe. Don't cross him at any time. By the by, what is your name?"

"I am Chataine Deirdre, daughter of Surchatain Galapos of Lystra," she recited almost as if to convince herself.

The old man paused in astonishment with food on his fingers halfway to his mouth. "You are! That is most strange. . . . Does Lord Troyce—the administrator who bought you—know that?"

"No, I don't think he does," Deirdre said.

"Well and good," he breathed. "Don't tell anyone who you are! If it were known, you would suffer greatly. Sheva hates Galapos with all the will she possesses. If she knew she had his daughter as a slave. . . . How did you fall into slavery?" The fingers with the mush went into his mouth now.

"I was kidnaped after my baby was born." Placing the bowl on the straw, she lifted the fussing child to her shoulder. "I was sold so many times, I lost count. . . ." She fell silent, and Josef eyed her keenly.

"God's hand is largely in this," he observed.

"How can you say that?" she cried. "Do you know how much I've suffered? What my father and my husband must be going through?"

He shook his white head resolutely. "The path you are walking now has been carefully smoothed and paved for you. I'm sure you have suffered, but look—you are unscathed. You are a slave, unfortunately, but under the kindest slavemaster who ever lived. No—God is protecting you on all fronts in this matter. You must trust His care." For some reason Deirdre thought of the would-be buyer who preceded Lord Troyce.

At that point, Sevter opened the door and said, "Josef, your duties wait." The old man nodded and got to his feet with some difficulty. To Deirdre, Sevter said, "I've arranged for you to do nothing but rest and nurse for a few days before your service begins."

Josef glanced back at her with a knowing smile, then turned to Sevter and said in a low voice, "We must speak."

Left alone with the baby, Deirdre lay down again wearily and tried to untangle her thoughts. Was God with her? But why then had He allowed her to experience such misery? Her thoughts ran together in confusion, and soon she was deep in sleep.

❖

Deirdre had a dream in which she was sitting alone and abandoned in the midst of a wretched grey wasteland. There was no sun in the sky and no living thing in sight. Strange, cold winds howled around her, blowing dead grasses and gritty sand. She huddled, frightened of some nameless evil in the air.

Suddenly Deirdre was aware of light coming from one side—there was warmth, too. She turned and beheld the most wonderful warrior she had ever seen. His face was hidden in blazing light. His clothes were white and his golden breastplate gleamed fiery red. In his right hand he carried a formidable, two-edged sword.

Her heart leaped when he held out his left hand toward her and spoke her name: "Deirdre." His voice was soft, yet so piercing that it reverberated through her. "Come walk with me."

She sprang to her feet to take his hand. He began to lead her down a winding, rocky trail that she had not seen from where she was sitting. "To walk with me, you must not leave the path," he said.

"Who are you?" she asked.

"I am Faithful and True."

As she walked at his side, holding tightly to his hand, she saw that he used his sword to clear the path before them. He brushed aside large, sharp rocks and hissing snakes. Yet when they came to a boulder that completely obstructed the path, they stopped. As Deirdre looked at that rock, it seemed to grow larger and larger, filling her vision until it threatened to crush her.

Terrified, she whirled to plead with the warrior. But she had hardly spoken when he bent down and lifted her over it effortlessly. Once past it, she looked back and saw that the rock was actually no larger than a loaf of bread.

Walking with him was pleasant, and soon Deirdre saw grasses and flowers growing tenderly along the path. Then she noticed that no matter how hard she peered, she could not see the road ahead more than a few feet at a time.

"Where are we going?"

"To the mountain." He pointed with his sword, and Deirdre saw in the far distance a shimmering purple mountain that radiated light and life. But the path unexpectedly veered away here and there to the left or the right.

"Surely there's an easier way to get there," she grumbled.

"There is no other way," he said.

Deirdre sighed and looked around. This was all well and good, but she was tiring. All at once she spotted a lovely willow grove on the shore of a lake—why, it was her lake! She so wanted to go lie down. But he had said she must not leave the path.

Timidly, she looked to him again, and as she gazed, she felt strength and refreshment flow from him as profusely as the light. She forgot the lake entirely. She never wanted to leave him.

From nowhere she heard a precious, familiar voice calling her name: "Deirdre! Deirdre!" Roman! He was standing just forty feet away, beside the willow trees.

"Roman!" She rushed to his outstretched arms. But instantly he and the grove melted away into black shadows. All was desolate again, as before, but now the shadows were dancing around her. "Roman!" she sobbed. "Where are you?" He was not to be found, only the shadows closed in on her.

She cried out and blindly reached for the warrior. As she did, she felt his strong hand take hers. Opening her eyes, she saw him shattering the shadows into pieces with his sword. Immediately she was back safely on the road with him.

"Why did you leave me?" she gasped.

"I warned you not to leave the path. Yet even then I did not leave you, but you didn't know it until you reached for me," he said.

They continued on, and Deirdre clung tightly to his hand.

Yet the cinders in the path were sharp and hurt her feet. And she noticed too that now, the warrior did not brush aside every obstacle. Some she stumbled over, others tripped her up, although he never let her fall. She complained, "My feet hurt! Why won't you clear the path for me?"

"Little one," he said, "if I remove every pebble in the path, there will be no road left for you to walk on. And look! Our destination is near."

Deirdre raised her eyes, and the mountain burned with a radiance that almost blinded her. She squinted and blinked awake as the sun struck her face through the shutters of the little room.

❖

Deirdre rubbed her eyes, trying to hold on to the fading brilliance of the dream, at the same time Sevter entered to unfasten her leg shackles. "You may go outside for a moment and have yourself a look around," he said. "Don't wander far, and don't hinder anyone's work."

She nodded, sleepy, stiff, and sore. But she found her legs still held her up, so she slipped shyly out into the corridor behind him, leaving the baby in the straw.

Outside, she blinked in the brightness of the morning. From this side of the servants' house, she could see stables and a barn, and pens for the animals. Servants buzzed all around, working. One girl left the henhouse carrying a basket of eggs to the palace. Several men were laying posts for another pen. Nearby, another fellow was butchering a pig.

Deirdre grimaced and edged away, in the direction of the palace. In the midst of the courtyard she caught sight of a massive gallows. *Someone must be scheduled for an execution*, she thought uneasily.

Shying away from that area, she walked to the front of the servants' house and looked over the fence on its northeast corner. An orchard! *How lovely*. And from where she stood she could see fruit hanging heavy on the branches. She slipped over the fence to the nearest tree and picked up an apple that lay under it.

"You want to be hanged, or what?" She wheeled at the surly voice behind her. A soldier reached over and plucked the apple from her fingers.

"I—I'm hungry," she said pleadingly.

"You won't ever be hungry again if they hang you. Don't be stupid, and don't steal food."

"I'm sorry," she said, the tears coming readily. "I didn't know it was stealing. I won't do it again."

"I'll be silent this time, kitten, but you owe me." He leaned over and gave her a solid whap on the rear before turning away.

Deirdre, shocked to her bones, stood immobilized as two servants with bushels passed her on their way to the palace, eyeing her velvets curiously. Then she roused and fled back to the little room.

Safe within its narrow walls, she plopped down in the straw. The baby jerked his arms outward and turned his face toward her. She leaned over him, then, to study him more closely.

Such a scrawny thing he was, with his tummy all distended. He had wide-set brown eyes and sparse, light brown hair. And so dirty! She moistened a finger and wiped a clean streak on his tiny cheek. "Poor thing," she cooed, touching his palm. His little hand closed on her forefinger and held it while she wriggled it back and forth delightedly.

Her eyes fell on the rags he was wrapped in. They were rough and heavy with imbedded soil. He sorely needed cleaning up. While she was pondering this, Old Josef poked his head in the door. "Are you resting, child?"

She leaned back toward him. "Josef, this poor baby needs to be bathed!"

109

His grey eyebrows arched as he considered this problem. "Let's see what can be done," he said, and was gone.

In a short while, he returned with a small basin and some rags. Water slopped out as he struggled to lower the basin to the floor without spilling it all. "I have brought you wash water, a cloth to wash him, and a new cloth to wrap him in." Leaving those items, he was gone again.

Deirdre gingerly unwound the dirty wrap and tossed it aside with disgust. She dipped the small bit of rag in the warm water and carefully rubbed the baby's splotchy skin. He waved his tiny arms and fussed, but she scrubbed him gently all over, until his whole body was clean and pink. Then she wrapped him up snugly in the large cloth and cradled him. He closed his eyes.

"Now you smell rather human," she declared, kissing the top of his tender head. Almost immediately she felt something warm and wet, and dismally looked to see that her accomplishment was manifestly short-lived.

Sevter creaked open the door to her little room and unlocked her leg chains. "Deirdre . . . it has been three days since you arrived. . . . I can no longer justify treating you with special favor. You must begin your service this morning."

He helped her rise, and Josef crossed the room crookedly to join them. "Sevter we can trust, and I told him who you are. But we must not allow anyone else the suspicion that you are someone of importance. It will be hard, I know, but your life hangs on it," Josef said gently. He gave her a plain little servant's dress. "You will need to wear this."

Deirdre regarded the servant's dress, then glanced downward at the tattered, soiled remains of her costly velvets. "What will you do with these?" she murmured.

Josef's face contorted in amused sympathy. "My child . . . they must be burned." She sighed.

Sevter left them, and Deirdre undressed behind Josef's back. Stoically, she surrendered the velvets and stepped into the thin, drab servant's dress. It was very similar to the little dress Roman had made her wear for their trip to Corona—*Roman! Forgive me for making you leave me at the lake!* she cried inwardly, momentarily collapsing with grief. But then she straightened and said, "I'm ready."

"Bring the child," Josef nodded before leading her out toward the palace kitchen.

On their way through the courtyard, she took a closer look at the gallows. A permanent structure, not built solely for one execution, it showed signs of wear and age. Noticing her gaze, Josef explained, "Sheva uses it often."

As they entered the buzzing kitchen she whispered, "What am I to do with this baby?"

"He is your first concern, over all your other responsibilities," he replied. "Here—I will set up a box bed for him in the corner to sleep while you work." Before doing that, he humbly approached a large woman in a large apron to ask permission. The kitchen mistress glanced at Deirdre and the baby and gestured her leave. Soon after Josef had found a discarded produce box and old cloths, the baby was tucked snugly in his little corner bed. Deirdre smoothed his sparse hairs lovingly.

"One more thing," Josef whispered. "Do exactly as you're told—don't argue or fight. If you just do your work, you'll get along fine. And remember—God is with you." He patted her arm before hurrying off.

Deirdre turned uncertainly toward the head cook, who was occupied pounding meats and barking at the other servants. While waiting for instructions, fidgeting nervously, Deirdre surveyed the kitchen.

It was a small room compared to the kitchen at Westford, having only a few tables and benches at which the servants worked. This kitchen was not intended for additional use as a dining hall. Its floor was good, smooth wood. Its walls were plaster, hung with many shiny pots and cooking utensils.

One whole side of the room was stone; it contained a large open fireplace and beside it a deep oven. There were shuttered windows for ventilation along the wall that faced the courtyard. Deirdre pressed her shoulder in anxiety against this wall as she waited.

After a few minutes, the mistress tossed a paring knife toward her and nodded at a large basket of potatoes: "You start washing and peeling 'em." Deirdre stared at the yard-wide basket. Tentatively, she picked up a spud and fingered it. Now how was this done? The head cook glanced at her and barked, "Don't dawdle! Get to it!"

"Will you show me how?" Deirdre asked politely.

The mistress glared at her. "Are you an idiot?"

"No!" Deirdre flared back. "I am—" she started to spill out what Josef had earnestly warned her to keep secret. Biting her tongue, she surrendered the last vestige of pride and said, "We never peeled them . . . we ate them whole . . . we were too poor to throw anything out."

The cook's anger dissipated, but not her impatience. She seized a potato and thrust it under Deirdre's nose. "This is a potato! You hold it like this, and wash it like this—" She plunged it in a basin of water and rubbed it. "Then you take the knife like this, and peel it"—illustrating with rapid strokes. "Then you rinse it again and put it in this basket. Can you do that?"

Her face burning, Deirdre said, "Yes."

"Yes, *what?*" the mistress demanded. Deirdre stared, uncomprehending. "Yes, *mistress!*" shouted the woman. "Say it!"

"Yes mistress!" Deirdre blurted. The cook turned away in time to catch another servant committing some incredible blunder, and Deirdre turned in shock to the potatoes. She began rinsing and peeling carefully.

As an afterthought, the head cook said over her shoulder, "Save the peelings. They're fed to the druds."

"Yes mistress," Deirdre answered quickly, having not the vaguest idea what a drud was.

After scraping clean the third potato, she timidly inquired, "Mistress, how many of these am I to do?"

"All of them, of course," the cook answered from her oven. Deirdre looked miserably at the basket. This could take her the rest of her life. Bleakly, she picked up another potato.

As she worked, she observed the kitchen bustle. At home she had never once helped prepare a meal—that work was utterly beneath her. But she did not wish to get tripped up by her ignorance again, so she covertly watched everything the others did around her.

The kitchen mistress was high-strung by nature and short-tempered with everyone. A lesser cook who came back from market with the wrong variety of grapes received a caustic lecture. A servant who had neglected to pluck the chickens thoroughly enough got a kick in the rear. No one did anything exactly to suit her.

As she was scolding another servant for his carelessness in handling the venison, the rear kitchen door opened and all the bustle suddenly stilled. The mistress turned. "Why, Lord Caranoe," she faltered in surprise. Deirdre raised her head and found herself staring into the sharp eyes of a wiry, dark-haired man. She deliberately resumed peeling.

"Come in, come in, lord," begged the head cook. Deirdre marveled at the change in her voice. "What do you wish, lord? Pastry, perhaps, or—" She was cut off as he raised his hand impatiently and stepped toward Deirdre.

"You have the garbage?" he asked Deirdre curtly. She had no idea what he meant.

But the mistress quickly collected all the peelings and skins and pits and handed a basketful to him. "That's all we have now, Lord Caranoe—you usually send someone for them later—"

114

"Then that's all they will get," he said coldly. "What is your name, Goldie?"

Deirdre glanced up and murmured, "Goldie. That's my name."

"You will come sleep with me tonight, Goldie," he ordered.

"Forgive me, Lord Caranoe," she sputtered, "but I have been charged with the care of the baby." She pointed toward the box bed. He glanced at the bed and pursed his lips, but did not make an issue of it—for now.

Taking up the basket, he strode out, and Deirdre relaxed in relief. She realized she had been holding her breath.

A short while later the baby awoke with a lusty cry for milk. Deirdre paused with a half-peeled potato in hand, looking uncertainly to the kitchen mistress. The woman jerked her head toward him and demanded, "Go make him be quiet!"

"Yes, mistress," Deirdre answered willingly, throwing the potato and the knife down in the basket. She sat with the baby in the corner of the kitchen to nurse him, whispering, "It's a blessing to have you, little one. Now, what shall I name you?" Her first desire was to call him Roman, but she could not even think the name without a heartache. Besides, someone here who saw her good clothes might know the name of the Commander of Galapos's army and question her choice of that name.

So she probed her brain for another good name. She recalled a boy from a time before Roman had become her guardian. He was the son of a tradesman who had been invited to the palace to show his craft . . . a handsome, smiling boy with bashful brown eyes. . . .

"Your name is Arund," she declared, breaking into a flirtatious smile. A moment's thought dispelled the smile. "You are Arund and I am Goldie—two sojourners in a wretched land," she sighed. Arund merely closed his eyes, utterly unaware of their perilous situation. Her warmth and milk provided all the security he needed.

As he nursed, a serving girl paused to watch. Deirdre did not look up until the girl squatted beside her and smiled. "So your name is Goldie. I'm Bettina." Deirdre nodded and the girl folded her legs beneath her to sit more comfortably. She had very curly brown hair, an angular face with a sprinkling of freckles, and blue-grey eyes. She was an attractive girl mostly because of her friendly demeanor.

"There's been a lot of talk going on about you," Bettina continued. "Some of the others were complaining that you weren't working. Not me, though. I remember how I felt when I first got here."

Deirdre smiled, as the girl did not look any older than herself. "How long have you been here?" Deirdre asked.

"Over a year. They conscripted my husband into Savin's army when they passed through our village. They brought me here."

Listening, Deirdre shifted Arund, then muttered in dismay to find that he had soiled his wraps again. "How do I keep him clean?" she complained.

Bettina smiled. "Wait here." She left Deirdre sitting in the corner and returned in a few moments with an armload of discarded cloths. "Use these." Deirdre removed the soiled wrap and wiped the baby clean, then Bettina showed her how to wrap a clean cloth more snugly around his bottom.

That done, Deirdre gingerly picked up the dirty cloth and began to toss it in a corner when the mistress stopped over her, glaring. Bettina quickly said, "No, Goldie—out here." She led Deirdre outside, telling her, "Pile the dirty things here until you have a chance to wash them out. Don't pile them in the kitchen—the mistress will slay you!"

Deirdre believed her. "Where do I wash them?" she asked.

"Here." Bettina took her around the courtyard to show

her a stream that formed a boundary to the palace grounds. Ten feet at its widest, and not more than a few feet deep, it nonetheless flowed with great energy toward the edge of the cliffs. There it cascaded down in a silvery waterfall several hundred feet to the Sea.

Deirdre knelt to let the water cover her fingers. "It's warm!" she exclaimed.

"It springs steaming from the rocks just inside the great wall," said Bettina, pointing to a source she could not see. "If it weren't for the springs, no one could live on these cliffs. The rains are frequent enough, but the water all runs down to the valleys. With the springs, though, they've made these rocks into a garden." She gestured again, and Deirdre looked out across wide, terraced fields newly harvested, thick orchards, and green pastures on the upper slopes of the mount. Across the stream, directly in front of her, she could see up close one of the many irrigation trenches feeding the fields from the stream. Deirdre was not sufficiently mature at this time to realize the amount of hard labor represented by such a scheme.

Bettina resumed, "Wash the baby's wraps here and spread them on the rock wall to dry, or dry them on the hearth in the kitchen if the mistress isn't there."

By this time, Bettina's kindness had melted all Deirdre's sense of superiority toward her. "Thank you for showing me these things. . . . I've never had to do all this at once, when I don't know how to do any of it." Her throat tightened as she considered her miserable state.

Bettina squeezed her arm in gentle understanding. "We'd better go back in now."

Deirdre stood by in the kitchen as the noon meal was quickly prepared for the palace courtiers. She gleaned that the Surchataine was out inspecting some property and not expected to return until the dinner hour.

Then Deirdre watched as servants took dishes and

goblets through large double doors leading into the banquet hall. By standing at just the right spot, she could see through the door to a room with whitewashed walls and silver wainscoting. The candelabra on the great table were also highly polished silver. From an area beyond the table, she heard the voices of those entering the hall.

"Goldie!" barked the head cook, snapping Deirdre's attention from the other room.

"Yes, mistress?" she asked meekly.

"Are the potatoes finished?" the cook demanded, standing over the quarter-empty bushel.

"They will be soon, mistress," Deirdre promised, quickly retrieving the knife.

As Deirdre resumed paring, Bettina joined her with a bushel of greens to wash. Deirdre murmured, "Is this going to feed all the courtiers and soldiers?"

"Oh, *we* don't prepare meals for the soldiers," Bettina said with condescension. "They and the servants are fed from their own kitchen, off the barracks. We fix only for the Surchataine's table."

"Oh," Deirdre said, wondering why it wasn't done that way at Westford.

When finally she dropped the last clean potato into the basket, she turned triumphantly to the head cook, expecting a word of approval on the work done. But the cook merely glanced over and ordered, "Now, finish plucking and cleaning the birds," jerking her head toward a dozen headless chickens sparsely covered with down. Deirdre stared at them in horror.

"Don't tell me"—the cook slapped down her ladle—"you don't know how! No, never mind, I can't show you now! Here—grind the flour—like this, you twit! Are you watching?" A red-faced Deirdre intently observed the cook's demonstration.

Deirdre's ignorance brought blessing, however, in that

the mistress quickly realized she must teach this girl everything from the most basic level. Once Deirdre learned to do a task, she did it exactly as instructed, and brought no more criticism down on her head. In that way she escaped much of the harsher treatment other servants received.

Also, Deirdre discovered that whenever Arund cried, she was allowed to stop whatever she was doing to attend him. No one interfered when she nursed him. Having responsibility for him gave her a measure of control in her strange new life, and as she found, a reason to accept the beginning of each day without sinking into despair.

The pace in the kitchen, along with the head cook's outbursts, intensified as the dinner hour drew near. Silver plates and dishes were carefully set out even before the first guest arrived at table. Deirdre strained to glimpse through the doors as sounds of voices and knocking chairs indicated the guests were taking their places. Then a serving girl appeared from the hall to inform the mistress, "The Surchataine is seated."

The mistress motioned to a manservant, who carried out a large tray with an assortment of rare wines and ale. Following him, two servants carried out bowls of soup and loaves of fresh-baked bread.

The mistress put finishing garnishes on two dishes and motioned to Deirdre. "Goldie—you and Bettina take these out one at a time, and set them before the Surchataine. Bow before you put them on the table and bow afterwards. Then stand behind her chair and wait for orders. Watch her closely—she'll only lift a finger or glance toward you. And do not presume to say a word!"

Deirdre nodded and carried out a large platter of seasoned rice. She was hungry, and its aroma steamed in her face. She paused apprehensively as her stomach rumbled. Bettina nudged her from behind, and they entered the banquet hall.

Twenty-five men and women sat around a long table, talking and laughing among themselves. They were all dressed in fine clothes, as she once had been. The candles burned cheerily, and the food smelled tantalizing.

Seized with unbearable homesickness for past happy evenings with Roman and Galapos, Deirdre closed her eyes. In an instant she saw herself rudely snubbing Roman at the table after his innocent comment. *Oh, my darling, forgive me*, she pleaded inwardly. Then sternly, she opened her eyes to face the present moment.

At the head of the table sat Sheva, the Surchataine. In Deirdre's cold estimation, she was an unremarkable woman—hollow-cheeked and brunette, with deep-set eyes. Yet her plainness faded to inconsequence beneath the majesty of her attitude and attire. Envy surged up in Deirdre to see her sit so cool and regal, wearing emeralds and a rich green velvet gown draped in plentiful folds. Deirdre bowed shakily, placed the dish in front of her, bowed again, and stepped back. Bettina did likewise.

As the Surchataine ignored the serving girls, Deirdre soon found the courage to take her eyes off Sheva and scan the table again. Lord Troyce, seated to Sheva's right, seemed to occupy most of the Surchataine's attention. Sevter was down the table, and Caranoe a chair down from him. Sevter glanced up at Deirdre to acknowledge her with a wink. Caranoe, to her relief, was directing all his energy toward a lady on his right.

After observing the guests eat for some time, Deirdre discerned that although they appeared to be enjoying themselves, at every pause they darted their eyes to the Surchataine, watching for a sign of her disposition this evening. Tension weighted every word and soured every laugh.

"Surchataine, may I speak?" implored a rotund little man a chair down from Lord Troyce. She nodded toward him. "May I say, Surchataine, how wisely and effectively you have ruled since the untimely demise of High Lord Savin. There has never been such food, such goods, such opulence in Diamond's Head!" A number of voices seconded this opinion.

Sheva only smiled. "You still wish control of the water mill, Brude?" He reddened and stammered affirmation. "I will consider it," she said.

"Thank you, Surchataine, thank you," he gushed.

"Surchataine," Lord Troyce addressed her quietly, and everyone else hushed. "Regardless of his motives, what Lord Brude says is true. You have increased our wealth considerably. Yet you must also be aware of the growing discontent and fearfulness of the population, caught between the usurers and the slave traders. I am certain my lady is aware that the slaves at the palace now outnumber the soldiers— are you not?"

"What of it?" she asked testily.

"It makes for a dangerous situation, Surchataine. There are constant rumblings among the servants—"

"You will talk to me of this later," she interrupted. "The overseers will ensure that there are no malcontents. That is the purpose of the gallows." So saying, she glanced warnings at Sevter and Caranoe.

This last icy remark hung in the air while Sheva threw a hand toward Deirdre. "Bring me the custard now." Deirdre flew to the kitchen to comply.

As she returned with a tray of desserts, her ears pricked up to hear a military official mention Galapos ruling in Lystra. Sheva impulsively uttered the vilest curse Deirdre's tender ears had ever heard. Stunned, she jiggled the tray over Sevter's shoulder, and he surreptitiously reached a hand to steady it.

Sheva was now saying, "I swear I will have vengeance on Galapos. He thinks to rule, does he? Well, he has not yet met my strength. When I am ready, Galapos will learn who is sovereign on the Continent!"

Deirdre managed to place the tray properly before the Surchataine, who took one and motioned it down the table. The custard was eaten in watchful silence as Sheva's temper cooled. Then she stood abruptly and all the rest hastily stood, whether they were finished eating or not. Lord Troyce kissed her hand while she dismissed the guests with a wave. They quickly filed out as the Surchataine and her administrator climbed the stairs together.

Deirdre watched them go until Bettina nudged her, whispering, "Better not dawdle. The mistress hates dawdling." Dazed, Deirdre turned toward the great table cluttered with dirty dishes and uneaten portions, which Bettina had already begun clearing.

"Oh!" With a breath, Deirdre hungrily snatched up a half-eaten roll from a plate.

Bettina grabbed her arm. "Are you mad? Don't touch anything!" she whispered, knocking the roll from her fingers before any of the other servants saw it.

"But I'm so hungry!" Deirdre pleaded.

"I am too!" Bettina whispered back, glancing around as she gathered plates. "But no one's allowed to eat what's left from the Surchataine's table!"

"What—what will be done with it all, then?" asked Deirdre. There was enough food left to feed ten kitchen servants.

"Whatever Sheva leaves is thrown out. No one eats it," Bettina insisted. "Clean," she ordered.

Moaning, Deirdre picked up dishes still half full of food only to throw the contents out the window, as Bettina showed her. It was the hardest exercise she had ever endured, for her stomach coiled with hunger pains. But no one dared touch the remains of the elegantly prepared dishes. Rather, Sheva's dogs clustered outside the window to snap up what they wanted and ruin the rest.

I can't believe this, Deirdre thought, watching the dogs

paw through what was too good for her to eat. *How have I been reduced to such a state? How can I endure it?* She clutched the windowsill, feeling too weak to survive another moment of this heartless exile.

But then Roman crossed her mind, and it occurred to her how proud he would be if he could see her doing this— if he could see her learning to work and taking care of Arund, suffering without complaining and staying alive to return to him someday.

She let go of the window and turned back to help Bettina clear the table.

On her second or third trip with empty plates into the kitchen, Arund let out a hungry cry. The head cook waved at her: "Go back to your room and take the brawler with you. You'll be no more use to me tonight."

"Thank you, mistress," Deirdre breathed. She gratefully bundled the baby up to take him to her little room.

Stepping outside, she met a blast of cold air. She clutched the baby tightly and ran for the shelter of the servants' house across the courtyard. She had reached out to grasp the door handle when she was shot through by a piercing cry on the open air. It intensified, then cut off suddenly. The unmistakable sound of another human in pain and death made her flesh crawl. It seemed to have come from across the field that lay beyond the stables.

She stood shivering in the gusting wind, listening but hearing nothing more. Urgently, she heaved the door open and rushed inside.

10

It was cold in Deirdre's little cell. She shook out the one thin blanket she had for herself and Arund, bleakly wondering how they would ever survive the winter there.

When Old Josef dragged in, she almost pounced on him: "Josef! It's so cold in here! How do you live here in the winter? How does anyone? Who else lives in this awful house?"

He wearily smiled at her string of questions. "The newest and lowest of the servants stay here—the others sleep in the palace. But as for us, we'll be taken care of. Sevter is coming with quilts. They're quite warming," he said. It was not until then that she saw the tray he carried held a bowl of cold soup, milk, and a crust of bread.

He set the tray before her, and she ate everything on it without wondering what he had to eat. "I wish the mistress would allow me to eat in the kitchen," she grumbled. "I get so hungry—and there is so much food!"

"Don't risk stealing, child. You'll be provided for. God knows your needs—you just must ask Him," he insisted.

Deirdre watched him settle down on the straw, rubbing his pathetic ankles. "Josef . . . at first I thought you were a madman. Now I know you're not—you really seem to have special knowledge, and you've been very kind to me. But . . . why do you keep talking about God, in your position? I mean, how long have you been a slave? And why doesn't God free you if He cares like you say He does?"

"First, Deirdre, I *am* free—freer than any ruler on earth. The chains you see don't really bind me, because I have accepted them as a means to serve my Master." At her bemused look, he explained, "I am a servant of the Most High God, Deirdre."

He shifted earnestly toward her. "Much has been happening here that you can't see, but God is about to do a mighty work, and I have been instrumental in laying the foundation for it. You'll see that God works wonderfully on behalf of those who trust Him. There is much I must teach you in so little time, because my service here is soon to end." As he spoke, he reached a rough, wrinkled hand underneath his bed of straw.

Deirdre watched him with a touch of pity before his last words sank in. "Oh! Is Sheva going to release you, then?"

"I don't know exactly how it will happen, only that it will happen soon." He withdrew a bundle of tattered pages out from under the straw and handed it to her as if it were a precious gift. "This is all I have, and it is not complete. But it is what I have been able to reconstruct from memory of the Scriptures."

She took the bundle from his trembling hand. "Read them—study them—as if your life hung on it. Don't let anyone but Sevter see them—Caranoe in particular has a hatred of the Word, and we do not wish to provoke an early fight with him. Study and pray in secret until God wishes to make known what is hidden."

The heavy door opened, and Deirdre quickly thrust the

126

bundle behind her back. But it was Sevter bringing two fat quilts. They were dirty, and smelled of dogs, but Deirdre accepted them anyway. Looking at Josef with his one thin blanket, she began to hand him a quilt but he insisted, "No—you must have both, you and the baby. This is all I need."

As Sevter fastened on his leg irons, taking care for his ankles, Josef told him, "Try to arrange for Deirdre to sleep in the palace through the winter—perhaps in the kitchen. The baby might not survive the cold." Sevter agreed, crossing over to fasten Deirdre's chains.

"Josef, what about you?" she asked anxiously.

"As I said, I will soon be done. You, though—I am burdened for your safety," Josef said. The cell was now so dark, she could hardly see his face.

"Caranoe wanted me to sleep with him tonight," recalled Deirdre.

Sevter drew up sharply. "How were you able to refuse him?"

"I told him I had been ordered to care for the baby," Deirdre said.

"Then you are the one he calls Goldie," Sevter muttered.

"Yes. I didn't tell him my real name," she said.

"Good. Good. But . . . I must go confirm your duty with Lord Troyce, so that Caranoe won't be able to force you into his bed at night. He has no patience with the squallers," Sevter said. As soon as he had Deirdre locked in, he left.

Josef turned to her again. "Child, I can't tell you how important it will be to trust God with everything—every threat, every need, every pain. Tell Him about it. Wait on Him to act."

Deirdre considered this silently. Remembering the hard hours of her trek here, she asked, "Josef, where was God when I was kidnaped? It was horrible—I was in such pain! I prayed, but nothing happened. . . ."

"Ask—continually—and you shall receive; seek—with perseverance—and you shall find; knock—repeatedly—and

127

it shall be opened to you. . . . Deirdre, what did you do when you prayed and received no answer?" he asked, a dark shape in the shadows.

She frowned, thinking. "There was nothing I could do but go on—and ask God why He wouldn't answer me!"

"Yes. You asked again and again. In your confusion and pain, you turned toward Him, stretched your arms out to Him, searched for His face. But when at last you will have emerged from this trial, you will find that you were given all the answer you needed: Himself. His silence will have brought you close to Him."

Josef shifted, and she could tell he was massaging his swollen ankles. "He is like a father teaching his child to walk. The day comes when He releases your hands and you are left to stumble about on your own. You are frightened and unsteady, but He stands close by, ready to catch you. When you do stumble exhausted into His arms, you will have begun to learn to walk. In the stretching, you grow. It must be so for your good, Deirdre."

She turned this over in her mind and suddenly thought of Roman, feeling an urgent compulsion to pray for him. But before she could, another thought intruded. "Josef, what is a drud?"

She felt him startle, then he said, "That is an insulting name for the field slaves. They belong to a race of people who come from the mountain country beyond Goerge—Polontis. They're a strong, hardy people, but unlearned in our ways, so Sheva has exploited them to slavery in her fields." He stopped, swallowing painfully.

"They have been large in my prayers. Though they are cruelly worked and suffer greatly, many have become believers. I pray to the Father every night to release them from their bondage, but the time has not been right. . . ." His voice dropped to a mumble. Then he added, "Their true name is Polonti."

"Oh. Why did they leave their country?" she asked idly.

"I don't really know. One day a few appeared in the cities, then more and more came. Many of their women set up brothels when they discovered men here consider them exotic and attractive. They were not slaves, however, until— I don't understand this—a group of them appeared one day at the palace. Sheva put them immediately into fetters. Then slave traders began bringing them by cartloads . . . more and more. . . ."

He lapsed into silence, and Deirdre realized he was quite weary. So she stopped asking questions and soon heard his raspy snore.

She touched Arund's soft cheek, overwhelmed by a rush of longing for home. She pictured her father, Galapos—winking, laughing, subtle, and cunning; her husband Roman— brown and serious, revealing only to her the fire in his heart; and the baby she had only glimpsed. Her last conscious thought that night was a wistful prayer for all their good.

The following morning, Arund awakened her very early, as he usually did, and she had finished nursing him by the time Sevter came around with hot mush and fresh milk.

"I have something extra for you," he grinned and produced a fat golden apple from his cloak. He handed another one to groggy Josef in his corner.

"Sevter, how kind!" Deirdre exclaimed. "How did you get them?" She relished eating it down to the seeds.

"They had an abundant harvest from the orchards this year. Troyce is allowing the staff to take what they want from the bushels."

Josef smiled sleepily as he ate his meal. "You know, Deirdre, that you must not tell anyone about this. As becomes him, Sevter is risking himself to benefit us. It is not permissible for him to give us extra food."

Deirdre stared in admiration and dismay at Sevter, who unlocked their shackles with a bit more authority than usual.

"It is a small risk," he argued. "Now to your duties, both of you."

On leaving, Deirdre paused. "Josef, I keep forgetting to ask you . . . what are your duties?"

He carefully hid his uneaten apple in a fold of his ragged shirt. "I tend the field slaves, Deirdre. I bring their food and salve their wounds and bury their dead." For the first time, she heard a note of bitterness in his voice. But he patted her hand and assured her, "God is working." They parted in the courtyard—he to the fields, she to the palace.

Deirdre placed Arund in his corner bed and shyly stood by it, watching the early morning bustle of the kitchen until the mistress should deem to instruct her. After sending a tray with the Surchataine's breakfast up to her chambers, the head cook came toward Deirdre carrying a large pan. "I don't suppose you know how to clean fish, do you?" she snapped.

Deirdre stared at rows of googly eyes and shiny bodies and uttered in disgust, "No!"

"No, what?"

"No, mistress," she quickly recovered.

"Well, come to the courtyard." On the steps outside, the mistress demonstrated scraping and cutting while Deirdre watched in dismay, then left her alone to finish it.

Deirdre worked slowly, keeping her head down because she hated the sight of the gallows. *This is horrible*, she thought. *What good is it supposed to be for me to do this?* It occurred to her that she was learning to walk, as Josef had said. She left that thought there and scraped blankly for a while, then stopped to watch the courtyard activity.

She observed that servants who worked together talked in constant, covert whispers. Those who passed each other whispered a few words or gave a discreet sign, all without pausing. If an official or soldier approached, they ceased their conversation as if it had never been.

She also observed a few servants whispering and looking her way. At that point, she began scraping again. Soon, a large-boned manservant ambled over with firewood, which he began stacking against the wall near her. Without looking up, he whispered, "Who are you?"

She startled. "Are you speaking to me?"

He stacked for a moment, then fetched more wood and began stacking that. "Keep your head down. Who are you?"

"My name is Goldie." She felt ridiculous talking to the fish.

"Where did you come from?" he grunted as he lifted an armload.

Feeling a twinge of alarm, she answered vaguely, "Lystra. Why?"

He almost stopped working. "You seem different. We want to know where you came from."

"I was kidnaped from my home in Lystra," she said evenly, looking him in the eye. "My husband is a soldier."

He gave her a long, hard look, then finished stacking his load and ambled away.

Watching him go, Deirdre began to flounder in feelings of vulnerability and helplessness. *Here I am, a slave, prey to any man's whims. . . .* Before her thoughts could carry her into hysteria, she spotted Josef coming toward her, and she calmed.

"Goldie, ask the mistress if there are any scraps left over from yesterday," he said.

"Certainly, Josef." She left the fish gladly and found the head cook over the kettle. "Mistress, Josef asks for scraps for the druds."

"Find what you can, and don't pester me!" she snapped. Deirdre searched all around, going from table to table, but collected only handfuls in her basket.

As she dismally turned to go out, the mistress glanced in the basket, then said, "Wait." Deirdre stopped, and the cook dumped a generous load of turnips and greens into her basket. "Take those. The Surchataine doesn't care for 'em. No sense in wasting 'em."

"Oh, mistress! Thank you!" Deirdre exclaimed. The head cook gave her a queer look, as if wondering at her joy, so Deirdre quickly sobered and took her booty to Josef.

"Good!" he said upon receiving the basket. "You can help me, if you will keep your eyes open in the kitchen. Don't let them throw out to the pigs what could be fed to the slaves. It may save a man's life."

"Yes, Josef." *What a burden he carries*, she reflected, watching him take up the extra weight on unreliable ankles. *Here I was feeling so badly for myself, never thinking how much they must be suffering. It must have been one of them I heard scream last night*.

Downcast, she sat to clean the fish again. Then she stiffened to see Caranoe come strolling through the courtyard, looking idly about for someone on whom to vent his general displeasure. Josef let the bushel drop as if he were having difficulty carrying it. She stood to help him, but he shook his head at her slightly. He began dragging the bushel while keeping an eye on Caranoe.

The slave master found what he was looking for. A lanky young man with a simple, smiling face was attempting to harness two horses to a large flatbed cart, such as the one Deirdre arrived in, when one of the horses balked and shied away. It bumped Caranoe, stepping on his foot.

"Damnation!" Caranoe shouted, hitting the horse, but the animal preferred standing on his foot rather than backing up to the cart. "Get this—blasted animal—" He was pushing and wheezing in pain as the horse calmly stood its ground. The servants in the courtyard worked at their chores earnestly, careful not to raise their smiling faces toward Caranoe.

However, the boy was not so careful. He coaxed the horse off Caranoe's foot, smiling stupidly all the while.

"Master Caranoe, I be sorry about that horse, he be such a mule—"

"You—idiot!" screamed Caranoe. "How dare you make sport of me! Will you laugh at this? You—" he jerked toward a nearby servant, "bring rope!"

All smiles disappeared, and the activity stilled. Josef moved a step closer to Deirdre. The boy stood as if awaiting instructions, and her heart constricted for what was coming upon him.

The rope was brought. Caranoe said calmly, "Tie one of his arms to one horse, and the other to the other." Grimly, the servant obeyed. Deirdre heard muttered, "Such a shame. He was a good boy."

Comprehending that evil was upon him, the boy screwed up his face and began pleading, "I be sorry! I be sorry!" Deirdre began to cry.

The horses were placed rear to rear, the boy between them, and two servants with whips at their haunches. "Now, boy, we'll see how hard you laugh," growled Caranoe.

He stepped back. Josef made a simple request in a low voice: "Lord Jesus, save the life of this boy." Only Deirdre heard it.

"Now!" shouted Caranoe. The servants flailed the horses, which immediately bolted in opposite directions, trailing the ropes tied to the boy's arms.

But the instant the ropes were stretched taut, they snapped with loud cracks. One winging end caught Caranoe in the face and wrapped itself around his wrist. He was jerked to the ground and dragged thirty feet in the dirt before he could disentangle himself. All this while, the boy stood in the same spot, dazed but unharmed, broken rope dangling from his hands.

While Caranoe slowly raised himself up, Lord Troyce came into the courtyard and surveyed the cluster of motionless, gaping servants. "Have we no one who does his work any more?" he wondered aloud.

The servants leapt to their chores. Then, eyeing the bruised and dirtied slave master coolly, Troyce observed, "If you are finished with your games, perhaps you, too, should see to your responsibilities, Caranoe."

"Lord Troyce," he muttered through gritted teeth, bowing.

As Caranoe limped out of the courtyard, Deirdre turned to Josef, beaming. "Josef! How—?"

He put his finger to his lips, smiling with delight. "The Lord Jesus has said that what we do to the least of these, we do to Him. He cares, child." Then he lifted the bushel and carried it away.

She was watching him go in wonder when the head cook stuck her head out the door and demanded, "Finished those fish yet?"

Deirdre whirled. "No, mistress, but—"

"Why, you've hardly touched them!" she exclaimed. "Never mind! No time now! Come in to serve the noon meal!" And her head vanished.

Deirdre hastily brought in the fish and washed her hands. She took the dish Bettina smilingly held out to her. "We're serving it early today," Deirdre whispered.

"Someone special is here," Bettina returned in a whisper. "Sheva's son. He won't be here long, I think." Deirdre nodded absently and carried out a large bowl of steamed clams with herbs.

As she set the dish before Sheva and stepped back, she heard the Surchataine saying, "But why must you leave today?"

A familiar voice answered, "Why should I stay? There's nothing here for me." Deirdre looked up with a gasp. Artemeus! Of course, he was Sheva's son—Savin's son! How could she have forgotten that? She had spurned Artemeus rather brutally at her betrothal fest.

Sheva replied caustically, "*I* am here, and you are to rule after me—are you not?"

Artemeus laughed bitterly as he broke open a clam. "Rule what? What has Galapos left you?"

If he sees me, my life is ended. Deirdre hung her head to hide her face.

"We are daily growing stronger," insisted his mother. "Galapos will be the one cut off. You'll see."

Artemeus ate quietly a moment, not looking at Sheva. "No, I won't," he at last answered lightly. "I'm going abroad. There are places across the Sea I want to visit."

"No! You must be at my side when we attack Galapos!" she cried, stung.

"No, I mustn't." He tossed aside a shell and fixed his grey eyes on his mother. Deirdre, directly behind her, began to quake. "I'm not going to fight Galapos," Artemeus said.

"Why not?" Sheva demanded.

He took the flask and filled his goblet himself while she waited for an answer. "I don't know whether Deirdre is still there or not, but in any case I won't cross swords with Galapos," he said.

"Because of her? She spurned you and insulted you, and you would spare her?"

In the tense silence that followed, Deirdre felt that her breathing was shaking the room. In a rare show of maturity, Artemeus evidently decided not to argue the point with his mother. He stood, taking up a handful of nuts. "Well, I'm off."

"You haven't even finished your meal!" Sheva cried. "Artemeus—" He rounded the table and gave her a peck on the cheek. "Please . . ." she pleaded.

"Goodbye, mother," he said, then crossed directly in front of Deirdre on his way out.

As he disappeared beyond the doorway, Sheva collapsed in grief and Deirdre sagged in relief. He had not recognized her. After the shock of relief had passed, however, she felt somewhat affronted that he had never even looked her way.

When Sheva left the table, Deirdre and Bettina began clearing it. Deirdre cleaned absent-mindedly, thinking that something could be improved at Sheva's tables. So she wondered, "Doesn't Sheva ever have entertainment at her table?"

Bettina paused as if perplexed by the question. "Entertainment? No. Why should she?"

"Well, if she's going to host anyone important, she should entertain them properly, with minstrels or magicians," Deirdre said, lifting a brow.

Bettina answered in a low voice, "I suppose she feels their greatest pleasure would be to look at her." As she said it, Bettina studied her until Deirdre grew uneasy. "Goldie," Bettina whispered, "who are you to know how important guests should be entertained?"

Deirdre bit her chatty tongue, then wondered if she shouldn't confide in Bettina. Surely *she* could be trusted. Deirdre opened her mouth to tell her when a serving girl popped her head into the room and said, "Caranoe is coming."

Bettina wiped her hands and passed through the doors into the kitchen. Deirdre stayed behind, purportedly to finish clearing the table. As Caranoe entered he caught sight of her beyond the doors, but she pretended not to see him as she went around gathering dishes.

From the table, however, she could hear Bettina say brightly, "Lord Caranoe, have you come again yourself for the trash? What happened to that old man you used to send?"

"Ah—" he began in surprise, then laughed loudly. "Yes, Old Bag o' Bones is nearly worthless, being so close to Hades. Why I keep him, I don't know."

"Your kind heart," Bettina laughed. Deirdre ground her teeth. There was a moment of silence, as he seemed to be waiting. Deirdre worked around the table with extreme slowness, determined to prolong this chore as long as he stood in the kitchen.

Then he snapped, "I'll not wait here all day!" Deirdre heard his angry footfalls leaving.

Bettina reentered the hall to take up dishes from the table. "You were rather nice to Lord Caranoe," Deirdre observed.

Bettina shrugged, "I hate him. We all do. But it's best to stay on everyone's good side."

Deirdre nodded, "Yes, that's best." *But it means I don't dare tell you my secret.*

Once the meal had been cleared away, Deirdre took Arund's wraps to the stream to wash them as Bettina had told her. She tentatively dipped one cloth in the water and swished it around. Lifting it out, she ascertained that it would need more vigorous rubbing to come clean, so she held her breath and plunged both hands into the water. Its pleasant warmth surprised her again.

As she scrubbed, she heard a mild exclamation behind her back. She turned her head to see a fat fuller woman watching. "What you washing?" the woman demanded.

"My baby's wraps," answered Deirdre.

"Ho—ee," the gap-toothed woman laughed loudly. "You not going to get them clean that way, stupid!"

"What?" Deirdre sat back on her heels.

"Here!" The woman slapped a small cake of something smelly down near Deirdre.

"What's that?" she wrinkled her nose.

Finding the question unbelievably funny, the woman howled before answering in gasps, "That lye soap, stupid. Use it on the cloths, to make them clean. Ho, are you stupid!"

Deirdre looked at that poor, hopeless fuller woman calling her stupid and felt nothing but pity. So she took up the cake and said, "Thank you." The woman stilled and weighed that response, then turned and padded away.

When Deirdre had finished laying the cloths out to dry, she returned to the kitchen to find Arund crying. So she carried him to the doorway leading to the courtyard. While he nursed, she wanted to relax and see what might be happening now.

The servants, free for a short time, had gathered to amuse themselves with a mock festival. Some of the women were prancing about with baskets on their heads and their noses in the air, in imitation of courtly ladies. The men strutted in front of them, brandishing kindling at each other at the slightest provocation. Then they selected partners to perform around the gallows a ludicrous pantomime of one of Deirdre's favorite dances.

Her attention was drawn in particular to one pretty housemaid who haughtily refused the offers of every male around. One man kissed her and she tweaked his nose. Another fell on his knees before her and she kicked him over. The servants watching were convulsed with laughter, and one rejected suitor cried, "Lady, whom will you have?"

"Him!" she declared, pointing at Old Josef, who was passing through the courtyard. He did not even turn to see the cause of the sudden groans and laughter.

Deirdre smiled wryly. "You don't know it, but you picked the best," she murmured. At once she recalled when she herself had played out that scene. "Roman," she whispered, her eyes tearing, "what are you doing now?"

❧ II ❧

Roman rode silently through a small village north of Westford. For safety's sake, he had stopped along the road and torn off the insignias of Lystra from his uniform. He was aware that this gave him the appearance of a renegade, but it could not be helped. To travel alone in Seleca wearing Lystra's colors would be suicidal. It hurt, at first, to see the village children run in terror from him, but gradually he ceased to notice. He relaxed as he passed from the village into the cover of forest. Somehow, the less he was seen the easier he breathed.

As he spurred to a canter, he kept up his spirits thinking of his mission—to get her back. Even thoughts of Deirdre herself were somehow secondary to the task of planning her rescue. Doggedly, he pushed aside recurring intimations that something was wrong about the whole venture. He had to find her, he argued to himself; he must follow every possible clue, no matter how questionable the source. Abruptly, he remembered once telling Deirdre—in reference to the witch, yet—that one must always gauge truth by the source.

Blankly, he stared down the road.

Before long, he came to another village, a tiny one, nestled in the shelter of great oaks and birches. Spotting a well, he dismounted to drink and water his horse.

While resting, he scanned the peaceful site. It was one of those dreamy little places that legends grow up around, where so much black earth, moss and ancient trees must house more than mere earthly creatures.

He turned the creaking handle, bringing up a bucket from deep in the well, and drank from the gourd cup hanging on a nail. It was good water and cold. He closed his eyes. *Deirdre, I wish you could taste this.*

"Thirsy? Getcha drinka water?" He opened his eyes and looked down at a toddler with round blue eyes and fawn-colored curls. She clapped her hands and laughed, "Getcha drinka water!" He smiled, so she scampered with astounding speed up the side of the stone well to reach for the bucket.

"Stop!" He grabbed her just as she would have tumbled into the well.

She laughed, "Gotcha!"

"Put the child down slowly, fellow," a menacing voice said. Roman, lowering the baby, looked up to see a Lystran soldier, obviously one sent by Galapos to protect the villagers. Beyond him was a young woman watching anxiously from a doorway. The toddler ran to her, laughing.

"I certainly would not harm her," Roman said coolly. "I am Roman, your Commander."

The man hardly blinked. "You're not wearing your colors, Commander."

"I cannot, at this time. I am riding alone to dangerous country," Roman explained.

"I see," the soldier said flatly. "Allow me to observe, Commander, that if you don't wear your colors, you had best be prepared to be taken for an enemy by everyone you meet.

140

It may be less dangerous to show yourself for who you are, perhaps finding friends, than to hide from everyone and chance a knife in the back from someone who doesn't know who you are and doesn't care."

Roman eyed him without responding, so he raised his sword to his face in a salute and turned away. Roman remounted and spurred from the village, forgetting even to water the bay. Why did he feel ashamed?

He cantered easily for a while, but found no pleasure now in planning his great mission. Then he slowed to a walk to eat some of the bread packed in his pouch.

Moments later, his hunter's senses alerted him that he was not alone on the road. Without hesitation he turned off the path and concealed himself and his horse in the brush. Then he waited in stillness, watching the road.

For long minutes he remained on the alert, but neither saw nor heard anything that did not belong to the forest. He began to wonder if his trusted instincts were now failing him as well. Yet, as a caution, he watched and waited still.

Finally, he became convinced his caution was groundless and left his hiding place. The instant he stepped onto the road again, two figures appeared on horseback from the trees, whooping and kicking their horses toward him. Roman had no time to run. He drew his short sword and held it ready under his cloak.

They were upon him recklessly, without considering that he might defend himself. The first one who jumped him was stopped dead with Roman's sword in his side. As Roman wrenched his blade free and wheeled to face the other, he was thrown off balance by a heavy net flung over his head. Writhing, he fell.

He struggled fiercely as he glimpsed the second approaching him cautiously. But the more he struggled, the tighter the net bound him. Helplessly, he watched the man raise a club and smash it down in the general area of his head. Roman collapsed, though still conscious.

He lay as if stunned while the attacker retrieved something from his horse, then carefully began untangling Roman from the net. The instant his sword hand was free, Roman thrust it upward into the other's chest. Then, his head still ringing from the blow, he deliberately worked himself free of the net.

Before he even looked to his assailants, he studied that curious net. It was six feet square, weighted all around the edges with lead pellets. The ropes of the net were interwoven with tiny curved barbs designed not to injure, but to catch in sleeves and cloak and effectively make a trap of one's own clothing. Oddly, these men had intended not to kill or rob, but to capture him. He turned to his dead attackers. Renegades. And the item the second had taken from his horse was an iron neck ring—the kind used on slaves.

Roman stood immobilized in the shock of understanding that they had intended to capture him and sell him as a slave. It was incredible to him that even renegades would attempt selling one of their own into slavery. Had they become so bold as to attack each other on the roads? And why had they taken him on first sight for such easy prey?

For a moment, he was shaken in his resolve to go to Corona. If the extent of their lawlessness had reached this point, he would never come away alive. In that moment, he stood on the verge of prayer. He even dared to lift his eyes to heaven and wonder where God had gone.

But no—his vision crashed back to earth. He had gone too far to turn back. He would not tuck his tail and run home. He had taken this upon himself, and he would finish it.

Grimly, he mounted again and headed north.

❖

When the head cook finally dismissed her at the end of day, Deirdre bundled Arund up and hurried out to the servants' house. She was anxious to see Josef. In this past week she had learned so much from him that made her life here bearable—not the least of which was his conviction that God had allowed her enslavement for a reason. She had a purpose here, other than caring for Arund, though what that might be was beyond her knowing. How much she would rather escape! But alone, in a strange country, she would never find home. And Arund—what would happen to him if she left to seek her own freedom? No—she saw no choice but to stay and work. So she kept alert, observing, learning, reading Josef's Scriptures, and listening to him explain them.

Holding Arund as she sat on her straw bed to nurse him, she fretted over the painful-looking rash on his bottom. It made him cry more, she was sure, but she was helpless to know what to do for it. "Lord, must he suffer with it?" she muttered, then smiled to herself. "Josef will have me praying over the ants on the floor next." *Not the ants, but Roman and Galapos*, a thought answered.

Roman. She had not prayed for him, had she? "Oh, what good would it do?" she muttered again. "He doesn't need me to pray for him. He doesn't need anyone's help to do anything."

He is suffering. At that thought, her heart broke a little. "Is he suffering without me?"

She glanced self-consciously at the door, and as neither Josef nor Sevter had yet appeared, she bowed her head over Arund and imitated Josef as best she could: "Father in heaven, please protect my husband, Roman. Enable him to bear the burden of my absence. Please—help him understand that everything will be well, and bring us safely back together again. And please . . ." she murmured, faltering, "keep safe my baby. . . ." She stopped then, unable to continue, as Josef entered with their evening meal.

As they ate, she sighed, "I don't see how you can live on such small portions. . . . How long have you been a slave, Josef?"

"Ten years this winter," he said, licking mush from his fingers. His hands were so chapped, they bled.

"Ten years? Somehow, I thought you were born into slavery," she said. When he looked up in amusement she reddened, realizing the thoughtlessness of the remark. "What did you do before you became a slave?" she asked.

"I was a tutor here—rather, in Savin's court. I taught a number of the children of the courtiers and officials," he said.

"Artemeus?"

"Yes, Artemeus, for a while," he answered.

"What happened?" Arund's lips loosened, and she gently detached him to lay him beside her in the straw.

"Well, Deirdre, one of my disciplines was philosophy. And in teaching it, I searched out the wisdom of the ages to draw upon—Amenemope, Homer, Cicero, Aurelius, and the Septuagint. There, in the Jewish law and prophets, I discovered a moving, breathing wisdom which walked with me in the day and waited by my bed while I slept.

"The wisdom I found there—no, which found me—held fast under every test I put to it, whether of reason or pragmatics or even time. And it gave rise to questions I had never considered. I was haunted beyond words by the prophet Isaiah's vision of the suffering of the Righteous One."

"The Righteous One . . . ?"

Josef closed his eyes and gathered himself to speak words of power, like a leopard readying to leap. Deirdre felt her scalp tingle. He began:

"Who has believed what we have heard?
And to whom has the arm of the LORD been revealed?

144

For he grew up before him like a young plant,
    and like a root out of dry ground;
he had no form or comeliness that we should look
        at him,
    and no beauty that we should desire him.
He was despised and rejected by men;
    a man of sorrows, and acquainted with grief;
and as one from whom men hide their faces
    he was despised, and we esteemed him not—"

"Why would the prophet bother about someone who was despised?" Deirdre interrupted, frowning.

"Because only sorrow and affliction can teach true wisdom, Deirdre," Josef patiently explained. "You do not understand the limitations of our humanity until you feel it here, and here, and here—" touching his head, his stomach, and his ankles. In spite of the dimness of the cell, she saw what he meant. "Most people think as you do: that anyone who suffers somehow brings it on himself. But the prophet makes clear that the Righteous One did not suffer because of anything *He* did, but because of what *we* did:

"Surely he has borne our griefs
    and carried our sorrows;
yet we esteemed him stricken,
    smitten by God, and afflicted.
But he was wounded for our transgressions,
    he was bruised for our iniquities;
upon him was the chastisement that made us
        whole,
    and with his stripes we are healed.
All we like sheep have gone astray;
    we have turned every one to his own way;
    and the LORD has laid on him the iniquity of
        us all."

145

"That's not fair!" Deirdre said indignantly. "It's not fair nor right to punish someone for something another person does!" The memory of Roman's whipping was fresh as ever on her mind.

"Who considers what is fair when the life of your beloved is at stake?" Josef demanded, and Deirdre startled, wondering how he could have known about Roman. "This is why He is called righteous, because He laid down His life willingly for us! For *us*, Deirdre! And God is not so unjust that He didn't notice, for the prophet further says:

"Yet it was the will of the LORD to bruise him;
    he has put him to grief;
When he makes himself an offering for sin,
    he shall see his offspring, he shall prolong
        his days;
the will of the LORD shall prosper in his hand;
    he shall see the fruit of the travail of his soul
        and be satisfied;
 by his knowledge shall the righteous one, my servant,
    make many to be accounted righteous."

This time Deirdre was silent. He went on, "Then I read Josephus and discovered there had lived a Galilean prophet who some believed was the fulfillment of this prophecy. I obtained the Gospels, and the writings of Paul and the other apostles. And I read of a life which, detail by detail, enacted the prophecies of old. Yet still I did not see, did not understand." He began to tremble.

"Then late one terrible night, after days of struggling to piece together the knowledge before me, I read from the Apostle Peter: 'Because Christ also suffered for you, leaving you an example, that you should follow in his steps. He committed no sin; no guile was found on his lips. When he was reviled, he did not revile in return; when he suffered, he did not threaten; but he trusted to him who judges justly. He himself bore our sins in his body on the tree, that we might die to sin and live to righteousness. By his wounds you have been healed. For you were straying like sheep, but have now returned to the Shepherd and Guardian of your souls.'

"This remembrance of the prophecy came from a disciple who saw his Master beaten, spat upon, crucified—and resurrected. In the reading of those words, the wisdom of the Septuagint and the prophecies of the seers came together and stood before me unveiled as what I had feared more than anything to surmise—a Person of the Godhead, the Word of truth made alive, the Master who frees the slaves, Jesus Christ. I was overwhelmed by the tide of knowledge that washed over me.

"With this revelation, I had no choice but to teach the truth I knew. I began to read Scripture to my pupils. Artemeus, reaching the age of insolence, reported this to Savin. He warned me to stop, and when I did not, he stripped me of my position and made me the lowest of the slaves."

"Josef," she murmured in dismay.

"Don't pity me, Deirdre," he insisted. "I have lost nothing I could keep, and gained riches I can never lose. Read now, child, while we have any light left."

She set down her bowl and wiped her mouth, digging out the pages from the straw. Holding them up to the faint light from the window, she found where they had left off the night before and began to read out loud: "Lo! I tell you a mystery. We shall not all sleep, but we shall all be changed, in a moment, in the twinkling of an eye, at the last trumpet. For the trumpet will sound, and the dead will be raised imperishable, and we shall be changed—" She slapped the pages down in frustration. "Josef, what does that mean? What trumpet? A battle trumpet? And how shall we be changed?"

He smiled patiently and motioned for her to settle down. "He is referring to the time when our resurrected Lord Jesus will return to the world a conquering warrior to claim His own. Those believers who have died before then will be raised to new life, and those who are alive will be changed to be like them, and like Him."

"How will they be changed?"

"I don't know exactly, child. But we will all be given new and glorious bodies that do not sicken or grow old. Read on—uh—" he stuttered and began to gasp. His eyes widened in pain as he clutched his ragged shirt.

"Josef!" She fell across the floor to seize his arms. His hands were cold. "Josef, what's wrong?" He tried to speak but could not.

She dropped his hands and rushed to pound on the door. A guard opened it. "Please get Sevter!" she cried. "Josef is very sick!" He motioned her back to her place as he moved off, and she hurriedly kicked the strewn pages under the straw.

"Josef." She returned to him helplessly. "Sevter is coming . . . what? I can't understand you . . . what?"

With a last effort he swallowed and gasped out, "Brightness . . . the glory . . . *shekinah*. . . ."

In a moment the door banged open as Sevter entered. He halted with an exclamation at Deirdre's side, and they watched Old Josef fall limply back into the straw. Then he was still. His friends stood transfixed.

Sevter put out a tentative hand to feel Josef's chest and face. He pressed both hands to the thin, grizzled neck. Then he looked toward Deirdre.

"No," she said, shaking her head in refusal.

"He's dead," Sevter said, standing.

"No!" she cried. "What will I do without him? How can I face this without him to help me?"

Sevter shook his head at her. "He said his service here

was to end soon . . . it has ended. I'm glad, and you should be also."

"But what will I do without him?" she moaned.

"What we all will do, girl! Carry on! Carry on!" His face was ruddier than ever.

She turned petulantly from him toward Josef's body. Seeing it, she sucked in her breath and grabbed Sevter's arm. He followed her eyes and blanched at the sight. Then they both inched closer in wonder to look at him.

They should have seen the wasted, cast-off shell of an old man. But they saw a sleeping god. The firm, muscled body stretched almost seven feet, extending over both ends of his straw bed. The skin had a smooth, translucent beauty. Lush golden hair covered the graceful head, and an aura of strength and peace surrounded the form.

Sevter suddenly peered into the face and swore. "It's Josef!" he whispered. "I recognize him!"

In disbelief, Deirdre touched the body. It was real, though dead. Sevter stepped back, wiping his face, and uttered a low laugh. "All this time, I see he was right. What is this but vindication of his life and his hope?"

Deirdre was still watching the body, almost expecting him to rise up. She hardly noticed Sevter leaving the room. "Josef," she murmured.

We shall all be changed.

Deirdre gasped, recalling the words with ringing clarity. Was this what they meant? Was this a hint, a foretaste of what awaited Josef, herself, and all believers at the coming of their Lord?

Sevter returned with two guards and motioned toward the body. "Bury him in the western field."

On seeing the body, they jumped back a pace. "Who in blazes is that, Lord Sevter?" whispered one.

"That is Josef," Sevter answered, watching their faces. "*Old* Josef. And he's not in blazes. He has entered heaven—

now bury his remains."

The guards gingerly picked up the corpse—it required both of them—and carried it out. Deirdre and Sevter stood watching them in tense awe. Then he blinked in sudden recollection and said, "I had news for you. I was just now given permission by Lord Troyce to house you and the babe in the kitchen for the winter. Starting tonight."

"Oh, Sevter," she stammered, "thank you."

"You will not be chained there. You'll have free run of the courtyard, too. But don't venture beyond the stables. You mustn't go into the fields," he said.

She nodded as she wrapped Arund in the quilts with trembling hands. "But may I still use the stream bordering the fields?"

"Yes. But that's as far as you go. Now come to the kitchen." He seemed anxious to be gone from that room.

"Yes, Sevter." She carried Arund out, then stopped short. "Wait! I forgot—" She returned to the straw bed and dug the pages out from their hasty hiding place. Then she concealed them in Arund's quilts. "Now I'm ready."

The empty kitchen was warm and quiet. She made a bed for herself and Arund before the low-burning fireplace and snuggled him down in the quilts. Wonderingly, she mulled over Josef's death. Carry on? Yes, certainly. . . .

As Arund slept, she picked up the pages to find where she had left off reading. By the firelight she read, "When the perishable puts on the imperishable, and the mortal puts on immortality, then shall come to pass the saying that is written: 'Death is swallowed up in victory.' 'O death, where is thy victory? O death, where is thy sting?'"

At those words, a thrill ran down her spine. She had witnessed victory, seen it, touched it. In quiet awe, sensing the immortal and imponderable all around her, she huddled close by the child to sleep.

12

In the morning Deirdre was awakened by a gentle prod-
ding. "Goldie. Goldie! What are you doing here?" She
opened her eyes to see a fuzzy Bettina.

"Sevter got us permission to winter here," she yawned,
then roused alert. "Bettina, Josef died last night."

"Oh. Poor old man," she muttered sympathetically, stok-
ing the fire.

"No, Bettina, it was good," Deirdre earnestly explained.
"He was a believer, and God just took him to a better place.
And his body was changed, like the Scriptures said it would
be, only later when Christ comes again—but Josef looked
like a beautiful warrior, only he was dead." She stopped, feeling it was not all coming out quite right, and Bettina glanced
her way with a puzzled frown.

"We have to pack the fruit today," Bettina said carefully,
lining up stone jars on the table. "Will you bring a bushel
from the storerooms, Goldie?"

Deirdre nodded and sighed. *I'll never be able to explain*

it to anyone. I'd best just keep it quiet. She went out of the kitchen and down the corridor to a nearby storeroom. Emerging with a bushel, she paused, startled by sudden nasty laughter.

She wheeled to look, but there was no one. Silence followed—was that a whimper?—and the laughter broke out again. Men's voices. She realized it came from a nearby storeroom. Setting the bushel down with a thump, she strode to the door without a thought and looked in.

Four soldiers stood around a very young, very frightened girl, teasing her, handling her, pushing her from man to man. "Stop it!" Deirdre demanded.

They did, looking at Deirdre with great surprise. The girl wilted to the floor. Emboldened by the events of last night, Deirdre announced, "The Lord Jesus does not like what you're doing."

Three of the men looked suddenly uneasy, but the fourth stepped toward Deirdre with eyes of seething malice. "Wait until He sees what I do with you, then."

"You can't do anything to me," she said. "Now get out of this room!"

He hesitated with widened eyes, then blew from the room like dry straw in the wind. The others followed hastily, crowding themselves to get past Deirdre without touching her.

Deirdre went over to the girl and lifted her, telling her, "Don't be afraid. Hide in God, and no evil here can touch you." Then she retrieved her bushel and carried it to the kitchen door, where she dropped it.

"What did I just do?" she gasped. "Did I do that?" Thinking of what she had said to the girl, Deirdre muttered, "Those words were meant for me. Oh, what am I in for here?" Apprehensively, she took up the bushel again.

When she came back into the kitchen, Bettina said, "Here. I forgot to give you this," and handed her a small bowl of tallow. "Smear it on Arund's bottom. It should ease his rash."

"Thank you, Bettina," Deirdre murmured, recalling in astonishment her halfhearted prayer about it. She knelt beside the baby, scooping up tallow with shaky fingers.

Later, after Deirdre had given Arund his midday feeding, she gathered his most soiled wrappings to wash. Briskly, she carried them out to her usual washing place at the stream.

As she plunged them into the warm water and began to scrub, she curiously noted a pile of large rocks on the opposite bank of the stream, only six feet away. Her washing was arrested when she sighted a field slave carrying a heavy stone.

He wore more chains than clothes—chains extending from his neck ring to cuffs on his wrists and more cuffs on his ankles. Only a loin girdle covered his body. Straining, he dropped the stone on the pile with the others, then collapsed beside the stream and plunged his face into the water.

Horrified, Deirdre yanked the cloths from the stream. She watched in disgust as he drank, then scooped water over his face and chest. His hands were bleeding. He lifted his head and looked straight at her. Expressionless, he just looked at her.

Startled, she at first thought he was the same man who had ridden with her in the cart—black hair, brown skin, husky build . . . but no, his face was different.

Then Deirdre saw another slave approach, lay a boulder on the pile, and shuffle off, the chain on his neck ring clanging. Black hair, brown skin . . . like Roman. . . . In a burst of stunning insight, she made the connection. Druds—the slave race—they all looked like Roman because *he* was one of them. Worse—a half-breed.

At this moment a guard walked up to her and said, "I see you often washing those filthy rags here in the stream. Why are you doing that? Don't you realize everyone draws water from this stream? Boil those blasted things over the fire!

153

Don't foul your own drinking water!"

In a crying fit, Deirdre seized the sodden cloths and ran for the kitchen. Mercifully, at this time of the afternoon it was empty. She threw herself in her corner, quivering, trying to think.

Roman's mother must have been one of the Polonti women who came down from their country and set up brothels. Roman, raised in the army, had escaped any threat from slave traders. How providential that Galapos had found him before they had! But these—all these field slaves—how many were there? Hundreds, she was sure. They were his kindred. They were her kindred, now. At that turn of thought, Deirdre stopped trembling and began thinking cogently.

Moments later, when the head cook came into the kitchen, Deirdre raised her face and brazenly asked, "Mistress, rather than foul the stream, may I boil my baby's wraps over this fire?"

The mistress glanced in her direction. "Yes."

"Then may I go draw water, mistress?"

"Go."

Deirdre ran to the stream opposite the rock pile, but the slave was gone. She focused across the field and saw in the distance a long, low wooden structure. That must be where they were housed. She drew the water, deep in thought. As she turned from the stream with her pail full, she was so preoccupied that she almost spilled her water on Caranoe before seeing him.

"Goldie." He reached out to her and she jumped back, sloshing water. His face was different than she had ever seen it. Smooth, open, beseeching—as she wondered at it, he said, "You're wrong about me. I'm not the villain you seem to think."

"Why would I think you a villain?" she asked cautiously, drawing away.

"Sevter seems to have filled Lord Troyce's ear with all

kinds of nonsense about how I might mistreat you," he said with reproach. "Why should you be afraid of me?"

Deirdre was so relieved to hear of Sevter making good his word that she admitted, "I've seen how you treat the servants, and I've heard how you treat the slaves."

"Only because they won't work otherwise," he said earnestly. "But those who trouble to make friends with me find me most kind and generous."

She studied him silently, and the thought occurred to her that perhaps Josef was wrong to regard him as an adversary. Perhaps, with tact and patience, he could be changed. Roman had accomplished that with her. Could that be one reason she was here?

She relaxed and smiled slightly at him. "I suppose I haven't given you much of a chance."

His face lifted. "I have one, now?"

"Well . . ." she hedged.

"Come," Caranoe said eagerly, taking her hand. "Put your bucket down."

"I can't—" she began, thinking of Arund.

"Just for a moment, to show you something," he urged. "Come."

She hesitantly set the bucket down and let him lead her by the hand. First, he took her to the kitchen and stuck his head in the door. "I want pastry for Goldie!" he demanded.

Happily, the mistress was not in to hear that. A little girl Deirdre had seen tending the sheep paused to wipe her hands and Caranoe bellowed, "Now, you little goose! Get it now!"

The girl ran to a work table and grabbed a handful of newly baked cakes, upsetting the tray and spilling the rest on the floor. Deirdre winced, knowing how long it took to prepare those cakes and that now it would have to be done all over again.

"Lord Caranoe, please, I don't really want pastry," she

protested in spite of the fact that she was continually hungry.

"Of course you do," he insisted, handing her one and popping another in his mouth. "C'm'ere," he mumbled, blowing out crumbs.

She devoured the pastry, uneasily allowing him to take her hand and parade her through the courtyard before the servants and guards. When he took her to a footbridge spanning the stream, she objected, "Lord Caranoe, I'm not allowed to leave the courtyard."

"You can go anywhere with me." His eyes tended to squint when he got impatient or angry, so that he was forever squinting.

"But, my lord, I must be nearby to tend the baby's needs," she reminded him.

"The brat can wait," he snapped. Deirdre's stomach tightened. Somehow, this was going all wrong.

He led her to the edge of a field where they could watch slaves harvest rocks from the treacherous cliffs. "I am the master of all these men," he said arrogantly, and Deirdre dropped her shoulders in dismay.

"My lord, isn't that reason to treat them with kindness?" she asked gently.

He laughed. "That's reason to treat them however I please. The weaker are ruled by the stronger. That's the law of the universe." He looked at her with laughing contempt, and his eyes revealed that, to him, she was only another slave to exert power over. She saw he *was* stronger than she, for the goodness in her was not mature enough, not disciplined enough to overcome the attitudes entrenched in him. No—reforming Caranoe was not the task for her.

She turned. "I must return to the kitchen now."

He held her arm. "No. Not yet."

"Lord Caranoe, if you don't let me go, you'll get me trouble from the kitchen mistress. Is that how you show your affection for me?" she asked pointedly.

Pouting, he followed her back to the courtyard, where she took up her bucket of water. "I'd show you plenty for your time with me," he argued. "What do you like, Goldie? Rich food? Gold rings? Dresses and soft shoes? I can give you all those things."

She looked down at her bare feet, only too aware that once she had all those things. "I don't want any of that."

"No? What do you want?"

She looked past Caranoe, past stone walls, past fields to the west, and said, "My husband and my home."

"Fool!" he spat, grabbing her wrist. Her bucket spilled over their feet. "I say you will come with me now!"

"No!" She steeled her legs.

A voice behind them said, "Caranoe, you will excuse us while I speak with this servant."

They both pivoted to face Lord Troyce, two large hounds with wagging tails at his side. Caranoe released her and bowed stiffly to him. Then with a threatening glance at her, he strode away.

Lord Troyce waited until he was out of earshot before gesturing toward her spilled bucket. "Draw your water."

Deirdre bowed unsteadily and fumbled for the bucket. He stepped closer and said quietly, "There is a rumor afoot that Old Josef's death was somehow extraordinary. Do you know anything of this?"

Deirdre held her breath. Dare she try to tell him? "A little, my lord," she murmured.

"Yes?" He stood waiting.

"After he died," she faltered, "he seemed to change . . . I mean, his appearance. He looked different." Lord Troyce raised his brows. Deirdre explained, "That is, he looked very young and strong and healthy in death—so different than he looked alive, though Sevter said it was indeed Josef."

"Sevter saw it also?" he asked.

"Yes. And the two guards who buried him."

157

Lord Troyce was silent as Deirdre drew the water and set the bucket on the ground. Then he asked, "What do you make of this?"

"My lord . . . I don't know."

"You shared quarters with him. You knew his beliefs. How would you account for what happened to him?" His intelligent eyes narrowed as he waited for her response.

Deirdre nervously patted one hound. "Lord Troyce, I really don't know. But the power of God was with him. Sevter said it proved he was right all along."

He smiled. "You think, then, that God did it?"

Deirdre hesitated. Dare she ally herself with miserable, lowly Josef before Lord Troyce, who had the power to release her? She inhaled and said, "Yes."

Troyce smiled faintly, glancing around the courtyard. No one else presumed to listen in. "I'm glad to hear that . . . because, you see, I was one of Old Josef's first converts."

"You?" Deirdre almost knocked over the bucket again.

"Yes." He looked back toward the palace. "I must go now, but we'll talk more of this later. Meanwhile, this much I can do for you: I will prevent Caranoe from harassing you further." He nodded curtly and was gone, Sheva's hounds padding after him.

Deirdre hauled the bucket into the kitchen and dumped the water into a large iron kettle over the fire. As she dropped in the rags one by one, she darted a look toward the head cook. "Mistress . . . I noticed the—the druds taking rocks from the cliffs and piling them next to the stream. Why are they doing that?"

"The Surchataine needs more fields. They are terracing the eastern slopes for cultivation. That's what the rocks are for," the mistress answered in a brittle voice, picking up ruined pastries from the floor. "Do you know who did this?" she demanded.

"Lord Caranoe was in here earlier, helping himself,"

Deirdre replied lightly.

"Ohh—that man—" the cook muttered under her breath.

Watching the water boil, Deirdre wondered aloud, "Why were they stacking the rocks by the stream?"

"Because that's where they were ordered!" the cook snapped. "Now be quick with those things so you can help me make more pastry for tonight!"

"Yes, mistress," Deirdre sighed, dumping in all the rest of the rags at once.

As Deirdre helped Bettina serve dinner that evening, she watched Lord Troyce from under her brows. Sheva leaned toward him, placing her hand on his arm. "I wish to go falconing tomorrow. Did you see the new hawk Brude gave me?" she asked as if baiting him.

"Yes, my lady. She's beautiful," Troyce agreed unemphatically, and Brude beamed.

Sheva paused, watching Troyce with a slight, calculating smile. Then she asked prettily, "What do you think, Troyce? Should I give the water mill to Brude?" Those at the table listened with interest, especially Lord Brude.

Troyce hesitated, wiping his mouth with his cloth. "Lord Brude would certainly manage it efficiently," he observed, "but we must remember that it has belonged to Oral's family ever since being built by his great-grandfather. As Oral is loyal to my lady, and pays his taxes, I do not see that we should strip him of his inheritance."

Brude said quickly, "Permit me to point out to my lady's administrator that Oral pays taxes of only thirty percent. Since I could operate it at a greater profit, I would most gladly pay taxes of forty percent . . . if given the opportunity."

Sheva's face shone with approval. "Wouldn't it be prudent to give it to Brude, Troyce?"

He tightened his lips, and Deirdre could see perspiration forming on his forehead. "It would not serve justice, my lady," he said, eyes on the table.

"*I* am the only one you should be concerned about serving," she pointed out. "You may have the mill, Brude." It was almost as if she spurned Troyce's counsel solely as a demonstration of her power.

"Oh, thank you, Surchataine!" Brude breathed in adoration. Troyce chose not to take a stand over Oral's inheritance and remained silent.

"Go write up the proper paper," Sheva ordered him. "We will give it to Brude before he leaves tonight." Troyce slowly rose with downcast eyes while Brude gushed his gratitude to the Surchataine.

Troubled, Deirdre watched Troyce go up the stairs. He had said he was a believer. Yet he obeyed Sheva in whatever she demanded, and even Deirdre could see that her goals had nothing to do with Christ. Troyce certainly seemed to be a mule pulling two wagons.

As he returned with the legal paper, his eyes happened to meet Deirdre's over Sheva's head, and his quickly lowered. *Whom do you really serve, Troyce?* she wondered.

After the guests had left, Deirdre and Bettina began clearing the table. Having eaten nothing but the pastry all day, Deirdre looked down at the honey-glazed ham with tears in her eyes. She looked up toward the window where Bettina was tossing out the sauce. *Lord, throwing all this good food to the dogs isn't right! Have mercy on those who are hungry here!* Deirdre pleaded inwardly, without even realizing that she wasn't praying just for herself anymore.

Bettina turned back toward the table and stiffened. "Yes, mistress?"

Deirdre turned to see the kitchen mistress standing at the doors. "You may go, Bettina. Goldie will finish clearing the table," she said curtly.

"Thank you, mistress," Bettina gave a little bow and left without a second look at the large, cluttered table. Deirdre slowly resumed gathering plates.

The mistress stood at the door until Bettina had gone. Glancing up, Deirdre saw that all the other servants had retired as well, leaving her alone to clean up the table and kitchen. Strangling a complaint, she resolved just to get it done.

Still the mistress stood there. Deirdre glanced up. "Yes, mistress?"

The woman shifted, then in a very low voice said, "You are hungry."

"Yes," Deirdre breathed, "so very hungry—!"

"Shh!" The mistress cut her off, glancing over her shoulder, then she grumbled, "I don't slave all day to feed dogs. Eat what you want from the table, then gather all the rest and place it under the stairs out back. Someone will come 'round for it tonight. But if you're caught, Goldie, you're on your own!"

"Thank you, mistress! Thank you!" Deirdre breathed with all the gratitude in her being.

The mistress eyed her almost in satisfaction, then nodded and retired herself for the night.

That evening Deirdre feasted on ham, beans, and dried fruit compote. To allay any suspicions, she put out enough for the dogs to be seen eating outside the window. Then she gathered bowlfuls of leftovers, covered them tightly with cloths, and stealthily slipped them under the wooden stairs out back of the kitchen.

Full and happy, Deirdre nestled Arund in her corner of the warm kitchen and peeked through the shutters. It had begun to snow—the first of the season. She smiled. What providential timing for her to be allowed to sleep and eat here, with Josef gone and winter arriving. Inwardly, Deirdre knew it was not happenstance. It was beyond her even to guess what God might do next.

⁂ 13 ⁂

Roman sat on his horse and looked up at the high, grey stone walls. The massive wooden gates still hung in pieces around the battering ram, the wheels of which had sunk deep into the earth. Evidently, the machinists had been unable to unlock the mystery of its mechanism. He wondered vaguely if they had given up on it. They were not here now.

The robe was there, however. That splendid golden robe was still suspended between heaven and earth. No man had dared to remove it from the post on which Galapos had tossed it.

With stinging eyes, Roman surveyed the deserted outpost, remarking the detailed preservation of their last battle scene. It stood as a mute testimony of a mighty answer to a desperate prayer.

At that, he bit his lip and looked down. He knew what he should do. But if he humbled his spirit and prayed, he felt sure God would send him back to Westford. And he could not—he just could not—give up now. He had not yet reached his end.

He directed the Bay Hunter through the rubble of the gates. At least the outpost would provide shelter from the night. He stabled the horse, then listlessly wandered through the cool stone corridors until he found his former quarters. *Old habits die hard*, he thought ruefully as he sat on the hard cot to eat his bread. Then he lay down, fully alert, to try to sleep.

His mind raced ahead to speculate on his meeting with Karel. How would he handle the old Surchatain?—assuming he was indeed alive. As the possibilities occurred to him, he grew distraught. Karel must not be allowed to depose Galapos, yet . . . to kill the old ruler outright . . . he could not. He still had that much respect for the man he had known for so long as Deirdre's father. Yet, what if the old Surchatain had been corrupted beyond hope? And what if he was corrupting Deirdre . . . ?

When at last he slept, he dreamed weird and troubling dreams. He was in a lonely forest, following Deirdre's footprints on a path. On the way, he saw the mists before him come together to form an unheard-of creature with fangs and oozing, slimy skin. It puffed itself up to block his path, then extended its green neck toward Roman to fasten its jaws on his arm. Crying out with the pain of it, he plunged his sword into its soft underbelly. The monster opened its jaws, but only to laugh, then with a flick of its tail knocked Roman farther down the path.

Straining to see in the gloom, he found her prints again and raised himself. Derisive laughter sounded before him, and he jerked his head up. There in the mists stood Tremaine. "I owe you this, guardian!" he declared, lifting his sword.

"No! You're dead!" Roman insisted.

"As you are now!" Tremaine promised with a mighty

swing. Helpless, Roman felt the sear of metal through his throat, and he was choking on blood. He felt himself fall as dead, but his mind did not cease or rest. From where he lay, he could see the prints. He picked himself up to follow them once more.

As the mists began to coalesce again into a form, he gripped his sword tensely. But there before him stood Galapos in shining mail.

"Galapos—father—" moaned Roman.

"Worthless scum! I'm not your father!" retorted Galapos. "You are a stupid, cowardly fool, and I will have nothing more to do with you. I wish I had left you to starve on the streets or be hanged! You are removed from your post as Commander and banished from Lystra. Go!" With that command he seized Roman by the neck and flung him down the road.

Blinded by tears, Roman wandered farther until he looked up to see himself before a grand palace. The guard at the gate, dressed in finery like the Cohort, looked down at him and said, "What do you want, peasant?"

Gathering the vestiges of his will, he replied, "I have come for Deirdre."

"Really?" the guard smirked, but he led Roman into the great audience hall. There on a glorious golden throne sat Karel, draped in the golden mantle. Deirdre sat perched on his lap with her arms around his neck. They both looked up in amusement as Roman approached.

"You think to have my daughter?" laughed Karel. "You? A common, bastard soldier?" At which came peals of laughter from invisible faces.

Roman held out his arms, pleading with his last breath: "Deirdre, my love—"

"You ugly thing!" she declared, wrinkling her nose. "You're a fool to come after me this way. Leave me alone!"

Roman awakened sobbing and shouting, bruising his fists on the frame of the cot. When he realized it was only a dream, he lay down again, empty and aching, to seek what he needed in sleep.

In the morning, he awoke already weary. He got up and prepared himself to ride reluctantly, for a man on a mission. After eating a light breakfast from his provisions, he paused to think through his objectives again. Why was he hesitating? His determination—or stubbornness—alone impelled him out of the gates on a northward course.

The plain was still scarred and trashed from the battle months before. Roman noted a broken water pot, a reminder of their deliverance, but turned his eyes away and wrapped his cloak more tightly about him. It had turned much colder overnight.

He rode watchfully through the Pass, but all was dead or still. Even the forest beyond appeared empty and void. Its deadness seemed to seep into his mind, for soon he rode without thinking or seeing. He went on for hours in this state, traveling for the sake of traveling, marking time by the state of his horse's weariness. There was no sun in the heavy grey skies to guide him, and the day did not brighten as it progressed.

His dullness began to clear away as he drew close to the outskirts of Corona. He formed a tentative plan: If Karel was here, he would certainly be occupying Tremaine's palace. Somehow, Roman would have to gain entry and . . . what? He did not know.

His senses came to full alert as he rode into the jostling crowds of Corona. The disintegration of the city was woefully apparent. Most of the legitimate businesses had been vacated but left standing to be overrun by squatters. Yet the streets were bustling with business. A dirty prostitute, spotting Roman, motioned to him and opened her bodice in supposed enticement. He recoiled in disgust and pity.

As he rode up the thoroughfare, he witnessed a casual murder and open looting. A few renegades on the street eyed him, but he stared back stonily and no one accosted him. With difficulty, he directed his horse around a drunken group attempting to batter down a door. Then he found the side street that led to the best inn he knew. For now, he needed hot food and drink. Then he would consider how to deal with Karel.

The inn was still open. Roman stabled the bay but took his gear with him into the dining room. It was crowded and stuffy, occupied by a few wary-eyed merchants and jaded women, but mostly men of unknown occupations. Roman was ignored by the proprietor and serving girls, so he got up and leaned over the bar.

"I want stew and ale," he told the proprietor.

"Twenty-five pieces," the owner said. Roman, shocked at the price, handed him a royal. He slopped a bowlful from an iron kettle and shoved it and a mug toward Roman.

"You owe me some money," Roman reminded him. The proprietor grudgingly returned him his change.

Roman took his bowl and mug to sit at a table nearer the door. He took a swig of the ale and found it watered. The stew smelled old and greasy. He ate slowly, tense and alert, listening to every voice and movement around him.

Two renegades passed by him on their way out. They were dressed in good leathers and carried royal broadswords. One was laughing, "Did you hear about old Gerd? Says he got hold of one girl who swore she was a chataine. Sold her to—" the slam of the door as they left cut off his voice.

Roman bolted to the door and collided with such force into another renegade that both of them went sprawling. The soldier got up swearing and swinging, but Roman ducked his fists and stumbled outside.

They were nowhere to be seen. He was peering down the street when he was grabbed from behind by the fellow he had run into. Roman impatiently knocked him to the ground again and ran up the road to look farther. But the two soldiers had been swallowed up completely by the street life.

Crushed and dizzy, Roman felt the burning flush of insight. Of course! That's what had happened! Deirdre had been captured and sold into slavery. That explained all the riddles of her disappearance. He felt nauseated and giddy at once. He would find her now. He would find where she had been sold and trace her. It could be done.

With new hope and confidence, Roman strode back to the inn and sat to finish his stew. He went to the bar again to tell the proprietor, "I want a room for the night."

Grunting, the owner wiped his hands on his dirty apron and led Roman past the bar to a dank corridor. He stopped at the second door and set a lamp down in a small, windowless room that contained a bed and a dry washbasin.

Roman moved to step inside, but the owner stopped him with a hand on his chest. "Two royals," he said. Breathing a disgusted sigh, Roman paid him again. The proprietor stopped him once more from entering. "You want company?" he asked.

"What?"

"A girl," suggested the owner.

"No," said Roman, then reconsidered. "Wait . . . yes, I do. But not just for the night, nor just a village girl—someone special. Who would sell me that kind of girl?"

"As a slave?"

"Yes," Roman choked out.

"Well," the proprietor took on an informative air, "the best slaves are usually in Fark's market. He takes care of his property, he does. But you better have a lot of money, and keep a tight hand on it. He's a clever cheat, and his friends'll stab you in the back for a few royals."

Roman turned to leave. "Where is it?"

"Ah, it differs from day to day. In the morning, I'll find out from the boys where he is now. I wouldn't go at night anyway, if I were you."

Roman nodded unhappily and tossed his pack down in the room. He cast an inquiring look to the proprietor, who still stood in the doorway. "So—you want a girl tonight?" the owner persisted.

"No," Roman said.

✤

In the morning Roman rose eager and determined. He entered the dining room, nearly empty at that hour, and sat at the bar. The proprietor set a plate of ham and bread before him. "Have you heard where Fark's market is?" asked Roman.

"Yep. North of here, near the abandoned mill. He's already set up this morning," he answered amiably. Roman gulped the breakfast and stood, taking up his pack.

"That will be two royals," said the proprietor.

"Two royals? For what?"

"Your lodging."

"I paid you for that last night," Roman said, watching him.

"I said, that will be two royals." The proprietor raised his voice and a couple of scruffy soldiers looked up. "Are you refusing to pay your bill?" The soldiers stood and ambled over to stand behind the owner.

Roman gritted his teeth and produced the money. "Have a safe and pleasant journey, sonny," the proprietor called after him, cackling, as Roman stalked out.

He reached the inn's stables in time to see a young man leading out a balking Bay Hunter, saddled and bridled. "Let go of that horse before I break your hands," Roman growled.

The boy jumped and sputtered, "He is—I was readying him for you."

Unconvinced, Roman checked the cinch, then mounted. The boy held out his hand, smirking, "That will be two royals for the care of your horse."

"I paid the proprietor for your services. Go claim it from him," Roman said, kicking the bay sharply.

As it happened, he needed no directions to find Fark's market. Heading north, he simply followed the trail of slave traders leading their merchandise to market.

The abandoned mill was located in a grassy meadow a few miles outside of Corona. But the mill was hardly visible for the activity around it. Pulling his horse to the side of the road, Roman stonily took in a scene he had never before witnessed: Hundreds of slaves stood in the open field, chained together in rows of thirty to forty each. The rows changed like tides as new slaves were added and purchased slaves removed.

Roman dismounted with extreme wariness and moved closer to the field, leading his horse. He listened, incredulous, as a trader outlined the features of a slave to a buyer: "Look at his color—you can see he's healthy. And strong—he'll pull for you what a mule would!"

"But he's blind in one eye," the buyer observed in dissatisfaction.

"That's why the good Lord gave us two—the other eye sees perfectly! And for that little defect, I'll give you a reduced price of only one hundred twenty royals."

Someone tapped Roman's shoulder and he jumped. "See anything you like, soldier?" A steely-eyed trader was watching him.

"I must look more closely," Roman mumbled, and he began leading his horse down the rows, looking for a blonde head.

He intended only to scan the rows for her, but found himself instead looking into faces—faces blank from misery; frightened faces; hateful, angry faces; tender, innocent, suffering faces. Yet they all shared a common stance of hopelessness. They were chattel, something less than human, because no one cared or was able to redeem them.

Deirdre—are you enduring this somewhere?

He walked the length of the field, and she was not there. He found the trader again. "I'm looking for someone especially . . . a girl, with blonde hair, whom Gerd might have brought in. She—she might have claimed to be daughter of a surchatain."

The trader laughed hoarsely. "Now that's a selling point I hadn't thought of! No, I dare say we haven't had a chataine here."

"Do you know Gerd?"

"Sure. Buy a lot from him," the trader admitted.

"Where does he live?" Roman asked.

"Gerd? Nowhere. But he works mostly in southern Seleca." The trader kept a wary eye on his merchandise as he talked.

"Where can I find him?" Roman pressed.

"Wherever he is, soldier. Whether you ever find him depends a lot on what you want from him." The trader eyed him with amused malice, and Roman looked away, thinking. Then he asked, "Are there other slave markets in Corona?"

The trader laughed again. "Are there fleas on a dog?"

"How many are there?"

"Who knows? It's a profitable business, and everyone wants to try his hand at it. They come and go in the night," replied the trader.

Roman stared at the shifting rows before him. "I'll search until I find her," he vowed to himself, mounting and riding to seek out another market.

It was a short ride away. Again, it was an open field with slaves chained in rows. He stopped to look. There were fewer here, and their condition was generally worse.

But there, toward the back, was a blonde girlish head tucked in slender arms—his heart raced as he ran toward her. He lifted her abruptly to peer in her face, and the little girl cringed away from him, crying.

His disappointment at finding her not to be Deirdre was overshadowed by pity and outrage. Why, this was just a child! She looked no older than Deirdre had been when he first became her guardian.

"Unhand the merchandise until you pay for her, soldier," growled a trader at his side.

Roman released her, gulping, "How much?"

"Eighty royals."

Eighty royals! he thought. *I can't pay that—it's almost all I have, and I would have nothing left to redeem Deirdre when I find her.* His conscience asked, *Will you leave this child in slavery, then?*

Roman stepped back a pace in dismay. *I can't free every slave I find,* he protested. *It's impossible.*

"Well?" the trader demanded.

Roman reluctantly drew out his money bag and paid him. "Tell me . . . do you know Gerd?"

"Yeah. Sure. What's he to you?" the trader muttered suspiciously.

"Has he brought in a girl to you—a blonde girl, claiming to be a chataine?"

"Let me tell you something, soldier. You go asking questions about Gerd, and you'll find him at your back with a knife." The trader unlocked the girl and shoved her toward Roman.

He led her to his horse, where he halted uncertainly. "Listen . . . I don't wish to use you. I only wanted to free you, but I can't ward you—"

She looked up at him wide-eyed. "You're going to free me?"

"Yes—" he began, but before another word fell from his lips, the child kicked him with all her strength in a tender place, seized his money bag, and ran for her life.

When Roman finally picked himself up from the dust amid the guffaws of the traders, he grittingly thought, *So much for my good deeds. If I find Deirdre now, I'll have to free her by force.* He mounted with a gasp and rode to find another market.

But locating the next one required a longer search. When he thought he saw a girl being led in chains, away from the other markets, he followed, but found himself stumbling into an ordinary tin shop. There was no one inside but craftsmen.

He stepped outside again, puzzled. He searched around the shop to see if she had been taken someplace near it that he had not seen. But there was nowhere else she could have gone.

Then he noticed that the building was rather large for a tin shop. He considered . . . the larger slave markets operated in the open, as they had the numbers to defend their merchandise from anything but an army. But a smaller operation, not so well manned, would need a cover. . . .

Roman entered the tin shop again and looked toward a rear door. One of the craftsmen stopped his work to peer at him. "Need something, fellow?"

"I want to buy a slave," said Roman. The other appraised him a moment, then went to the rear door and knocked a code on it. It opened, and Roman stepped into a dark back room.

Here, among tin scraps and tools, were about fifteen girls chained to rings in the wall. Three renegades who sat around a table, drinking, looked up. A fourth shut the door behind him.

None of the girls was Deirdre. "Are you here to buy, fellow?" one soldier demanded.

"Not one of these," Roman answered. "I'm looking for a particular girl, one who claimed to be a chataine."

"Oh, well, there she is," said another renegade, gesturing to a plump girl behind him.

Surprised, Roman said, "Ah—no, she's not the one—"

173

"She's a chataine," the renegade insisted defensively.

"Nonetheless, she's not the one I wanted," Roman answered. "The one I'm looking for is—"

"Well, how about this one?" the fellow pointed to another. "She happens to be a chataine also!"

Roman inhaled. This was turning into a carnival. "I'm looking for a girl Gerd might have sold—"

"What's wrong with our chataines?" the renegade demanded, standing while the others snickered. "Are you saying you don't like any of our girls? Why, they're ALL chataines!" he exclaimed, flapping his arms to encompass the whole room. "You're an idiot if you can't see that!"

The others fell from their seats laughing, and he added, "Rufus, get the idiot out of here." The fellow behind the door opened it and shoved Roman out.

He retreated outside under the tinworkers' curious glances. There, he paused to eat the last bit of bread from his pouch and think. With no money and no more provender, how would he stay in Corona and search through the winter?

Roman was pondering this dilemma when a voice at his back said, "Try for a royal, fellow?"

He jerked his head around to see a ragtag drifter holding up three walnut shells and a gold royal. "Find the pebble, and the royal's yours, eh? If not, you pay me. Hey, fellow?"

Roman looked interested. "How is this done?"

The drifter squatted to the ground and laid the three shells in a row. Then he placed a pebble beneath one. "You just tell me which shell hides the pebble, and I pay you a royal," he said, moving them around. He lifted the middle one to expose the pebble. "There, see?" He replaced it and switched them around again. Then he lifted an end shell. "There it is again! Easy, huh?"

"It looks easy," admitted Roman.

"But if you don't find it, you pay me," said the gambler.

"Very well," agreed Roman.

With a flourish, the fellow set the shells down and moved them so swiftly they blurred. He sat back on his heels and demanded, "Now, where's the pebble?"

Roman looked down at the shells a moment, then up at the gambler. "In your right hand," he answered. He reached over to open the drifter's fingers and show him the pebble. "You owe me a royal," Roman said.

The gambler gave it up to him, laughing, "Say, you're good at this! Try it again, and win another!"

Roman stood. "One from you is enough." He lifted his foot to the bay's stirrups.

"Wait!" demanded the drifter. "You've got my money!"

"You lost it fairly—" Roman began, but was yanked from the saddle by a second drifter who started beating him savagely with a short wooden club.

Roman struck him solidly in the throat, and he fell right away. Then Roman wheeled back to the first, but he had vanished. So he climbed back on the Bay Hunter, muttering, "Hardest royal I ever earned." From there he continued his quest.

14

Galapos sat absent-mindedly drumming the table. Seated across from him, Basil was examining marked and smudged maps with satisfaction. "You've done well, Surchatain. The villagers will be overjoyed at your generosity in dividing your land among them."

"Perhaps, Counselor. I think more likely, however, that they will bitterly complain about the taxes of a tenth I will require for the privilege of owning their own land." He rose and impatiently stalked to the window.

Basil laid the maps down, quietly observing, "You are troubled for your children."

Galapos snorted. "Troubled? Because Deirdre has disappeared from the inhabited earth and Roman is off on an addled search for her? Why should that trouble me?" Basil remained silent and Galapos breathed out heavily, turning toward him. "Forgive me, Counselor. My tongue runs of its own accord at times."

"I'm not offended, Surchatain—I know the trial you're

enduring. But has there been no word from the scouts you sent out?"

Galapos shook his head. "I received a negative message from Karl and Joel in Calle Valley, and a negative message from Perin and Lari in Goerge. From Marc and Varan I've heard nothing."

Basil walked over to the window to scan the countryside himself. "Roman may yet find her. He is a born hunter, and his sense of direction is uncanny."

Galapos said, "Yes, but this time his compass is off." He looked intently out over the land as if searching into the streets of Corona.

A knock. "Enter!" called Galapos, turning determinedly from the window.

A sentry opened the door. "Dinner, Surchatain."

"Well timed, at that," Galapos muttered.

In the dining hall, Galapos, Kam, Basil, and a few others sat down at one end of the long table. Kam made a disgusted face at the watery, lumpy pottage set before them. "If you were able to pay the cooks, Surchatain, perhaps they would treat us with greater kindness at mealtime."

Galapos smiled wryly. "They do the best they can, considering they are soldiers who think a pan is for smashing on heads."

Kam looked up at a soldier who ambled in with a bottle of ale and an armload of goblets. "You are the ugliest serving girl I have ever seen," he declared with feeling.

"You're no delight to gaze upon, yourself," the soldier griped, dragging up a chair.

"Gentlemen, please," Galapos laughed, "we must make do with each other until such time as more people can be brought into the palace. Peace, fellows."

Kam sullenly ate his soup, dribbling a little down his black beard. "Any word from Roman?"

"No." Galapos's smile faded.

"Corona is a sorry place to carry out a search in winter," Kam continued. Basil's look warned him to stop, but he did not see. "I think we ought to send an outfit to bring him back. He was just not thinking aright to go there."

"No, he was not," Galapos acknowledged. "But to bring him back against his will would not straighten his thinking. That task falls to a higher power than mine. Roman will return when he is made ready." Kam pursed his lips skeptically, and the party ate in depressed silence.

At length, Galapos looked around and muttered, "What I wouldn't give for some entertainment now."

A sentry entered while he was speaking and whispered to him, "Surchatain. A traveling minstrel asks you to hear him."

"Send him now," Galapos agreed in surprise. "A traveling minstrel," he explained to Basil.

"We haven't had one pass through since before Tremaine," said Basil, and those at table straightened a little in interest.

A pleasant-faced young man came in and bowed low before Galapos. "Surchatain Galapos, I am honored you receive me. Your name has been on the lips of men from Goerge to Calle Valley as the deposer of the tyrant Tremaine. A long life to you, Surchatain! And now, if you allow me, I will sing a song in your honor, which I just now composed."

"Sing if you will, when you discover I cannot pay you for your song," Galapos said wryly. "But you may eat your fill at this table tonight."

"You honor me beyond measure, Surchatain." The minstrel bowed again. "Now hear me." He took up his guitar and began to strum boldly.

From places far I've heard a tale
Of glorious victory;
When raving death pressed hard around
This man rose up to be—

179

Conqueror!
Deliverer!
Hail to the Surchatain
Who rules in splendid wisdom;
God watches all his deeds.
God makes his store increase.

We trembled, fainting at the sight
Of armies from the north;
Prayers were made to Him above,
And God sent this man forth!

Conqueror!
Deliverer!
Hail to the Surchatain
Who rules in splendid wisdom;
God watches all his deeds.
God makes his store increase.

And though you rule a shattered land
Of we who were brought low;
Our eyes now see and hearts perceive
The heavens all aglow!

Conqueror!
Deliverer!
Hail to the Surchatain
Who rules in splendid wisdom;
God watches all his deeds.
God makes his store increase.

Now father, let no doubting cloud
Your purpose and your worth.
Your faith will stand, and from that act
Comes joy to us on earth!

Conqueror!
Deliverer!
Hail to the Surchatain
Who rules in splendid wisdom;
God watches all his deeds.
God makes his store increase!

As he ended in triumph, those at table sat soaking up the song's note of hope. Galapos turned to the sentry. "Olynn, bring this fellow the best we have left in the kitchen."

While the minstrel sat eagerly, Galapos asked him, "And how did you come to compose that song, my boy?"

"To admit the truth, Surchatain, it just came into my head, and I wanted to sing it for you."

"It's a good song. But you should know that you didn't get it quite right. The Conqueror you praise is Christ, not I. Nonetheless, you've encouraged me, and I thank you for that." The minstrel raised his goblet in acknowledgment, and talk at the table suddenly turned lighthearted.

"Sure, things aren't so bad," Olynn said, setting a plate before the minstrel. "It's not dainty fare, but at least you're eating."

"And drinking," added a soldier, lifting his goblet.

"He does plenty of that," muttered a third, below Kam's hearing.

Galapos laughed, but Basil said thoughtfully, "That is strange, Surchatain—every day I can't see how we will possibly put food in front of all these men, yet every evening we seem to have exactly enough. Last week the deer ran themselves into the very ravine the men were hunting. Yesterday we found all that barley in a forgotten storeroom. And I can never remember the currants bearing so late in the year. I don't know where it all comes from, but somehow we always seem to have enough."

181

Galapos's eyes glazed slightly. "What was it I just read . . . ? Something about the birds of the air and the lilies of the field, how God feeds and clothes them, so how much more He will provide for you, if you seek Him above these things. . . . It appears to be true, Counselor."

Basil arched his brows, and Olynn passed around the bottle.

Shortly afterward, Galapos rose from his seat, but bade the others to stay or go at their will. He climbed the stone stairs alone and came to the nursery door. The nursemaid, seeing it was him, nodded cordially and withdrew to the adjoining room.

Galapos pulled up a chair beside the cradle and smiled down at the sleeping baby. "Hello there, fellow. No need to get up—it's only me again. What? Oh yes, I do enjoy coming to talk with you. Since your father left, I need someone to talk with, and you listen just as well." He snorted mildly, shaking his head and studying his fingertips.

"I've been thinking about your father much lately. Let me tell you about him, my boy. Headstrong as a mule for sure, but straight as the pines, with a heart as pure as the northern brooks." His voice wavered and his eyes grew distant. "I found him once a starving boy, and I watched him grow into the finest man under my command. Not that I did anything—oh, no! I see now that it was God, shaping him day by day into greatness. And he will be great, if he—" He cut off and closed his eyes.

In a moment he resumed, "And let me tell you about your mother, my boy. Child of my own body, and I did not know it. . . . Beautiful, willful child who grew into a woman so fast my eyes never saw her in between. . . . Did you know she was at one time ward of your father? Dear Lord, the more he bled for her, the more he loved her—" He spread his hand over his face and wept for his children.

❖

From the shelter of a vine-laden oak, Roman observed three renegades eating around a campfire. Standing near them, chained together, were two shivering young women and an older man. Roman listened in on the conversation of the renegades:

"Phew! Eulen, you idiot, this mash isn't fit for a dog!" One turned and threw the contents of his tin place into the brush behind him.

Eulen replied, "It's more than *you've* brought in, you pig!"

Retorted Pig: "Yeah? What about them?" He jerked his head toward the captives.

"You'd never have managed them without us. That old lady almost took your head off."

"Huh," snorted Pig. "She'll never do that again. But I still say you should've took the tools."

"Who's going to buy milk cans and butter molds in Corona?" Eulen demanded sarcastically. "And how were you going to carry a plow?"

"Not those, fool. The leather tools!"

Eulen opened his mouth, but the third renegade, who had sat silently all the while, held up his hand and looked toward the tree that hid Roman. The others turned around to look also.

Roman stepped from his hiding place, leading his horse. He made his face solid rock and said, "I am looking for Gerd."

The three glanced at each other, then the third said, "Why?"

"He sold a girl who claimed to be a chataine. I am looking for her."

Pig's face turned a pale green, and he rose unsteadily, eyes darting to their horses. "Who are you?"

"I am the one sent ahead to find her," Roman answered,

playing on Pig's fear.

Eulen rose also, scanning the trees around them nervously. "We don't know Gerd, and we don't know this girl," he said gruffly.

The third kept his seat. "You play a dangerous game, interfering in other people's business when you are obviously alone."

In a bold bluff, Roman put his fingers to his lips and whistled. As it happened, the sound startled an unseen covey of quail resting nearby. They fluttered up with such an alarming commotion that the renegades lunged in panic for their horses. As quick as vipers, they were gone.

Roman leaned over to get the pouches they left behind, muttering, "That's one way to gather provisions." He came across an iron key and raised his eyes to the shaking captives.

He unlocked them, then tossed a dropped money pouch to the old man. "Get yourselves home as best you can," Roman said.

The old man gripped the pouch with white fingers. "You think money can repay my loss?" he choked out in anger. "Do you know what they did? *Do you know?*"

Roman eyed him with reserved compassion. "I'm sorry," he said.

"Sorry! Phoo!" And he spat venomously on Roman. Then he grabbed the girls' arms and hustled them away.

Roman quietly repacked the renegades' pouches and swung up on the Bay Hunter, feeling that another small piece of himself had died.

He rode down a little footpath that he thought might lead to another barely visible slave market. But it ended in the clearing of a small cluster of huts.

This was not even a village, really. There was no well and no farrier's hut. Actually, there was not a moving thing anywhere. He dismounted to have a look around, fearing the renegades had already visited this place.

184

But suddenly a girl appeared in the doorway of one hut.
A very pretty girl, with long, clean brown hair. Her dress hung
loosely off one shoulder. She smiled at Roman from the doorway, and immediately his mind went blank.

As he remained by his horse, she left the doorway to
come over to him, looking up at him through thick lashes.
"You look tired," she said softly, taking his hand. He blinked.
"Come in and rest. I have some very good ale. Come," she
urged, and he let her lead him by the hand to her hut.

At the doorway, he came to himself enough to check
that the Bay Hunter was close by outside. Then he darted a
look around the hut. There were some simple furnishings,
but no one other than the girl pouring ale into two cups.

"Do you live here alone?" he asked, alarmed that she
would be so accessible to the renegades.

"All alone," she smiled, holding a cup out to him. He
took it, and her fingers left the cup to touch his bearded
face. Then she leaned up against him and pressed soft lips to
his.

He allowed her, because it felt good and he ached to feel
something good again. She let off from his lips, sighing, and
led him to sit on the bed beside her. She put her cup to her
lips, her green eyes inviting him to drink also.

He raised the cup, then lowered it, frowning, "But how
do you live?"

"I sell to the merchants of Corona," she said softly, taking
another sip.

Looking around the hut, he saw no merchandise, just
some crockery dishes and a few small jars on a high shelf.
"No, I mean, how do you defend yourself, all alone?"

"No one bothers me," she replied innocently, drinking
again.

Shrugging, he put the cup to his mouth, but his eyes
were drawn to the little window in the back of the hut. One
small corner of the covering was hanging awry, caught on

the wood, and Roman could see out the window several large mounds of newly dug earth. They looked like . . . graves.

He dropped the cup and stood, gasping, "Graves!" He stared at the spilled ale, which was uncharacteristically red. Then he looked over at the girl, and her face went hard with wily caution. "You're a match for any renegade, girl!" he swore.

He ran from her hut and jumped on the Bay Hunter. Leaving at a run, he muttered, "Forgive me, Deirdre—I will never touch another girl but you. Fire and ice! No wonder she has no trouble with renegades—she poisons them, then plants them in her garden. And I was almost there, but for the grace of—" he stopped and grimaced. He knew who, but could not bring himself to say it.

15

A few days following her conversation with Troyce, Deirdre was ordered to the courtyard to help unload a cart of vegetables and fish bought at market.

Exiting the kitchen, she noticed three menservants standing beside the cart, whispering fervently. When she approached, they hushed and began to unload bushels of onions, garlic, and squash. She did not really feel curious to know what they had been discussing; she had noticed other servants whispering among themselves and had assumed it was a common form of entertainment.

She carried a basket into the kitchen and returned to the cart. One of the servants kept glancing at her, then at another servant, as if asking permission to talk to her. The other shook his head. Deirdre smiled in a superior sort of way to herself. *As if I cared to know their little secret.*

When all the baskets were unloaded, she proceeded to hang a bushel of onions for drying. This was one of those frequent days when Sheva was gone on an excursion, and there was not much activity in the kitchen.

Bettina entered and came beside her as if to help, but only stood fingering the onions. Deirdre, turning to smile at her, noticed the distracted, anxious look on her face. "What—?" began Deirdre, but Bettina waved her silent. Bettina waited, watching the corridor leading from the kitchen until she was satisfied it was empty.

Then she turned back to Deirdre and whispered, "Goldie, I'm afraid. I've been hearing rumors of an uprising by some of the servants. They're going to try to escape."

"Good!" said Deirdre. But at Bettina's horrified look, she added, "Isn't that good?"

"No!" exclaimed Bettina, then glanced at the corridor again and spoke in a lower tone. "They've tried it before, and it never goes right. Then Sheva executes many of the servants at random as punishment. Even if they did some-how escape, the ones left behind would suffer for it. I fear for our lives, Goldie!"

Deirdre inhaled and squeezed her arm. "Don't worry, Bettina. We'll be taken care of." *Won't we, Lord?*

They worked silently when the head cook entered the kitchen to begin making bread. But she was called away by a summons from Caranoe for pastry. "Bettina—you come over here and finish this bread," she instructed over her shoul-der as she hurried out with the pastries.

There was silence a while longer, then a manservant entered the kitchen with an empty basket and set it down. Deirdre noticed he was the leader of the group who had been whispering at the cart. He had a scar on his forehead much like Roman's, except this man's scar gave his face an air of defiance rather than vulnerability. She turned her back to him, but he crossed the kitchen warily, as if listening, and stood beside her.

He took note of Bettina across the room, then whispered to Deirdre, "You've been chosen to come with us."

"What?" she whispered back.

"We're leaving this place," he uttered.

"How are you going to do that?" Deirdre did not bother to whisper.

He gritted his teeth. "Keep your voice down." He handed her a small bag of powder. "Tomorrow early, put that in the food of the overseer and all the guards who eat here. A few hours after they've had that, we can walk away from here."

"What is it?" she asked.

"Deadly poison," he replied.

Deirdre gasped and dropped the bag. "I won't do that!"

He snatched the bag up from the floor and shoved it back into her hands. "If you don't, I will kill you myself," he promised.

She started to tremble. "Are—are you going to free all the slaves?"

"Any who can walk away can leave," he said coolly.

"What about the ones who are chained?"

"This is every man for himself. I'm not crossing Caranoe," he said.

"But—if he is poisoned—" she stuttered, confused.

"Not him, stupid. Sevter! Poison Sevter and his guards!" he hissed.

"No!" Deirdre shouted, shoving the bag back at him.

He jerked it away. "Then someone else will, and we'll see to you later!" He stalked out, and Deirdre turned in time to see a corner of the kitchen mistress's skirt disappear in the corridor.

Bettina, blanching, fell toward Deirdre and cried, "What will we do?"

"Be still, be still," Deirdre urged, rocking her, but her own eyes burned and her throat was stretched taut.

Moments later a tower bell sounded an alarm. Guards rushed into the kitchen to lay hands on Deirdre and Bettina. Other guards ran into the courtyard and began yanking servants away from their chores. They were all herded into the courtyard beside the gallows.

And there they waited. The leader of the insurrection had been seized also, and as he stood he glared at Deirdre in a promise of revenge.

Lord Troyce appeared in the courtyard. He pointed to the leader and said, "Him." Then, swinging a finger of doom, he pointed to other servants one by one. "Him. Him. And her." The rebels were being bound and lined up as the gallows was made ready. Bettina was wailing, and Deirdre thought miserably, *Who will take care of Arund?*

Mercifully, Troyce finished his litany and did not point to Deirdre or Bettina. But when the leader saw that, he shouted, "Those two! Those two serving girls were in with us!" Troyce halted and looked at Deirdre in surprise.

Incredibly, the head cook, standing at the kitchen door, spoke up. "Pardon, Lord Troyce, but that is a lie. As I told the guards, Goldie here refused to help them. And since you know how expensive domestic slaves are nowadays, my lord, I am sure you will have pity and spare my kitchen help."

Troyce nodded, and the two girls were not touched. Then he waved a signal. Beginning with the leader, the soldiers hanged twelve insurrectionists. Deirdre and Bettina fled to the kitchen as the first was being fitted with the noose. But even there, they could hear the terrible creak and bang! creak and bang! of the rebels' executions.

When it was over, the head cook returned to the kitchen. In utter self-forgetfulness, Deirdre grasped her hand and fell on her knees before her. "Oh, thank you, mistress, for speaking up and saving our lives!"

The mistress pursed her lips and waved Deirdre off. "If I had let them hang you, look at all the time I would've wasted in teaching you everything you know. And then they would have given me another idiot to start all over with."

Deirdre could only smile, and the cook added, "You're

lucky this broke when Sheva was away. Lord Troyce executed only the guilty. She would've sent the lot of you to the gallows, and then some. And no one gainsays her sentence. Now get to work on those onions!"

❖

Weeks passed as winter closed in on Diamond's Head. During this time, the buzz in the kitchen rose to a high pitch as the staff labored to stock the storerooms adequately for winter. Deirdre learned to work as she never had before. From faint sunrise until late in the night, she dressed game for curing, made compotes and jams, peeled scores of bushels of produce for drying. She learned to milk and make bread and to cook savory spiced meats over hot coals. For a time, she forgot all else but working and following instructions.

Yet every night, when the work was done and the head cook left her and Arund alone, Deirdre would dig out Josef's pages to read. She clung to them as a bridge, a link between herself and him, and the wonderful power of God in him. In her longing for Roman, she put all her hope in that power to reunite them.

Mostly, however, she just worked at the chores assigned to her. As of late, she perceived that, perhaps because of her willing attitude or pleasing appearance, she was often given the least offensive tasks. Early one morning as the servants lined up to receive their assignments, the mistress directed them one by one to varied duties until only Deirdre and another girl remained—a plain, large-boned girl.

"Now," the kitchen mistress spoke to herself distractedly, "the nuts must be shelled, and the slaughter room floor must be scrubbed." As she glanced at the pair, Deirdre put on her tenderest face. "Goldie, you sit here and shell the nuts. Almetta, take the brush and pail and scrub the slaughter room floor. There must not be a drop of blood left. Now go!"

Almetta obediently took up the pail, and Deirdre sat smiling. *Things are getting easier here. At least I'm above some things now*, she thought.

At that moment a guard put his head in the door and exclaimed, "Almetta!" The head cook, Almetta, and Deirdre all looked. "The Surchataine's favorite hound is whelping and something's gone awry. Lord Troyce sends for you straightway."

"Go," directed the cook, and Almetta hurried off. Then the mistress turned to Deirdre and said, "You go wash down the floor. I'll shell the nuts." Deirdre, stunned, hesitated, and the mistress thundered, "Go! And make it shine!"

Deirdre grabbed up the bucket and brush and ran to the slaughter room. She stopped dead at the door, observing the mess of blood and entrails, pieces of bone and—she retched violently. She dropped on all fours, sobbing, to plunge her hands into the pail. "How long must I endure this?" she sobbed. "I am nothing here, nothing but a wretched slave, above nothing and no one."

Shaking in misery, she cleaned with forceful abandon. One floorboard at a time, she gathered the refuse, threw it out to the dogs, and scrubbed the boards fiercely with water and lye soap.

When finished, she calmly stood. The floor glistened. No one could have cleaned it any better. *I am beginning to think I can do anything*, she decided. *If I must be a servant, I will be the best there is.*

Something Josef had said recalled itself to her as if he himself were saying it: *You are a servant of the Most High God*. Deirdre walked out of that slaughter room as if she were draped in gold and jewels.

She returned to the kitchen to find Arund fussing. Having just nursed him an hour ago, she doubted he was hungry. When she knelt to pick him up, he held his head steady to look at her. "How big and strong you are getting, my little man," she murmured. His skin was pink, his eyes were clear, and his bottom was—very messy. Still, the rash had long since disappeared.

Deirdre laid him down to remove the dirty wrap and patiently clean him. As she wrapped him in the last dry cloth she had, she asked, "Mistress, may I boil Arund's wraps now?"

"Is the floor clean?" the head cook demanded without raising her face from the bushel of nuts.

Deirdre stood. "It is spotless. You may inspect it yourself."

The mistress looked up then, surprised at the note of pride. "Very well. Go draw your water."

Deirdre stepped out of the warm kitchen with her bucket and hurried through the courtyard to the stream. Glancing up, she startled, seeing the stream shrouded in a thick, eerie mist. She relaxed upon coming closer, realizing it was steam from the warm water into the cold air. She lowered her bucket into the stream, then checked herself as a field slave approached the other side and knelt to drink as before.

It was the same one she had seen earlier—she was sure of it. Yet she was appalled to see that, in spite of the deepening cold, he wore only a ragged tunic over his brief rags. She cast a cautious eye around, then braced herself to speak to him.

But he raised his face out of the water and said softly, "You were with him."

She startled. "What? Who?"

"Josef. Is it true?"

"Is—is what true?" she stammered.

"His face was like an angel when he died. Is it true?"

"Yes! But more than that. His whole body had changed—he was young and strong again. He—"

He had no time to chat about particulars. "Yes. And you have his holy Scriptures."

"Yes," she answered slowly.

"We want them," he said flatly. "We want to read where it says that Messiah came to free the prisoners."

"But—" Deirdre fought to find a base for her objections— "can you read?"

"Not I. But Volne reads. He will read to all of us."

"But . . ."

"Will you give them to us?" asked the slave who had nothing.

Her heart sank as she found no ground to refuse him. "Yes. But how?"

He stood. "Tonight, bring them to the northwest corner of the field house—" He jerked his head toward the wooden structure Deirdre had seen. "Tap on the wood." Then he swiftly moved off as she rose in panic.

"Wait!" she whispered loudly. But he was out of earshot. "I can't leave at night—or cross the stream—how do you expect—wait!" In despair she watched him disappear, then she tensely drew her water and ran to the warmth of the kitchen.

As she put the water on to boil, she shook her head. It was impossible. She could not risk it. She would just have to explain to him—suddenly Arund began crying and she knelt down to attend him. Finding him wet again, she muttered to herself in exasperation. Her bowl of tallow was empty, as well.

As Deirdre rolled him over on the quilts, his little flailing hand found Josef's pages and scattered them. Flustered, she began gathering them up lest the mistress see, but stopped in mid-motion when her eye caught this passage: "The Spirit of the Lord is upon me, because he has anointed me to preach good news to the poor. He has sent me to proclaim release to the captives and recovering of sight to the blind, to set at liberty those who are oppressed, to proclaim the acceptable year of the Lord." Her heart pounded as she read. Sighing, she slid the pages under the quilt and leaned back. Somehow, she had to do it.

The remainder of the day Deirdre was an exemplary serv-ant, somehow hoping to stave off trouble that night by per-forming well at her duties during the day. When Almetta returned, Deirdre volunteered to help her finish shelling the nuts. It was tedious work, cracking and cracking until her fingers were sore, but it ate up hours.

That completed, preparations for dinner began. "What are we serving tonight, mistress?" inquired Deirdre.

"The cod, with onions and potatoes, the exotic fruits and herbed bread, barley soup, and shrimp," she thought out.

"Shall I clean the fish, mistress?" Deirdre asked.

Open-mouthed, the mistress answered, "It has been done already."

"The shrimp?" Deirdre asked crisply.

"Ervie is drawing out traps now," the mistress replied, frowning.

"Then the potatoes must be peeled." Deirdre marched to the storeroom while the mistress stared after her. She returned with a bushel and promptly set herself to washing and peeling them.

The mistress watched her bemusedly a moment, then muttered, "Hmmph. Someone taught you well." She then poked her head out the door to scream for Ervie.

Hours later, the sumptuous dishes were served to Sheva and her court. It seemed to Deirdre that they ate with excru-ciating slowness. As she stood waiting behind Sheva's chair, the Surchataine said without preface, "Why didn't you tell me of the uprising while I was away, Troyce?"

He appeared caught off balance for just an instant. "Frankly, Surchataine, it was so insignificant it slipped my mind. A minor disturbance."

"Did you hang the offenders?" she demanded.

"Certainly, my lady."

"And how many were hanged?" she asked suspiciously.

"Twelve, Surchataine."

"Only twelve?"

"As I said, it was a little thing," Troyce answered lightly.

"If you are so concerned about the number of slaves here, perhaps you should have hanged more," Sheva purred.

He replied, smiling, "Those slaves cost my lady much money, and I did not wish to waste her wealth by hanging servants who had proved themselves loyal and hardworking."

Without deigning to look at him, she said coldly, "I wonder whether it was the loyal ones you spared, Troyce." His face froze.

By the time the Surchataine finally arose from the table, Deirdre was taut as a bowstring. She ate handfuls from plates as she swooped down the table, cleaning, then took out the leftovers before the mistress had even vacated the kitchen. Shortly thereafter, the mistress took her candle and nodded goodnight to Deirdre. She and Arund were alone. Deirdre waited as long as she could stand it for the general activity to wind down. She even let the fire die down low, to hide her absence. Then she decided it was time to go.

She sat still in the darkness a moment longer, calming her heart to pray, though she had no idea what she should ask of God. "Just help me do this and live," she whispered. Gathering Josef's Scriptures, she tied them in a bundle. She wrapped a thin shawl around her shoulders, kissed the sleeping baby bundled in his box, and inhaled courage to open the kitchen door and step into the cold night.

Her chest tightened as she heard the crunch of her feet on frozen ground and saw the steam of her breath in the bright moonlight. A scene flashed before her mind of every guard in the palace being alerted by the noise and surrounding her at the gallows.

She crouched in the shadows until the solitary guard lolled by, then she ran to the stream, encased in its billowy shroud. She located the little footbridge in the mists and crossed over on feet nearly frozen.

From there she ran through an open field to the huge black shape of the field house. It was farther away than it appeared, and by the time she reached the safety of its shadows, she was utterly winded. Now, the northwest corner. Or was it northeast?

Exasperated, she thumped her head. Northeast or northwest? She steadied herself and studied the building in relation to the palace and cliffs. Northwest. It had to be. That was the corner farthest from the palace.

She slid along the field house, remarking its size, until she reached the corner. Nervously, she tapped. A board popped out and a manacled hand gestured her closer. She hesitated, then put her head in—

And gagged. Packed in long, narrow rows were slaves, chained by their ankles to iron rings set in the ground. They lay or sat on dirty straw, without even the accommodation of stalls. Just men and chains and dirty straw.

Deirdre reeled back from the stench and gasped in clear, stinging air. Steeling herself, she leaned in again and held out the bundle. The slave nearest her, the one from the stream, took it as all the slaves strained to see. He turned it over in his hands, then handed it to another slave, who passed it to another, who passed it on.

The first turned back to Deirdre. "We will not forget this."

"Neither will I," she gasped.

"I am Nihl."

She paused. "I am Deirdre."

He nodded, and there was something in his face that made her ache for Roman. She drew back and pushed the board in place from the outside. She ran stealthily to the stream, crossed, and started across the courtyard. Then she stopped dead at a low growl.

She turned, very slowly, to see one of Sheva's hounds baring his teeth at her. "Good boy," she whispered, glancing around for the guard. "Good boy." She crouched and cautiously extended her hand to pat the dog's head. He sniffed her fingers, then licked them, wagging his tail. She smiled at this unforeseen benefit of working in the kitchen.

She gave him a farewell pat, then crept to the kitchen door just as the guard came around again. Holding her breath, she slipped into the kitchen and sank in relief beside Arund.

Sleep was unthinkable as she turned over and over in her mind what she had seen. Suddenly she sat up, aware of a perplexity. She had seen the slaves from one end of the building to the other. But she should not have been able to see anything. It should have been utterly black inside.

Probing her memory, Deirdre finally decided that there must have been smudge pots among them. *How perilous*, she shuddered, adding wood to the fireplace. One single straw set aflame would turn that field house into an inferno. She lay down again. They must want the message of those pages badly to risk being torched alive.

Then a new revelation stunned her with its simplicity. They did not like slavery. They did not accept their condition as slaves any more than did the domestic servants who revolted. They, too, considered themselves worthy of freedom, regardless of what others called them. What stunned her even more was realizing that somehow she had assumed they shared her hopeless resignation—that they would not change their condition even if it were in their power. How could she have overlooked the significance of those chains?

And yet, Josef had said he accepted his chains, and he seemed right in doing so . . . so what was the difference between him and them? She struggled mightily to understand this, and soon the answer came.

Josef was a man on a special mission. He had voluntarily taken upon himself the degradation of their condition in order to serve them, to do them good. He was where his

Lord wanted him, doing what his Lord needed him to do. And when his work was completed, the Master had appointed him to nobler service in higher realms.

But these slaves were serving no one but Sheva, and hating it. Josef had agonized over their enslavement, petitioning the Lord continually for their deliverance. . . .

Deirdre lay down in the cool satisfaction of insight. At last, she knew her purpose here.

At daybreak, she left Arund in the kitchen and deliberately tarried in the courtyard, shaking out rugs and sweeping the steps, until she spotted Sevter. He saw her at once and pointed: "Goldie! There are loose chickens in the servants' house. Get in here and get them out!"

She hastened behind him to the room she had shared with Josef. "Sevter—"

"Deirdre, how are you faring in the kitchen? And the baby? Has Caranoe molested you?"

"No—we are well—all is well. Sevter, did you know that Lord Troyce is a believer?"

His forehead crinkled. "No. Are you certain?"

"Well, he said he was . . . and he was asking about Josef's death." She caught up one hen and threw it out the door.

Sevter asked hesitantly, "Did he declare himself so in front of others, or to you alone?"

"Why, only to me. But what difference does that make? Why would he say he was if he weren't?" she asked.

"I don't know, rightly." Sevter gazed absently as she shooed out another few hens. When she came back to his side, he said, "Just be careful, Deirdre. There's unrest all over—the recent plot was just a hint of the trouble at hand. There are rumblings of a possible overthrow of the Surchataine—by Troyce or Caranoe, most likely. Just . . . be careful who you commit yourself to." He took her hand and looked anxiously into her face.

She returned his gaze and asked, "Would the slaves be

freed in the event of her overthrow?"

Sevter blinked. "No, of course not. Caranoe certainly would not free any of you, and Lord Troyce—who knows his mind?"

Deirdre diverted her gaze into space, and a moment later murmured, "The domestic servants are free of chains, at least during the day. Are the field slaves always chained?"

"Yes. The irons on their arms and necks are never unlocked. At night, each is chained in place in the field house. I fear to think what they would do to this place if they were ever released!"

"Who has the keys to unlock them?"

"There is only one key that unlocks their field-house fetters, and Caranoe carries it with him at all times."

Deirdre's brows contracted in puzzlement. "With only one key, it must take ages to unlock them every morning."

"No," said Sevter. "There are two long chains passed through their anklets and the ground rings. Those two chains are all that must be unlocked. And the keys that open their neck rings are hung above the doorway of the field house— to taunt them, I'm sure."

Deirdre stared up at Sevter with such cold determination that his eyes widened in alarm. "Deirdre—what are you thinking?"

"Nothing," she said, turning her eyes away and smoothing her face. But he continued to gaze at her, holding her hand. She looked back at him and asked, "Sevter, where is your wife?"

"I have none," he said lamely.

"Why not? You should," she observed.

"Sheva allows none of her officials to have wives," he said bitterly, releasing her hand. "We may have lovers, yes, but not wives."

"Why?" she demanded, shocked.

"To prevent divided loyalties. She must have the whole

man. I believe she is more interested in keeping Troyce tied to her than any of us. But we are just as bound." Deirdre avoided his angry eyes, remembering with discomfort a certain maid named Angelina, who had once loved Roman.

❖

As the days passed, Deirdre found herself watching for Caranoe, observing his movements and habits. One morning, she made as if to pass by him in the courtyard when he brusquely blocked her path.

"Listen quick, Goldie," he snarled. "I don't know what influence you have with Troyce or why he's protecting you, but you're as good as dead now. I gave you your chance, and if you were smart you would have sided with me. I could have made your life here sweet and given you fine things. But no—you made your choice, and when these cliffs fall down around you, wench, just remember I could have saved your life!" He spat the last words in her face and stalked toward the fields.

16

Galapos stood gazing out the window at the wintry white. Each day he had come to the window like this just to look—and hope. But in his innermost heart he did not believe he would ever see Roman riding up the winding road toward the palace.

Releasing a heavy breath, he let his eyes fall to the nearest field, covered with a silky white blanket. Almost three months had passed since Roman's headstrong departure to Corona, and in that time he had sent no message to Westford. Moreover, the whereabouts of their beloved Deirdre was as dark a mystery as ever.

Galapos was still gazing at the whiteness when Kam quietly approached. "Surchatain."

"Yes, Kam?"

"A message has arrived from the Surchataine of Goerge—Sheva. She invites you to come feast with her and discuss the future of your provinces."

"As the spider invited the fly," Galapos snorted. "I wonder

what deviltry that witch has in mind."

"Shall I send a refusal, then?"

Galapos continued to rest his eyes on the white purity. "If we don't face her down, then she schemes behind us. No, I'll go. And you will accompany me, Kam, but that is all," he said in a subdued voice. Kam's mouth opened in argument, but Galapos anticipated him: "Without numbers, we must have cunning, my friend. You will forgive me if I dress you as a servant."

Kam bowed. "You may dress me as a woman if it will serve your purpose. But I'm a poor substitute for a body-guard of soldiers, High Lord."

"Don't call me that. And you'll serve me well. Send an acceptance to Sheva, then come back here. We have much to plan."

Kam sent back the messenger carrying Galapos's accept-ance, then returned as ordered to the Surchatain's cham-bers. Basil was already there, seated.

Galapos motioned for Kam to sit as he himself paced the room and thought aloud. "Counselor Basil—I am charging you with the rule of Lystra in my absence until the return of Commander Roman. When he comes back you will confer upon him the authority I have given you and tell him of our whereabouts. He must not follow us—that is a command. He must take charge of Westford and await us here. If I do not return, he is to be made Surchatain."

"If he's here," Kam muttered. Galapos ignored him.

Basil asked, "Surchatain, do you suspect Sheva of evil designs on you?"

"Unquestionably."

"Then, forgive me for questioning, but—why are you going?" Basil asked.

"Your question is entirely proper, Counselor. Let me explain it thus: Once in a soldier's life he may be issued a challenge that he knows he cannot win. But if he refuses the contest, then the challenge may be turned upon others less ready to fight than he. In accepting it, at least he diverts the enemy's strength long enough to give his weaker allies a chance to strengthen their hand and, if all goes well, defeat their common enemy."

Galapos lapsed into silence, then resumed, "I believe I've done all I can here. The homeless have land, the villages have peace, and the palace is functioning as well as it can, due to your efforts. What we need now—men, and the means to pay them—I cannot produce like a magician. But perhaps by accepting Sheva's invitation, I can direct her energy away from the hapless towns around her. I will go in prayer."

"Surchatain," Basil hedged, "I'm an administrator, not a ruler. I don't know that I can do what you ask."

"Yes, you can, Basil. I ask only that you see to the affairs of the palace and settle the disputes of the people until I return, or until Roman comes to rule. You have wisdom aplenty to do that."

Basil, still troubled, spoke his mind: "Surchatain, it must be said. What if . . . neither of you returns?"

Galapos stilled at the mention of the unthinkable. "In that event," he said slowly, "I charge you to rule with all the wisdom God gives you. Safeguard the life of my grandson, and teach him, and when he is of age, put him on the throne."

Basil stood to bow. "I swear it shall be done as you say."

Galapos then turned to Kam. "You and I, my friend, will depart day after tomorrow if the weather holds. And I hope, before we reach Diamond's Head, that I will have a strategy for us. Now, gentlemen, you will excuse me. I have yet another charge to administer." He left the two men staring at each other in his chambers.

He went to Deirdre and Roman's vacant room and removed an item hanging in the wardrobe. Then he entered the nursery. The plump, healthy nursemaid nodded to him and rose to leave, but he said, "Please stay, Gusta. You'll need to hear this."

He pulled up a chair beside the cradle and addressed the baby. "My child . . . I, too, am leaving you. I do not know if I will return. And I do not know that your father will return. I do not have the authority to bequeath to you title of Surchatain—that right belongs to your father. But this I give you." He held up the gold medallion given to Roman long ago by his father.

"This has become something of a symbol to our family that our life and rule are preserved by God alone—not by our own strength. It is a reminder to us that if we cease to walk in His ways, we forfeit His protection and become prey for every evil on the earth. And it is a token to us that God delivers those who call on His name. I charge you to continue in the faith of your father and your grandfather and to serve the only Lord who can save you."

Galapos bent to kiss the baby, who gave him a delighted, toothless grin. Then Galapos stood and gave the medallion to the nursemaid. "I charge you to keep this for him, and to repeat those words to him every day of his life that his father is gone. If Roman returns, tell him my words."

The nursemaid bowed, brushing a blonde braid away from her tear-streaked cheek. "Yes, Surchatain. I swear to do this," she said softly.

That night, after a subdued dinner, Galapos retired early to his chambers. He removed his coat and washed his face in the marble washbasin, then paused to survey the room in which he stood: the rich purple velvets draped over the windows and the bed; the plush, intricate rug that let no space of bare floor show; the elaborately carved mantel above the polished stone fireplace and the dancing fire; the tapestries of vibrant colors depicting royal life.

He stood up close to one needlework to examine the detail. The whole was composed of many tiny threads painstakingly woven together to create a complete work, each small stitch representing a moment of someone's time. In the overall scheme, most of the stitches made up the background and were of one or two colors. Only at selected points was the background broken up to allow a figure, or a flower, to emerge. If it were not so, he mused, the scene would be a hopeless confusion of competing focal points.

So in a life . . . in the completed tapestry of a man's lifespan, each moment of time spent waiting had its purpose—to provide background and reinforcement for the occasions one is called upon to act.

He turned from the tapestry. Now was a time to act, and there was no way around it. He could pray that Sheva would not have the men or means to take Lystra from him, but unless he rose to her challenge and confronted her, how would he know if his prayer had been granted? He would spend the remainder of his days fearfully watching the road from the east.

Where he stood, he sank to his knees. "Lord God Almighty, I'm scared. I'm scared of this woman and what she designs. I'm scared for this wobbly little state and those people who have entrusted me with their lives and the lives of their children. And I fear for my own children, Roman and Deirdre—are they even among the living?

"Further, Lord, I'm scared for the helpless, innocent baby who sleeps within these walls. What will become of him if neither Roman nor I return? Lord God, I beg you to stretch your hand of protection over us all. I beg you to go with me on this visit to hell I am preparing to make. God! Give me the strength and courage to act!"

He stopped and looked up. A burning log collapsed on the grate. Galapos did not see it, for his eyes were drawn to the stone walls. They were ordinary grey stone walls. Yet something about their weight, their strength, their solidity, was an illustration to him that his prayer had been heard.

207

As he lay down to sleep, snatches of the minstrel's song ran through his mind: *Your faith will stand, and from that act comes joy to us on earth. . . .*

❖

At the appointed time, Galapos and Kam set out for Diamond's Head. At first they agreed to make a straight path for the city, passing the remains of Outpost Three and arriving at their destination by nightfall. But when they measured their progress through snow drifts and ice patches, they saw the impossibility of making it in one day. Therefore, they opted for the somewhat longer route through Bresen to afford themselves the shelter of its inn overnight.

At dusk, after a day's mute ride in biting cold and searing wind, the two travelers welcomed the sight of bustling Bresen with its crackling hearthfires and cooking pots full of savory stew. Their relief evaporated, however, as they drew into the city and saw the nature of its commerce. Even into the night, merchants and buyers were gathered around a large slave tent. Galapos's eyes grew fiery, and Kam uttered curses.

"This is a new business since I last was here," Galapos muttered.

"If we only had an outfit with us, we'd shut their shop down fast," declared Kam.

Galapos bitterly agreed. "I wonder now whether I was mistaken not to bring them." They rode slowly past the tent, noting every person around it. "Three traders and six renegades that I can see," Galapos whispered.

Kam added, "A seventh just left the tent."

"Too many for us two. And look—there's one I would be pleased to garrote—old Gerd." Galapos gritted his teeth.

"What can we do?" Kam asked in an angry breath of steam.

Galapos sat so long thinking that a few renegades began

to watch them suspiciously. He finally gave up: "I can think of nothing for now, but to return with men when we're able."

They found the inn and stabled their horses, then stamping and blowing, entered the warm glow of the dining hall. Galapos gestured to a serving girl, who brought them two large plates of beef hash, barley cakes, and ale.

As they ate and drank, their minds sharpened and they turned their attention to planning a two-man assault on Diamond's Head. "When we get within the gates of the city," Galapos instructed, "you will fall away from my side. I wish you to become a part of the crowd on the outside of the palace."

"Surchatain! Leave you to go inside alone? Why?" Kam asked, pained.

"If Sheva is planning mischief to me, you will be able to carry tidings back to Westford and organize our meager defense accordingly. Otherwise, if you remained by my side, Sheva would certainly silence you."

"Will Basil command our defenses, Surchatain?" Kam could not suppress the sarcasm in his voice.

"Roman must return soon," Galapos answered straightforwardly. "And when he does, he'll need you." He did not say out loud, *If he does not return, we are lost*.

Kam nodded reluctantly, then stiffened. "Surchatain . . . that woman over there . . . she studies you intently."

"I noticed. Perhaps the matron does not believe we are good for the bill," Galapos said wryly, swigging his ale.

"Good thing the Counselor was able to sell some of the Chataine's jewelry," muttered Kam.

As if she had somehow overheard their conversation, the woman glanced about furtively and approached their table. "You are Galapos, ruler of Lystra?" she whispered.

"Yes, lady." He eyed her in surprise.

"I have news for you. Privately."

"My servant here is utterly trustworthy, matron. Have

your say," Galapos replied.

She hesitated, weighing their eyes. "Your daughter Deirdre passed through the slave market here some months ago, while it was yet autumn. Lord Troyce bought her for the Surchataine's service in Goerge. I promised her I would tell you this if ever I had the chance. I have kept my word." And glancing around again, she retreated to the kitchen.

Galapos and Kam sat dumbstruck. Kam shot up from his seat. "Surchatain, we must ride back to Westford and gather every soldier—"

"No." Galapos reached out a hand and sat him back down. "We will go with our original plan."

"You cannot mean—"

"Kam, listen! You know we don't have the resources to attack a fortress in rock cliffs. Strength would not help us here, even if we had it! And there are crucial questions yet to be answered: *If indeed* this matron speaks the truth, does Sheva know that she has my daughter as a slave? Or is her invitation merely a coincidence? Use your reason, here, Kam! We must tread warily."

Kam hunkered down on the bench. "You are treading into fire and brimstone."

"In which case I will tread ever so lightly," Galapos winked. He called the serving girl for more ale, then continued thoughtfully, "Kam, you were with us at the outpost." The other nodded. "You saw the nature of our victory—how it came without my help or even my knowledge. Now, since God can work so great a deliverance as that, can't He do whatever He wishes with this Sheva?" Kam looked skeptical.

"Besides," Galapos added, "how do I know that God hasn't sent me just this way for Deirdre's rescue? If He can bring Tremaine's whole army to ruin to save one man who prayed, can't I trust Him with my life as well?"

"It may cost you your life," Kam said dully.

"Everyone's life is spent in time, Kam. The question is, on

what? But if this is my appointed time, then I trust that God will bring good even from my death. It must be so." The conviction in his statement left no space for debate. But Kam's eyes were clouded with doubt.

❖

That very evening at Westford, a troubled Basil rose from his bed, unable to sleep, and walked in the courtyard to let the cold night air shake him of his burdens. He was walking, and thinking, when his vision was suddenly blocked by the sight of a beautiful woman with long black hair. He pretended not to see her, for he thought he was imagining things.

But she took a step toward him and said, "I salute you, wise Counselor Basil." She lowered herself to the ground in a bow.

"Who are you?" he exclaimed.

"My name is Varela, and I have come to announce that you will soon be the new Surchatain."

He startled. "That's impossible," he sputtered. "Galapos is the Surchatain, and he is only away for a time. But even if he does not return, his Commander and son-in-law Roman has been appointed—"

Varela shook her flowing blue-black hair. "Galapos and Roman will not return, Counselor Basil. They are both dead men. I have seen it."

Basil began to tremble. "I don't believe you. Who are you to know such things?"

"I have special sight to guide you in your rule, Surchatain. Historians will record your reign as the greatest on the Continent."

He struggled inwardly. "No," he said. "The babe is next in line to rule."

"Can a babe rule?" she laughed. He was silent. "And babes

pass away from us for no reason, sometimes," she whispered. "They are so easily removed—"

"Silence, woman!" shouted Basil. "You speak murder and treason! Be gone from me!" Instantly she vanished, and Basil fled to his chambers, bolting the door behind him.

17

Roman, grim, unkempt, drew back the tent flap and halted, allowing his eyes to adjust to the darkness. A figure moved toward him, and Roman gripped his sword under his cloak. "Speak quick your purpose, fellow," the figure uttered.

"Have you slaves here?" Roman demanded, glancing around as his eyesight returned.

"A few. What's it to you?" The fellow crossed his arms, and Roman instinctively knew he had closed his hand over a breast knife.

"I am searching for a girl whom Gerd might have sold—"

"Ah ha!" laughed the other, uncrossing his arms. "The legendary seeker! Tell me, how did you lose a chataine?"

Roman's heart thumped in hope. "Have you seen her, then?"

"Well, perhaps," he answered evasively, moving to one side. An alarm sounded in Roman's head. "The question is, do you have enough money to buy her?"

"I will do whatever is necessary to release her," Roman promised, watching him. The inner alarm rose to a shriek.

"You will, eh?" the other considered, but then committed the error of flicking his eyes from Roman's face to a point behind him. Roman leapt sideways the instant a trader at his back knifed the air.

Roman rammed his sword into the man's side and spun back to the first, placing his bloody blade firmly at the trader's neck. "Answer me straight—where is she?"

"I don't know!" the trader cried, throwing his hands up.

"Then how did you know I searched for a chataine?"

"It's all over the camps—I just heard of you from the other traders! I swear I haven't seen her!"

"If you have heard of me, then you have heard of her. Who bought her from Gerd?" demanded Roman.

"I don't know, fellow—I swear it! We all laughed about it because no one knows of this girl you search for. You're chasing a ghost!"

"No!" Roman shouted. "It isn't so!" and he raised his sword to punish him for saying it.

The trader whipped out his knife in meager defense and suddenly Roman saw in his stance the attitude of the slaves—hopelessness, helplessness. This man was a slave himself, to a most cruel master. *Will you slay the captives, now?*

"Oh, Lord, no," he moaned, withdrawing his sword and backing out of the tent.

Blinking in the brightness of the winter sun on snow, he thought he saw two men standing beside the Bay Hunter. But when he looked again, there was no one, only the horse.

He felt himself suspended in the blustering cold, aching for home, aching for fear that the trader was right and Deirdre was dead. But he could not accept that. "I will never accept it until I see her myself, cold and still," he swore. Weeping with the tiredness and the pain, he mounted to continue his quest.

But as he rode forward, his heart would not go on. It knew that the trader had not lied. He had not heard of her. No one had heard of her. She was either dead, or. . . . He stopped and slowly dismounted, gazing at the palace of Corona in the distance.

He leaned up against his horse in soundless despair. How stupid, how futile this search had been. All the time that he had been searching the slave markets, she had probably been right here—in this palace. With him. With Karel, the old Surchatain, ruler of old Lystra. The man who had once sentenced him to death. Fury surged through Roman. *If I do nothing else on this futile mission,* he swore, *I will kill him.*

Choose righteousness, pursue it more than any beautiful woman. Were those words his? They echoed from a long-distant past like a warning.

Ignoring it, he mounted savagely and kicked his quivering horse toward the palace. He thundered up the path through the abandoned gates and forced open the massive doors to the vast audience hall where he had once stood with Deirdre to meet Tremaine.

It was dark and stale. The once-brilliant mosaic on the floor was obscured with debris and dust, and the chandeliers above hung empty of candles. Crude torches placed near the front of the hall betrayed habitation, however. The massive throne, stripped of its gold and jewels, still stood on the backs of four carved lions.

Roman drew his sword and warily advanced. His footfalls echoed like a drumbeat in the emptiness. He gained the throne and peered at the thick, musty curtains behind it. He had begun to draw them aside gingerly with his sword when an echoing rustle in the hall drew him about instantly.

Rollet, son and Chatain of the late Tremaine, stood in the center of the hall grinning maliciously. At his sides stood four glowering soldiers. "Have you lost something, guardian?" Rollet sneered.

215

Roman gripped his sword tighter. "Where is she?"

"Oh, how I wish she were here," Rollet sighed sarcastically. "I would display her to your eyes before I gouged them out!"

"Where is she?" Roman repeated, louder, to drown out the discomfiting ring of truth in Rollet's words.

Rollet only laughed and lifted his sword. As a man, the five of them advanced to encircle Roman. He backed up to the throne as his only defense. But the greater battle was already raging within him. Was he mistaken? Had he been wrong from the start?

The answer seemed to come in the fierce blows from Rollet's swordsmen. Roman warded them off and struck back as best he could, hampered by the necessity of keeping his back to the throne. They could not all reach him at once, but as soon as he tired. . . . His thoughts evaporated in the concentration of fighting for his life.

He saw Rollet step back and allow the others to harry Roman while he rested. "Save the kill for me!" Rollet ordered. Roman lunged unexpectedly and wounded one of them. The others pressed him all the more intently.

He parried their strikes, but could not stave off his own thoughts. *I have been wrong; I have been all wrong, and I will die for my error.*

It occurred to him to cry out to his Savior, but he refused. *He won't help me now—I forsook Him.* His own words after the battle at the outpost rang in his mind: "Lord God, my strength and my Redeemer!" *No, it's too late for me*, he thought as he felt his strength slipping away.

Then Rollet motioned to the soldiers, who backed off. As he stepped up to Roman and lifted his sword, his face burned with the intensity of his hatred. "It will give me great pleasure to send your body back in pieces to Galapos," he uttered.

Roman raised his sword in utter weariness and whispered, "Lord God—"

He did not have a chance to finish. The soldiers behind Rollet dropped in quick succession. Rollet wheeled to meet his end, cursing.

Roman blinked to see two of his own men, Marc and Varan, wiping their blades and grasping his arms. "Commander, thank God we reached you in time!" exclaimed Marc.

Varan added, "We thought we had lost you for sure in that last trader's tent—but you came out whole after all. So we knew we had better follow you closer after that. Then the blasted door jammed on us, and we had to go around to get in!"

Roman shook his head stupidly. "How is it . . . that you . . . ?"

The men glanced at each other, then Marc said carefully, "Commander, the Surchatain instructed us to follow and watch you. . . . We were not to interfere unless your life was in peril."

Roman hung his head and murmured, "Thank you for the foresight of dear Galapos." Then he raised beaten eyes to the men before him. "You have certainly saved my life. Your faithfulness has earned you a substantial reward on our return to Westford. And we must return immediately. . . . I fear I've already been diverted too long."

He closed his eyes in pain, or grief, and Varan reached a hand to steady him. Roman gripped it and said, "Please return to the horses and wait for me there. I'll be out straightway." Marc and Varan exchanged dubious looks, but Roman insisted, "I'm all right now. There is one more thing I must do here. Go." They saluted and turned away, their boots echoing retreat in the great hall.

Roman watched them vanish beyond the door, then he turned away from the bodies on the floor and knelt before the throne. "Lord God," he murmured, his voice cracking, "thank you for rescuing me, though I left in disobedience, taking the word of a witch over my own father Galapos. And though I have spent these months denying you and going my own way, still you answered when I cried to you. How little I understand your mercy. . . . Forgive me for my wandering, for my wasting time. Now, Lord, I relent. I know you want me to return to Westford, and I will." He stopped to wipe his face.

Struggling, he continued, "And Deirdre—oh, Father! If she is indeed dead—if I must live my days without her, my jewel, my dove—then—then—" he jerked up his grimy, tear-stained face to the throne and cried, "So be it! But oh, Father—you must enable me to bear it, for without you and her I would die." Collapsing, broken, at the foot of the throne, he wept as he had never done before.

A few minutes later he stilled, then quietly rose. His mind was settled and quiet at last, the brokenness healed. He straightened, cleaning off his face, then calmly stepped over the bodies to depart the hall. Reconsidering, he paused to retrieve the good swords Rollet and his men had carried.

Marc and Varan were seated on their horses with the Bay Hunter between them, waiting. As he approached, they eyed him with concern but did not question him. "We're going to have a hard ride ahead of us," he said matter-of-factly. "We'll take these swords as payment for our provisions. I hope you're not too weary, for we're going to ride through the day and night until we reach Westford."

"Is time so short, Commander?" wondered Marc, thinking of the months they had trailed him.

"Yes. I may be too late as it is."

They rode to the inn at which Roman had stayed his first night in Corona. As he entered, flanked by his men, the talk in the dining room hushed. Roman plopped the swords on the bar before the proprietor and said, "I want good stew and good ale for myself and my men, fodder for our horses, and bread and meat enough for a three-day journey. These swords are worth ten times that, so *don't short me*."

The proprietor blustered, "Yessir—certainly, my good man. Here—sit here—best seats in the house. We'll serve you directly." So saying, he rapidly wiped a large table and gestured nervously for them to sit. A serving girl promptly appeared at his wave and poured three large goblets full, then left the jug.

The hall was silent as the three quietly drank and broke apart the loaf of bread that had been brought them. Then a renegade near the bar turned lazily in his chair toward them. "Those swords have Tremaine's crest," he drawled. "Where'd you get them?"

Roman raised dangerous eyes and looked him over. The renegade shifted a little. Then Roman answered, "I took them from five men who tried to kill me." All over the hall, eyes darted and heads cocked a little, but no one else spoke.

The proprietor brought out a large kettle of rich stew. Roman, Marc, and Varan ate until they were satisfied as the quiet hall observed their every bite. Then the proprietor returned with three leather bags stuffed with provisions. Marc looked through them and nodded. They rose to leave.

Then a stranger rushed into the hall and, not perceiving the atmosphere, exclaimed to a fellow near the door, "I just been by the palace, and Rollet's been cut up like a leg o' lamb!"

"Dead?" startled the other.

"Dead as a rat under a cart wheel!"

A hundred eyes fastened on the three Lystrans. "Why, we have the murderers right here," said the renegade near the bar, standing. Others began to stand. "I think they ought to pay for it," he said. "What do you say?"

Swords were unsheathed. "Yeah!" "Make them answer for it!" "Murderers!" Chairs scraped the floor, and a mob came together.

"You lawless dogs!" spat Roman. "You murder and rob every waking moment and you would judge me? Get out of my way!"

The men between him and the door dropped back as Roman stalked through their midst, never even having bothered to draw his sword. Close behind him, Marc winked at Varan, who shook his head.

Outside, Varan muttered, "Oh, no." For the thick grey clouds had opened up and begun to pour snow down upon the city like white ash. Roman noted it with a shrug and mounted. The three rode out of Corona due south.

After an hour, the snowfall lessened and then cleared away. By the time they came upon the mountains, the clouds had lightened to a creamy white.

On the edge of Falcon Pass, they halted. Individually, they studied the high, heavily laden peaks. The stillness around was profound. "Doesn't look good, Commander," whispered Marc.

"We can't go around," Roman returned in a whisper, shaking a thin layer of snow from his hood. "No talking past this point until we're well onto the plain." The men gingerly spurred their horses, and they advanced at a cautious walk, barely breathing, through the treacherous whiteness.

They had almost made the plain when a snowshoe rabbit dashed under the legs of Marc's horse. Startled, it reared and neighed. The sound echoed up to the mountaintops, and the horrified men watched great cracks appear in the immense white slopes.

"Ride!" Roman cried. But they could not possibly outrun the avalanche. It thundered down the mountainsides, gaining on them by the second. Marc shouted above the roar, gesturing toward a large crag in the Pass. The three pushed their horses desperately for the shelter of the jutting rock just as the snow and ice crashed down the mountains around them.

In seconds it was over. The men looked dumbly at each other, amazed to be alive, and Roman uttered, "Thank you, Father, for the rock." They rested long enough to stop shaking, then urged the horses on.

18

Roman had not been exaggerating when he warned Marc and Varan of a hard ride. Coming out of the Pass, they met up with a vast expanse of white that had been the plain. They spurred to a bumpy gallop, the horses seesawing through the snow. When Varan's horse landed both front feet in a camouflaged hole Varan did a perfect flip over its head, disappearing into a man-shaped indention in the snow. Roman and Marc reined up, looking down at the hole in astonishment.

Varan slowly rose up out of it, shaking off a coat of snow while his horse staggered up onto firmer footing. Marc snickered. "Are you hurt?" Roman asked.

"Uh . . . no, Commander," Varan answered, grabbing for the loose reins.

"And the horse?"

"He's laughing, too," Varan observed, shooting a frosty look at Marc.

These slowdowns were frequent. When they came to

the cover of forest where the snow was not so deep, the ground was frozen and slippery. Edgy horses balked at galloping and, when they attempted to run, went slipping into the nearest tree. After barely an hour the men were forced to rest and calm the horses.

Marc passed around a small loaf, and they ate handfuls of snow while standing. Into the quiet of the forest, from some distance, came an echoing howl. The men looked up apprehensively, and Marc's horse whinnied. A second howl, closer, answered the first. The men went for the horses. "No need to gather such unpleasant company as wolves," remarked Varan.

"That settles any question of sleeping in the forest," added Marc. Roman nodded as if expecting it. They reseated themselves and rode in formation. As they rounded a bend, they abruptly found themselves facing an impenetrable wall of trees and underbrush.

"What—?" Roman uttered. "How did we—?" He spun around to look at the ground.

"We're not on the road. We've lost the road," groaned Varan.

"Backtrack. Carefully now," said Roman, and they turned on their own tracks, searching the ground and trees. From very close came a hungry howl, and Marc's horse began to hop like a rabbit.

"Easy. Easy now," Marc soothed it, muttering under his breath, "from now on I'm leaving you home for my wife to ride."

"Here's the road," Roman said suddenly. "We just got a false start." Letting down in relief, they took it at a canter.

Throughout that day and into the night they rode, guiding themselves by instinct when they lost the road in fields of white. Time and again they were forced to maneuver around obstacles hidden by the snow or to backtrack when they could not move forward at all.

At daybreak, after they had ridden through the whole long night, they stopped in an abandoned hut to eat and sleep a few hours. But when Marc, on watch, heard the cry of wolves closing in, they stiffly roused and began to ride again.

As urgently as he felt the need to see Westford, Roman accepted the various dangers and setbacks without question or complaint. They were the natural consequences of his stubborn venture. Thoroughly humbled by the destruction he had nearly brought on his own head, he was genuinely grateful to at least be moving in the right direction. He would not presume to question Providence now.

But the relief of seeing the towers of Westford rise in the distance caused his eyes to water. He pushed his faltering horse to a gallop through the snow and plunged down the winding road to the front gates. The guards greeted him with a surprised hallo, but he hardly paused to wave as he fell from the horse and tossed off the reins.

"Galapos!" He ascended the stone stairs in leaps.

Basil met him at the head of the stairs. "Roman! You've come home!" He impulsively embraced the grimy, sweaty soldier in relief and joy.

Roman pulled away. "Where is Galapos?"

"He's not here," Basil said, sobering. "He accepted an offer to meet with Sheva at Diamond's Head."

"Sheva?" Roman repeated in alarm. "How many soldiers did he take?"

"One. Kam alone."

"Only Kam? He went to Diamond's Head and took only Kam?" Roman protested, pained. *I should have been here. I should have been here.*

Reading him, Basil answered, "That is what he wished. It would have been no different had you been here, for the Surchatain left instructions for you to rule Westford in his absence. If he doesn't return, I am to proclaim you Surchatain."

He paused to gauge Roman's reaction, but the other's

face was hard and unmoved. "It's good you're here now, Commander," Basil continued, formality masking his fervor. "I can run the business of a palace, but have no mind for defending it in war."

Roman nodded, thinking. He had turned to speak to Marc and Varan standing behind him when a commotion in the audience hall below drew their attention.

There, a young man in a well-worn, bulky cloak was scuffling with two soldiers. He was demanding, "I must speak with him! I must!" Looking up, he caught sight of Roman on the stairway and shouted, "Roman, hear me! Please! It will profit you greatly!"

Roman motioned to the men to release him and came slowly down the stairs, peering at the young man. His face was vaguely familiar, but who . . . ?

The young man was saying, "For months now, ever since I came to Westford, I've been waiting for you and watching for you—I would speak with no one else. I know only you here, and I knew you would hear me out rather than kill me—" at Roman's bemused expression, he pleaded, "Don't you recognize me?" Roman shook his head. "I'm Colin, son of Corneus."

A soldier behind him snarled, and he exclaimed, "Wait! Here me out! Will you hear me, Roman?"

"That is the Commander you're addressing," Marc said coolly.

"Yes, so I heard. An honor well deserved," Colin said sincerely.

"You may speak," Roman nodded.

Colin inhaled and began, "Last winter, when you brought my father the offer of an alliance with Galapos against Tremaine—I was there, remember?" Roman nodded firmly.

"I was so eager to be a part of it all and fight with you that my father allowed me to ride at his side, preparing our defenses and overseeing the army. He was pleased with my performance, so that he began to entrust me with greater and greater matters. Eventually, he handed over to me knowledge that he withheld even from Jason. One of the things he taught me was how to gain entry to the palace treasury. It was such a great store that even its location was a closely held secret. Only he, my mother, and I knew it.

"However, when he made that treacherous counteralliance with Tremaine, I broke with him. Completely. It so angered him that he sent scouts after my life and I was forced into hiding. But when I learned what happened at your outpost, I returned to the palace at Ooster. There I found Jason and mother—dead.

"But the treasury is there, untouched! I have brought proof of that—" And he drew out a large, heavy pouch from under his cloak and poured out a stream of gold coins at Roman's feet. "That amounts to a thousand royals," Colin stated, and the soldiers standing around gaped. Even Roman looked stunned.

"There are many hundreds of thousands royals more— I don't know how much," Colin continued. "But the entire treasury is yours, Commander, if you will give me a place in your army and let me serve under you."

In the dumbstruck silence of all those around, Roman raised one eyebrow ever so slightly and said, "Done."

Colin breathed out. "Send with me a unit of your most trusted men, and I will bring you back a treasury ten times that of Karel's."

Roman addressed the soldier at his side. "Didn't I say you would be rewarded on our return? Marc, I charge you and Varan to select and lead a unit to Ooster tomorrow morning. For your services, I will appoint you a percentage of what you bring back."

"Commander!" Despite their depleted condition, they somehow found the energy to salute smartly before sprinting from the hall.

"Colin." Roman turned back to him. "I am grateful for your loyalty to the alliance with Galapos, even at the cost of defying your father."

"A good soldier stands by his word," Colin replied.

"You are that," Roman acknowledged. "Now, do you accept this charge: to defend Lystra and the Surchatain with your life, to execute the orders of your Commander, and to deal responsibly with the men under you?"

"I do, Commander." Colin stood straight-backed.

"Then I appoint you to the rank of captain in the army. Dub," he motioned to a soldier, "take Captain Colin to the captains' quarters and find him a uniform." To Colin he added, "Tomorrow early, Marc and Varan and their men will meet you at the front gates. When you return from Ooster, I will set you over a unit."

"Commander!" Colin saluted, as did Dub, and crisply departed.

Roman looked down at the mess of gold on the floor and said, "Counselor, it appears you've been repaid for the hundred royals you gave me. Gather these up for the treasury and begin settling accounts with the soldiers immediately. And yourself, of course."

"Certainly, Commander." Basil stooped eagerly, mentally computing.

Roman's return, and the good fortune attending it, led to a sudden transformation around the palace. Soldiers who had been slacking off, moping or drinking, all at once began repairing equipment and drilling again. Posts that had been abandoned were now attended by correctly dressed guards standing at attention. And when word leaked out that there was money in the treasury again, servants who missed the comforts of palace life returned in droves, seeking work. As Basil was inundated with requests for appointments, interviews, and considerations, he could not have been happier.

Roman himself had an interview that had been waiting

several months. Somewhat shyly, he opened the nursery door. The nursemaid raised her head and stood quickly. "Commander! You're back! Welcome home, Commander Roman!" Gusta restrained herself to greet him with the proper respect, although her face shone.

He nodded distractedly to her and began, "Where . . . ?" She pointed proudly to the bed, where a black-headed baby lay enthusiastically whipping a heavy medallion about. "Is that the infant I left?" Roman gasped. Pausing to watch him quietly for a moment, Roman remarked the similarity he saw in the baby's features to Deirdre's—the shape of the eyes, the curve of the lips.

Then he crossed over and picked up the child. As the baby whacked him in the face with the medallion, he took it from the little fist and asked, "How did he get hold of this?"

"Commander, the Surchatain gave it as a bequest to him before he left, as he seemed uncertain of ever returning. And he gave him a charge, which he instructed me to tell you on your return." She pursed her lips to get her memory in order, and Roman watched her intently.

"He said, the medallion is a symbol to the Surchatain's family that your life and rule are preserved by God. He said that if you fail to walk in God's ways, you forfeit His protection and become prey for any evil on the earth. He said it is also a reminder that God delivers those who call on His name, and he charged the baby to serve God as did his father and grandfather."

Roman nodded slowly, closing his eyes. "Galapos is a wise, wise man. . . . Have I lost them both, now?" As he gazed at the child, the nursemaid grew anxious at the sad look in his eyes.

"Commander, he's a strong, healthy baby," Gusta said brightly. "He'll make you so proud! But he needs a name! What will you name him?"

Roman stared into the baby's face, then sighed and shook

his head. "I can't even think now. I will have to think of what she would have wanted to name him."

He looked up out the window toward the northern hill country, and his drawn face darkened. He handed the child to the nursemaid, saying, "I have one more task that remains before I can rest."

As he left the nursery and trotted down the stairs, reservations flooded his mind: *You're tired—you've ridden almost two days and a night just to get here. You've done well; you can rest and take care of the other later*.

Looking up, Roman replied to the air, "If I delay, you will escape and come back to cause trouble later."

Downstairs, he strapped on his sword and called for a fresh horse. Basil met him at the door, anxious. "Where are you going, Roman?"

The Commander stopped briefly. "There is an evil that I've allowed to remain too long in Lystra. I am going to remove it without further delay. I'll be back before nightfall, Basil—if I live." Baffled, the Counselor stepped aside to let him leave.

Roman took the waiting horse's reins from the errand boy, who grinned up at him, "Welcome home, Commander."

"Thank you, Kevin," he smiled wearily. But he lifted himself onto the horse and resolutely headed toward the hills. Stride by stride, he prayed with grim intensity. He feared what he had to do. But she must be dealt with.

As he rode, he looked down at the horse's hoofs, crunching the snow. It was virgin white all around, but for tiny prints of hares or birds. Roman found himself warily scanning for large animal tracks. Despite seeing none, he threw back his cloak to ride with one hand on the hilt of his sword. He would not be caught unaware.

He paused at a ravine to gauge his direction. Her hut was farther north—yes, that was the way. He dismounted to lead his horse down into and up the far side of the rocky,

230

icy ravine. Topping the crest, he had scarcely glanced up before a mammoth black wolf crashed into his chest, fangs lunging for his throat.

The momentum of the attack threw man and wolf back down into the gorge. Painfully, but fortunately, they landed in a tangling mass of frosty briar. In the precious seconds the wolf needed to free itself, snapping and snarling, Roman had gotten to his knees and drawn his sword. At the wolf's next lunge, he held the sword steady with both hands and the beast blindly impaled itself on the blade. Then it sank dead before him.

Staggering up, Roman stared down in unsteady wonder at the monster. He had never seen a wolf like it before. It was large beyond belief—almost the size of a small pony. It had thick, blue-black fur and abnormally long fangs. And strangely, it had no tail. The putrid smell of its blood drove Roman back a pace. At length, he shrugged off the mystery of it, climbed out of the ravine, and remounted. He would not be deterred.

He reached the witch's hut, holding his newly stained sword at the ready. Smoke wafted up from the crude chimney. Breathing a final prayer, he slid from his horse and approached the door. "Come out to me, Varela!" There was no movement in reply. He braced himself and shoved open the door.

He saw the rough table cluttered with herbs and utensils. A large book lay open on it. A fire burned in the grate. A chair lay overturned by the table. She had apparently gone in haste, intending to return soon.

Roman stood a moment, undecided. Should he wait for her? No—the idea was abhorrent to him. But he would make certain she had nothing to return to.

He gingerly lifted a burning branch from the fire and set it to the book on the table, then to the table itself, the chair, the sides of the hut. Stepping outside, he tossed the branch up onto the thatched roof. Then impassively he watched the flames consume the hut and melt the snow around it in a widening ring.

As he witnessed the fire burn fiercely and then die away, he felt the conviction that he had done all that was required of him.

19

"Goldie, please decorate these cakes for me," Bettina whispered. "I can't do it like you, and the mistress will slay me if it's not done just right."

Deirdre smiled and took the tray of pastries. "The mistress is especially edgy today."

"Someone important is dining with the Surchataine, and she has promised the gallows for anyone who fails in his duties." Bettina hushed as the kitchen mistress harriedly approached.

"Goldie—here—you serve the wine tonight. No, no—no need to take that stinking ale Caranoe likes. He is not at table tonight. He is ill in his room. Here—go on!"

✛

Within his chambers, Caranoe stood whispering instructions to an armed soldier. "You will station your men at every exit and behind every curtain. We will allow them dinner.

Then, after the meal, I will enter the hall and make my accusations against Troyce before Sheva and everyone present.

"Your signal will be the word *traitor*. When you hear that word, you will attack and kill everyone. If you let anyone escape, you will pay for it! Make certain you slay Sheva first, then Troyce, then all her bodyguard, servants, and court. When all is done, I shall announce at large that I quashed an attempted takeover by Troyce, and that I am the new Surchatain. If you execute my instructions to the letter, you will be Commander of my army. Now go!"

❖

Deirdre stepped gracefully into the dining hall with the silver decanter of wine. She noted with approval the boughs of evergreen decorating the room. But as she looked from the evergreen on the table to the faces above it, her breathing stopped and her legs turned to water. There, seated at Sheva's left, was Galapos, dear Galapos, her own father. He wore his Lystran uniform like a proud bear surrounded by scruffy dogs.

For an instant she was ready to drop the decanter and fling herself upon him. But somehow she was restrained and woodenly advanced with the wine. *He must see me; he must see me*, she thought as she poured the Surchataine's wine.

Now she was pouring his wine, leaning close to him, almost in his face. She even dared to spill a drop in his lap to make him look at her, even in anger. But he did not raise his head. Perspiration beaded on her forehead as she filled Lord Troyce's goblet, across from him. *He must see me*. But as she worked her way around the table, Galapos never looked toward her.

"I was somewhat surprised by your invitation, my lady," he was saying. "Knowing you were allied with Tremaine, I did not think we had much to discuss. So what is it you wish to tell me?"

"Galapos, you offend me," she protested sweetly. "*I* had no desire to see Tremaine rule the Continent, but Savin chose to join with him, and what choice does a woman have but to go along with her husband? Your victory, however, allows each of us to rule our own sphere as we ought. Will you allow me to rule my little plot, my lord?" she beseeched him.

He eyed her shrewdly. "If you obey and enforce my laws, Sheva."

She lowered her eyes to hide her anger. Then she casually said, "I must confess I was surprised to see you brought no soldiers."

"Why should I?" he returned easily, reaching for his goblet. "One ruler visiting another by invitation should have no fear for his life. You know the value of protecting the office."

"But, how dangerous for a ruler to travel alone. . . ."

"Not for me. Somehow, I find friends in every corner." He gave her a meaningful look. "My soldiers are where I need them, Sheva."

The Surchataine shifted uneasily. The other guests hardly stirred, watching this interchange with consuming interest. Brude, though, stared at Galapos in blatant hatred. Galapos matched his stare with cold blue eyes until the other looked away.

Deirdre finished pouring and had to step away from the table behind Sheva. Still he did not look. Then she realized sickeningly that he had not recognized her. He would eat and carry on business and leave, never knowing his only child had served him wine at Sheva's table.

The despair of the situation almost strangled her. Blackness passed momentarily before her face. But from out of the mists, she heard Galapos saying, "There is, however, one thing we lack desperately at Westford, my lady, and that is pretty serving girls. You seem to have an abundance. In your generosity, perhaps you would allow me to buy one or two from you?"

Sheva recovered, amused. "And which one catches your eye, my lord?"

"Why," Galapos straightened and casually looked over the serving maids who entered and exited. "Your wine bearer is comely, though sloppy."

The Surchataine shifted to regard Deirdre, who stood motionless for fear of screaming or fainting. Then Sheva turned back and deliberately placed her elbows on the table. "I never knew you had such an interest in serving girls, Galapos." The softness of her voice accentuated her contempt. Lord Troyce glanced in furtive embarrassment at Sheva.

"Well," Galapos winked, "it certainly makes a pleasanter dinner to have one like her around."

Sheva smiled. "And what would you pay for her?"

"What would you require, my lady?" Galapos returned.

Sheva's eyes gleamed with fanciful greed. "Your life, Galapos."

A gasp went around the table. But when Galapos said, "I will pay it," even Sheva was silent.

Then she sputtered, "Are you a fool, Galapos? What is she to you? Don't you know that your word before me is irrevocable?"

"I know, Sheva." Deirdre had never seen him so calm and sure. "But I require a bill of freedom to assure her release after my death."

Sheva spun to Lord Troyce. "Go write up the proper paper immediately—bring it and—"

"Surchataine!" cried Lord Troyce. "There *is* no proper paper for such a thing! To require the blood of a ruler to free a slave is—is absurd! You must not even consider—"

"*Do as I say!*" Sheva screamed. "Or pay the price yourself!"

For a moment he sat frozen. Then he rose, knocking the table, and hurried from the hall.

Deirdre was struck immobile in horror and hope. The guests at table watched Sheva and Galapos. Sheva calmly resumed her meal; Galapos sat contemplating.

In minutes Troyce returned, carrying a paper. "Sheva, I beg you—"

"Read what you have written," she commanded.

He swallowed and coughed. "Bill of Freedom. This bill authorizes the release from the service of Sheva, Surchataine of Goerge, one maid known as Goldie. This bill is effective upon the death of Galapos, Surchatain of Lystra, and assures the freedom from bondage of said maid to the day of her death. Signed with the Surchataine's seal this tenth day of the sixth month of the first year of her reign."

Sheva turned to Galapos. "Is it satisfactory?"

"Yes."

"Then bring the candle," she instructed Troyce. Helplessly, he handed her a lighted taper. She dripped it on the document, then pressed her signet ring into the wax.

The Surchataine stood and held the bill out to Deirdre. "Claim your freedom, girl."

Her anguish broke. "No! No! Galapos, no!"

"Child—Goldie." He addressed her by that silly name in a voice of quiet authority. "Take it. It must be so."

To refuse such authority, so graciously expended on her behalf, was arrogance. Trembling, Deirdre accepted the document.

"Guards." Sheva was radiant with unexpected triumph. "Escort our guest to the gallows."

There was upheaval as the guards took hold of Galapos and led him out. The dinner guests rose of one accord to follow and watch. Deirdre forced herself as far as the door that opened into the courtyard, then leaned in despair on the doorjamb as the others brushed past her for a better view.

By this time Kam, outside as instructed, had found some logs to split behind the servants' house. He was working undisturbed by the servants and guards, who were occupied with their own chores. "Look there!" the smith said suddenly, pointing his hammer toward the palace.

Kam could not see around the corner of the building, but others near the smith stopped their work to watch. "Who's that?" asked one.

"A dead man, now," another answered bitterly. As other servants were coming around the building to look, Kam dropped the axe and joined them.

In horror Kam watched as his ruler was shoved toward the gallows, then bound there. Kam descried the Surchataine in her royal dress and her administrator beside her, talking rapidly. He could not hear Troyce saying, "Sheva, this is madness! Consider the consequences of murdering a Surchatain!" Kam could only watch in furious impotence as Galapos was taken, unresisting, to the platform and fitted with the noose. The Surchatain stood at attention, eyes straight ahead as if fixed on something compelling. A hood was brought up, but Sheva waved it away.

The guards began backing off. Sheva stepped up to the gallows and said something to Galapos. He made no reply that Kam could see.

Suddenly Kam roused from his shock: *Kam, you idiot, do something!* Sheva raised her hand, and Kam lunged toward the courtyard. A guard stopped him with a blow to his chest. He fell to his knees, breathless, as Sheva dropped her hand and Galapos dropped through the platform.

Kam struggled, unable to breathe, to move, to tear his eyes from the horror of the scene before him. When at last Kam's breath came in a rending gasp, Galapos was still.

In a loud voice, Sheva ordered the body taken down and thrown over the cliffs into the Sea. Kam, on his knees, pressed his forehead into the dirt, utterly unable to believe what he had just seen. It was not real. It could not have happened to Galapos.

But the servants around him began to disperse and return to their chores. They had witnessed it, and it meant nothing to them.

Then Kam remembered his orders. He rose and quietly slipped from the milling crowd. He slid unnoticed through the fence, retrieved his horse from the stables of Diamond's Head inn, and rode like a madman out of the city gates.

❖

At the palace, Sheva bade all her guests back into the dining hall to finish their meal. Passing Deirdre, she looked over the pale, frightened girl and said contemptuously, "You have your freedom. Now get out of my palace."

Deirdre flung herself into the courtyard. The guests passing her stared and Brude spat. The last one to pass her was Sevter. His face conveyed his wretched helplessness and grief, then he too returned with heavy steps to the dining hall.

Alone beside the gallows, Deirdre threw herself on the ground and began to weep. But then she had another thought. Galapos had spent his life to free her. It must not be in vain.

She jumped upright and ran from the courtyard into the kitchen. "Bettina—!"

"Goldie, what happened out there? Who was hanged?"

"Bettina, if I die today, promise me you will care for Arund!"

"Goldie!"

"Will you take care of him?" Deirdre demanded.

"Yes, but—"

"Good. Now tell me where Caranoe's quarters are."

"Goldie!"

"Where is his room?" Deirdre shouted.

A servant who had been listening interrupted, "I'm taking

239

his dinner to him there. Follow me." The girl picked up a tray of roast quail and left the kitchen. Deirdre followed her up stone stairs and down a passageway to a door.

The servant knocked, entered with the tray, and came out empty-handed a moment later. "He's in there, and he doesn't look so sick to me," she whispered in passing Deirdre.

Standing in the corridor, Deirdre shoved the paper into her sash and tried to think. *Lord, what do I do? How do I do this?* She took a long breath and knocked on the door.

"Enter!" His voice sounded muffled. She opened the door and walked into his chambers.

Caranoe was standing fully dressed and armed in the center of the room, devouring the bird with one hand. When he saw her, the surprise on his face gave way quickly to a leer. "So you changed your mind? Smart girl," he mumbled around a mouthful.

"No, Caranoe," she said. "I have come for the key to the chains."

At this assertion, he burst into roaring laughter. But only for a moment. Suddenly he gagged and grabbed his throat. He spat out his mouthful but something was caught. Deirdre watched in shock as he reeled and gouged and fell to the floor choking. Soon he lay motionless, hands still clutching at his throat.

When she could make herself move, she reached shaking hands toward him, pulling from his tunic a golden chain bearing an ugly iron key. Grasping it tightly, she ran from the room, down the passage and stairs, through the courtyard, and across the footbridge into the fields. Finished for the day, the slaves had been locked into their house for the night. Even now she could not help but notice that the setting sun had colored the palace a blood red.

She fell at the northwest corner of the field house and pounded on the boards. A plank popped open, and she shoved the key in to Nihl. "Free yourselves, then come to my aid in the dining hall!" she gasped.

"Wait for us!" he urged.

"No—just come as soon as you are able!" She was on her feet again, running back to the palace. She stopped at the courtyard entrance only because she was too winded to run a step farther. Gaining her breath took only a moment, however. She was delirious with courage, impelled to see her actions through to the end.

Brushing aside servants and guards, she walked into the dining hall where Sheva and her court were still seated. The conversation hushed, all eyes looking toward the redeemed slave. Deirdre announced, "Sheva, I have come to call you to account for the murder of my father, Galapos."

The statement shook Sheva herself. Before she could respond, Lord Troyce stood. "I also, Sheva, renounce your actions as reprehensible and criminal. I will no longer serve you." He walked the length of the table to stand by Deirdre.

At this point Sevter rose. "I am with you also, Chataine Deirdre."

As he went to Deirdre's side, Sheva bolted up in panic or fury. "Traitors! Traitors!" she screamed. "I am—" At once soldiers sprang from every doorway, slashing their swords. Sheva was the first to fall.

Neither Sevter nor Troyce was armed. But before a soldier could reach them, the three were surrounded by a wall of slaves who appeared carrying swords, clubs, and even tools for weapons. As more and more slaves poured into the hall, the soldiers backed off from them to fight against Sheva's bodyguard instead.

The tower alarm sounded. Deirdre suddenly realized there was fighting in the kitchen. "Nihl!" she shouted. He was right beside her. "Save Bettina and the baby in the kitchen!"

He motioned, and several slaves dispatched themselves

as a band to the kitchen. In moments they returned, herding a large group of panicky servants. Bettina rushed to Deirdre, handing her a screaming Arund.

They stood in a tight group, watching as Sheva's guards and Caranoe's rebels battled each other. It was a wicked, confusing fight, for the two sides wore identical uniforms and could not be certain in the frenzy who was friend or foe. So they killed each other without discretion, too inflamed or afraid to stop.

The moment came when there was only a handful of soldiers left alive and fighting in the great hall. Suddenly a spirit of sanity seemed to return to them, and they paused with lifted swords to stare at each other. Then several dropped their swords and ran. Only four soldiers remained, blank-faced and gasping.

Slowly, one of them turned toward Deirdre and her retinue of slaves. Dragging his sword, the soldier approached her and dropped to his knees. "Chataine," he said miserably, "I have no choice but to beg service under you. If you will not have me, I beg you to deliver me swiftly to death. But if you let me live, I swear my life in allegiance to you."

Deirdre's heart broke at the despair in his voice. "I accept your offer of allegiance, and I promise you will come to know pride in your service," she answered. He gazed up at her in wonderment. Promptly the other three soldiers offered their allegiance, which she also accepted.

At this point, Troyce turned toward Deirdre and sank to his knees. "My lady," he began, "I have thrown away all honor and title I ever possessed, and have no more to offer you now than any one of the slaves who stands behind you. But if you can accept such a foolish administrator into your service, I will serve you and God to the end of my days, as did your father, Galapos."

Deirdre's eyes misted and she felt suddenly drained. "You may come with me, Troyce."

"You'll take me also, won't you, Deirdre?" It was Sevter.

"You will oversee all household activity at the palace," Deirdre said warmly.

"You have an army to command," Nihl said to her, gesturing to the hundreds of slaves who now filled the hall and courtyard.

"Yes," she said eagerly. "Nihl, get them bathed and clothed and fed. Instruct them to take from the palace all the food and livestock they can handle. We'll need it all when we get to Westford—"

Westford! Roman! The thought of seeing him again— and her baby!—made her spirit soar in joy.

There was a rustle in the crowd around her. It parted, and the kitchen mistress came before her and fell at her feet. "My—my lady," she faltered, and Deirdre looked down at her.

"What do you want?"

"If you could find it within your heart—to take me also— I will serve in the lowest place on your kitchen staff—"

Deirdre sighed. "I wouldn't presume to run a kitchen without you—what is your name, by the by?"

"Merry, my lady," she answered, raising her face.

"Merry!" Deirdre and Bettina turned to each other, bursting into laughter. Turning solemn, Deirdre said, "You may have charge of the kitchen, Merry, if you swear not to slay your staff."

"Oh, I swear, my lady," she vowed in dead seriousness.

Deirdre laughed again, shaking her head. Thoughts of Roman crowded out every other thought. "Troyce, how soon can we reach Westford if we leave tonight?"

"My lady," he answered carefully, "in this cold, we should wait until morning to travel. Then it will take two, well, three days, if the weather is calm. Is there a lord who awaits you?"

"Yes." It came out with such intensity. "He does not know it yet, but he is the Surchatain."

Deirdre bathed that night in Sheva's bath, and dressed in Sheva's robes. She bent over Arund, snuggled in his box, now lined with clean quilts. Then she nestled herself between the downy covers of Sheva's bed.

Warm and grateful, she began to ponder the events of her deliverance, and Galapos's costly sacrifice. "Oh, Galapos—Father—" she murmured in new grief and wonder. "How could you have done that for me? Am I worth such a price to you?" As she drifted to sleep, the answer came with conviction: The simple fact that he had paid it made her worth such a price.

❧ 20 ❧

Early in the glistening morning Deirdre met Troyce, Sevter and Nihl at the palace gates. They had readied Sheva's own horse for Deirdre, and she mounted, marveling, "How different is my going out from my coming in!" She wore Sheva's velvets, her fur cloak and hood. Sevter handed Arund up to her, and from her saddle she looked on the rest of the assembly.

The slaves—soldiers, now—were arranging themselves in ranks for travel. Dressed appropriately in uniforms and cloaks, each carried a pack and a weapon. Several had taken charge of driving the livestock. A number rode horses— among them, Nihl.

Deirdre remarked to him, "Your men are so orderly and disciplined! How can that be? I was led to believe that if you were ever unchained, you would wreak havoc."

Nihl smiled grimly. "You misunderstand us, Chataine Deirdre. Our chains did not make us animals. No—they made us willing to learn discipline from Josef. The men have agreed to obey me as their leader. But more," he said, drawing a bundle from his coat, "God has avenged us, as He said." Nihl held up the bundle so she could see it was Josef's Scriptures.

As Deirdre stared at him in admiration, her eye was caught by a large mound of ordered stones. Several former slaves were cooperatively lifting a large, rounded rock to top the pile. It stood beside the entrance of the palace gates like a monument. "What is that?" she pointed.

"That is the stone of help, which we have raised as the prophet Samuel did. For the Lord has helped us also."

"Yes," she murmured, "and in ways I could never fore-see. . . ."

Troyce addressed her: "My lady, if we march in a straight northwesterly path, we may see Westford by the third day."

Deirdre began to assent eagerly when the memory of a prayer she had once prayed seized her: *Lord, save the children. . . .* "No," she said slowly. "We can't. We must ride through Bresen."

"Why?" Troyce frowned. "That will mean another day of travel."

"You'll see. Nihl, we'll need the service of your soldiers," she said. He nodded in response. Thus the caravan of hundreds of soldiers and servants set out behind Deirdre, Troyce, Nihl, and Sevter.

As they approached the township of Diamond's Head, Deirdre stiffened to see a mob forming along the thoroughfare ahead. Apparently word of the Surchataine's death preceded them. She shifted anxiously toward Nihl. "Must we fight the townspeople now?"

"I don't think it," he said. "Look again."

Sure enough, the shouts she heard were actually cheers, and the mob was made up of merchants and their families loaded up, ready to join the caravan. With the palace at Diamond's Head being vacated—for a time, at least—there would be no more royal purchases and no organized army to defend the township. So, many of the people were game for settling in Westford.

Deirdre waved, smiling, and they hailed her in response. The vanguard reached the deserted sentry posts at the great wall and found the gates standing open. As far as Deirdre knew, they were never shut again.

The day was favorable for traveling. The hazy February sun came out of hiding to warm them a little. The clouds opened in great blue gaps, and the wind blew lightly from the Sea.

For a large company, many on foot, they made good time. The expectation of a new life drove them on with laughter and songs all through the day, even when they grew weary and slowed their pace.

The first village they came to appeared deserted. But as the army passed through with their sheep and crated chickens and cartloads of playing children, curious villagers came out of hiding to look. When they gleaned the story from some of the travelers, many hastened back to their huts to gather their families and go. "I wonder why any would stay," Deirdre mused.

Sevter heard her. "The ones who are joining us have nothing to lose—no homes, no land. What I wonder is, how long those who stay will have them when it becomes known there is no longer any army here to protect them."

Through the day they passed a number of villages, and the scene was repeated with little variation. The caravan grew each time.

Toward dusk they stopped to make camp in the forest. Again, Deirdre marveled at the orderly manner in which the new soldiers divided themselves among the necessary tasks. She caught herself thinking, *Galapos will love an army already so disciplined*—then she remembered why they were all free.

The men with her expressed alarm when they found her

off alone, weeping. "Chataine Deirdre." Nihl touched her shoulder in concern. "What hurts you?" Sevter and Troyce came up behind him.

She answered in a moan, "Nihl, did you know my father gave his life to free me, and all of you?"

"I heard something of the hanging," he said carefully.

Deirdre straightened in a resolve to be callously truthful with respect to the whole story. She inhaled deeply, then began to relate the facts of her background—how she had lived in the midst of abundance and love, but through petty spite got lured away from her husband's protection. She told about giving birth in the cave, only to be taken as a slave: "I was sold to a renegade, who sold me to a trader in Bresen, who sold me to Lord Troyce," she said. Nihl looked at Troyce, and the administrator glanced away in discomfort.

Unaware, Deirdre continued, "He took me to Diamond's Head and placed me under Sevter in the room with Old Josef." She paused to reach appreciatively toward Sevter, who leaped forward to take her hand. "Sevter brought me a starving baby—Bettina holds him for me now—and Josef told me he had prayed for a nursemaid so the baby would live. I learned also that Josef served the field slaves—" nodding toward Nihl.

"Josef told me you were Polonti, and he agonized for your freedom. But what is more, I realized that my beloved husband is half Polonti—one of you!" Nihl's eyes widened. "After Josef's death, I knew I must somehow free you. I had no idea how.

"But yesterday, as I entered the banquet hall to serve the table, I saw my father, Galapos, sitting as Sheva's guest! I thought he didn't recognize me—but he did, and cleverly asked Sheva if he might buy me. She told him yes, but at the cost of his life. And—he agreed! He consented. But he made her have written a bill of freedom—" She drew it out of her belt and held it out to Nihl, before remembering that he could not read.

Deirdre continued quietly, "Then Sheva hanged him. It was horrible—they didn't even cover his head. And Sheva ordered me out of the palace. I wanted to throw myself off the cliffs where they had thrown his body, but then I thought of you—Roman's kindred. I ran back into the kitchen and followed a serving girl up to Caranoe's room. Strangely, he had said he was ill, but in his room he stood dressed and armed as he ate." She did not notice Troyce's face tighten.

"At any rate, I asked him for the key to the chains, and he started laughing at me. But a bone slipped into his throat and choked him to death. I took the key from his body and ran to the field house, where I slipped it to you. The rest you all know."

They sat silently mulling over the chain of circumstances that had led to their release. "I don't understand, though," added Deirdre, "why the soldiers fought each other and not us, nor why they killed Sheva."

"That was Caranoe's doing," Troyce said heavily. "I knew he was plotting rebellion, but I did not realize he had gathered enough malcontents to carry it out so quickly." In the weight of his pause Deirdre began to quake, recognizing how precisely the events had dovetailed between the fire of Sheva and the poison of Caranoe to the salvation of herself and those with her.

Sevter said, "Josef was right, in teaching the things of God. Every prayer he prayed was answered to the good. He was right."

Deirdre asked, "But Nihl—how did you come to be enslaved?"

He answered, "I was, in Polontis, leader of a band of hunters called the Forty. We heard of Tremaine—that he wished to conquer the Continent. So, too quickly, we gathered ourselves and traveled to Diamond's Head to join with Goerge in resisting him. We spoke to Sheva, not knowing that Savin was then warring at Tremaine's side. She seized us and put us in prison, but then thought we should be made to help in the harvest. As we are stronger than most of you southerners and used to hard labor, we suited her. She demanded more Polonti as slaves. Traders gathered up the unwary Polonti in the countryside like animals—"

"—And forced you to work her fields," Deirdre ended.

"Those who refused were hanged from the field house rafters as an example," Nihl continued. "Yet many chose this rather than slavery, until Caranoe made them suffer torture and starvation instead of a merciful hanging.

"But he blundered. He put Josef in care of us. Josef cared for us with such heart that just the sight of him coming in the morning made us able to work through one more day. And when he spoke comfort to us, we listened. He told us of a Lord in heaven who knew of our suffering and had died to free us. We chose to believe him. We staked our lives on the truth of his words."

Deirdre listened with a pounding heart. Josef had laid the foundation; Galapos had added stone and mortar—all because they placed the lives of others above their own. They loved as He loved, on whose message they had staked their own lives.

Sevter shook his head. "He was right all along."

Deirdre began shivering, and realized she was cold. The forest was already in the shadow of night. She pulled the fur cloak more tightly around herself and murmured, "How shall we sleep out here in this cold?"

The three men bestirred themselves at once, but Nihl reached her first. "Come. You shall be sheltered." He led her back to the camp where she saw that while they had been talking, the army had laid themselves out on blankets beside large, leaping fires.

"Wherever did they find so much wood?" she wondered.

"They brought it from the palace," Nihl answered as if it

were a respectable question, and Deirdre blushed at her empty-headedness.

He showed her a small sheepskin tent. It was warming by yet another fire being attended by a soldier on watch. The soldier was paying even greater attention to Bettina, who sat nearby holding Arund.

Deirdre peeked into the tent as Nihl said, "This is your bed tonight. I will sleep at the doorway to guard you in the night."

She nodded, smiling to herself, *All these Polonti have such strong protective instincts.* She turned to Bettina to take Arund, then opened her mouth to invite her to share her tent.

But Bettina anticipated her. "I have a place to sleep tonight, Goldie—er, Deirdre," she said, slipping off. So Deirdre knelt to enter the tent, laying the baby on the quilts beside her.

In the morning, she was awakened by the bustle of camp breaking. After nursing Arund, she peeked out to observe the soldiers loading the animals and snuffing out the campfires. Over her head, she heard Nihl's voice: "Do you wish breakfast, Chataine?"

She looked up to see him standing over her with a chunk of cheese and bread, which he handed her. "They are eager to be moving," he said almost conversationally, "so if you will stand here by the fire to eat, I will load your tent."

"Thank you, Nihl, but you needn't serve me," she said, emerging.

"It is an honor to serve you," he said.

As she ate and then strapped Arund to her chest, Deirdre reflected on how long it had been since anyone considered himself honored by her presence. With pain, she realized afresh that Roman had treated her with just such honor every day—and she had returned to him spite. "I'm ready to ride," she said humbly to Nihl.

251

Travel that day promised to be as easy and rapid as the day before. That small fact amazed Deirdre as much as anything—that she could ride for so long with so little discomfort. Yet she knew why. She was so much stronger now than she had ever been. The hard, sustained work required of her as a servant had actually endowed her with the stamina she needed now. In fact . . . she had begun to learn to walk.

Deirdre's army passed through only two small villages that day, but toward nightfall they spotted the cheery lights of Bresen. Deirdre glanced at Nihl, riding in the vanguard to her right. "Do you know what place this is?" she asked. He tightened his lips and nodded. "Alert your men, then. We're raiding it."

Troyce uttered a startled protest, but Deirdre ignored him. They halted the company on the outskirts of town, where she and Nihl selected fifty warriors. She left Arund with Bettina and instructed Sevter and Troyce to take charge of the caravan. Then the band stole group by group into town on foot and collected in the shadow of the inn.

"There is the slave tent," whispered Deirdre, nodding toward it. "How shall we do this, Nihl?"

"Surround it and attack on my signal," he returned. "Give all keys to the Chataine." His instructions were passed along in a whisper. To Deirdre he said, "Please stay by my side."

Like ghosts the men encircled the tent. Deirdre and Nihl approached from the front. Two renegades at the tent entrance stopped their idle conversation to look them over. Nihl drew within a few feet of them and stopped, smiling.

For an instant neither moved. Then one renegade came to life, swearing, and drew his sword. Nihl brought his own up with a sharp whistle, and his men leaped from the shadows onto the renegades and slave traders.

Such a lopsided contest lasted only a few minutes. The slaves within the tent, seeing only swords and torches, began screaming in terror of their lives. Nihl entered the stuffy tent and raised a torch, shouting, "Silence. Silence! Deirdre of Lystra is freeing you!" The men brought her every key they could recover, and Deirdre exultantly began unlocking prisoner after prisoner.

At first they stood dumbfounded. In his bewilderment, one of the newly freed slaves stumbled over a blanketed pile on the ground. Curious, he lifted the blanket to reveal five large money boxes. He seized one and began to run, but another freedman knocked him down. Others started to fight viciously over the remaining boxes.

Nihl shouted, "Stop! Release the money!" but they paid him no attention until the soldiers yanked away the boxes and piled them in a protected area at Nihl's feet. When order was restored, he instructed two nearby soldiers, "Count the money." Slaves and soldiers stood around in a tight circle as they counted out gold and silver pieces worth over twenty thousand royals.

Nihl had an idea, which he presented quietly to Deirdre as she paused over the chains. When she nodded her approval, he said, "Count out to each slave one hundred royals. The rest of the money goes into the Chataine's treasury." To the slaves at large, he said, "This money is recompense for your suffering. Take it and go peacefully." As the last sentence had the tone of a threat, many did just that.

Deirdre continued unlocking manacles. She released a child who clung to her, bringing her to tears. "Who do you belong to?" she asked him. He just held on to her more tightly. "But who takes care of you?" she persisted.

A slave nearby said, "My lady, that un's an orphan. Don't know where they picked him up, but he's alone."

She shook in anger. "Nihl!" Not far away, he came to stand beside her. "Nihl, find me a compassionate man from among you."

He cocked his head as if to check his hearing, then regarded the boy clinging to her skirts. Nihl turned and scanned the soldiers, summoning, "Wence, present yourself to the Chataine."

A giant of a man with a rough, black face stepped forward. After a moment of uncertainty, Deirdre cleared her throat and said, "Wence, this child is an orphan, and I wish you to ward him until we reach Westford and a family is found to take him in."

The man's black eyes looked down on the child whom she pushed forward. Wence bent until he was eye level with him and uttered deeply, "Do you like hoppy toads?" The boy managed a nervous giggle, and Wence said, "I have found a hoppy toad outside. Let's go have a look at him." So saying, he took the little white hand in his mammoth grasp and led him out of the tent.

Deirdre let out a relieved laugh and turned back to releasing slaves. They were straining forward now, reaching out, clamoring to get free. She grew uneasy at their pawing and shouting, but Nihl stood beside her to restrain them with the sight of his dripping sword.

There were other orphans among the slaves, and as she released them she pulled for them each a man from Nihl's ranks to act as guardians. She found not only Polonti among the slaves, but many villagers from provinces other than Goerge. She unlocked one prisoner who said calmly, "Deirdre of Lystra, I thank you." His voice had a Selecan accent.

"Are you from Seleca?" she asked.

"Yes, lady. I was taken from a village north of Corona."

"Why did they bring you so far, to Bresen, to sell you?"

"There are slave markets in Corona," he said slowly, rubbing his wrists, "but they are so crowded that many merchants found they could get more money here. Less dangerous here, too—until now." He took a breath. "Will you take another soldier, lady?"

She smiled and nodded toward Nihl. "Present yourself to your new Commander." A good number of the freedmen did likewise, and Nihl's band swelled. Yet other slaves who never had the benefit of Josef's teachings wanted more satisfaction than a hundred royals and service in Deirdre's army. They began to attack and plunder the town.

When Deirdre had freed all slaves and emerged from the tent, she gasped to see townspeople fleeing and screaming from the inn. Nihl's men, running inside to aid, suddenly found themselves in the unhappy position of fighting to defend the slave town against some of those they had just freed. Distressed by the absurdity of it, Deirdre watched freedmen battle freedmen.

Nihl's soldiers gathered up the looters and shook the citizens' property from their hands, then executed swift punishment on the offenders. Deirdre turned her head, unable to watch. But the remainder of the freedmen became considerably more tractable.

The band returned to camp with thirty new members in their ranks. Troyce and Sevter met them at once, faint with relief. "Chataine, I consider it a personal favor that you have come back whole," Troyce said, his face drained of color. Uppermost in his mind was the futility of returning to her homeland and husband without her.

She tried to look rugged. "Why shouldn't I?"

"Not doubting your ability, Deirdre, but we heard the commotion even here," Sevter said. "And it continued at length."

She sagged. "It was a mess."

"It was a successful raid," Nihl remarked.

"You're a good leader, Nihl," she said quietly. "I could not have known how to control those slaves. I'm sure Roman will put you in a position over the army."

"Thank you, Chataine," he said, looking as pleased as a stone-faced Polonti could look.

As Deirdre took Arund from Bettina, the maid asked, "May I speak with you, my lady?"

"Of course," Deirdre said, wondering at her formality.

"Will you tell me . . ." Bettina began hesitantly, "is there a place you wished me to serve in your household?"

"Of course!" Deirdre said brightly. "There will always be a place for you, Bettina." The girl looked down, and Deirdre thought she was going to cry. "That's . . . not what you wanted?"

"I was hoping you would release me from service," Bettina said, her face reddening. "There is a man who wants to marry me, but he will not marry a slave."

Deirdre stammered, "I didn't realize . . . I didn't consider you . . . of course you are already free, Bettina."

As Bettina bowed and turned away, Deirdre wondered, downcast, *How could she assume she's still a slave, after all that has happened?* Feeling strangely ashamed, Deirdre hunched down in her tent for the night.

She awoke at sunrise, as the camp was just beginning to break up. She herself was ready to ride in minutes, but with so many people and animals in tow, it required hours to get the caravan moving. Deirdre pressed them for speed, impatient to see home.

At last they moved forward and gained the road, with Deirdre, Troyce, Sevter and Nihl leading as before. They had traveled only minutes when they spotted a lone horseman riding toward them. Deirdre cried, "Nihl, look!" What she saw was a young woman trailing the horse, hands tied with a length of rope to the saddle.

Nihl's men were upon the renegade before he realized the danger. As they released the girl to join their company, she wrapped her arms around soldier after soldier, crying, "No one would look! No one would stop!"

"I know," Deirdre muttered, unheard. One soldier the girl embraced held on, and she remained with him until they reached Westford.

The caravan moved again. They had hardly journeyed

for half an hour before they spotted another traveler coming up the road driving a cart. He slowed, peering at the company, and as two of Nihl's soldiers spurred toward him he leapt from the cart and dove into the brush. His cart carried four slaves chained to the floorboard, all Polonti men. They were unlocked and freed. As they walked up to the vanguard, Nihl startled and exclaimed, "Asgard!"

One of the Polonti quickly looked up and, seeing him, said dryly, "You would have saved us some considerable trouble if you had sent word you were well, Nihl."

He dismounted. "How did they capture you, Asgard?"

"We allowed it, to find out what had become of you. I did not know you were gathering an army." He looked at Deirdre. "Who is this?"

Nihl answered, "This is Chataine Deirdre, and this is her army. Come ride beside me, and I will tell you an interesting story."

As Asgard was given a horse, Deirdre whispered to Nihl, "Who is that?"

"My brother, Chataine."

"Your brother! Posing as a slave? How clever! . . . Nihl, I can't believe all of the slaves—the number of traders! Who is buying all these slaves?"

Nihl raised his black brows slightly. "They use no servants at your palace?"

"Not slaves!" she insisted, then caught herself with a gasp. It was true, Galapos had prohibited slave labor at Westford, but under Karel . . . those servants had not been paid. Karel's fields had been worked by slaves. Her beautiful clothes and the delicious foods and the constant attendance on her person—all had been done by slaves, though they were not called such. Even Nanna was a slave, bought to love and nurture a child for nothing in return.

Deirdre dropped her head in shame. How ignorantly she had used those people, caring nothing for their needs or their pain. She had even tried to make slaves to herself of those who were free, like Roman. The way she had treated those around her, no wonder Bettina assumed the worst! *If I have learned nothing else from this, I will never again attempt to make anyone my slave*, she vowed.

And she was not returning empty. She looked down lovingly at Arund, strapped to her chest. "*Your* brother at Westford awaits," she whispered.

The company moved on. Nihl began recounting to Asgard the story of the Forty's trek to Diamond's Head and of their enslavement. While listening to him, Deirdre became aware of a sound she had been hearing indistinctly, without comprehension. Now that they were closer to the source, it sounded like a prolonged wailing or crying. Thinking it to be another slave, she said, "Nihl, lead the caravan. I must find out who that is."

Sevter said quickly, "Deirdre, I will go with you." Nihl nodded, gesturing a few soldiers to accompany them.

They broke from the road and followed the sound through the forest. Shortly, they came into a little clearing and a sturdy house. A woman was kneeling before a fresh mound in the cold earth—a tiny grave. Her grief was so intense, she was not aware of their presence at first.

When she did see them, she stood hastily and passed a hand over her face. "Forgive me . . . I see you are traveling. Be pleased to stop here and refresh yourselves," she offered in a shaky voice.

"Who are you grieving, lady?" Deirdre asked tenderly, without dismounting.

The woman tried not to look at the bundle strapped to Deirdre's chest. "It was . . . it was my baby that died," she said brokenly, her face contorting. "My husband is dead—the boy was the only one I had left in the world."

Sevter whispered suddenly to Deirdre, "I know this woman. I have bought woolens from her in Bresen. They say she is the only honest wool dealer in the province"—he paused and Deirdre knew the same thought had occurred to them both.

To drive it away, she asked the woman, "How do you live?"

"I sell woolens in Bresen," she replied, jerking her head toward a pen of sheep next to her house. "I do well enough. The merchants I deal with live close by here and their men watch out for us—me—as well."

Sevter dismounted and helped Deirdre down. His eyes were convicting. "You know what you should do," he whispered.

"No!" she protested. "Arund is mine! How can I hand him over to a stranger!"

"He is *not* yours—remember? Your son waits for you in a palace. What will become of this babe if you take him home with you?"

"I will love him and care for him as I would my very own—as I have been doing! He will be brother to my child," Deirdre insisted.

"In your eyes, perhaps, but no one else's. A child of unknown parentage would be given no quarter with the Surchatain's family."

Legally, he was correct. Deirdre glanced apprehensively at the woman, who, perceiving an argument in progress, discreetly kept her distance. "Roman would accept him," Deirdre said dully.

"Perhaps. But he could not force anyone else to. Arund would never gain the standing of your own son. Can't you see what kind of a life you are destining for this child if you insist on having him with you always? He would be no better than a servant. You've done well to care for him thus far, but you can no longer do him any good. Give him up, Deirdre, to someone who can!"

Apparently the woman overheard, for she seemed frozen

on the edge of an unbearable hope. Deirdre, loosening Arund's ties from her chest, forced her legs to walk toward the widow. "If I gave you the chance of another son, would you swear before God to care for him with your life and love him with your soul?"

"I—I would do all you say and more!"

Deirdre handed Arund to the weeping woman. "He was the child of a slave who died. He is your child now. His name is Arund." She turned quickly back to Sevter before her own grief escaped. As they spurred their horses to rejoin the caravan, the woman called down blessing after blessing from heaven on their heads.

᪥21᪥

A trumpet alarm rang through the palace at Westford as a lone rider pounded exhausted through the gates, calling hoarsely, "Basil! Basil!"

The Counselor met him at once. "Kam! What has happened? Where is Galapos?"

"Counselor—" Kam dismounted and then halted in surprise as Roman joined them. "You did return!"

"Where is Galapos?" Roman demanded. A crowd of soldiers quickly gathered.

"Commander—Counselor—that cursed Sheva had him hanged!"

The revelation stunned everyone to silence. Then cries of fury filled the courtyard. Roman stood planted in shock. When Basil finally gained order around him, he demanded, "How did she contrive to do that?"

"I don't really know, Counselor. We'd heard a rumor that the Chataine was in slavery to Sheva, so Galapos made me up to mingle with the servants. I never did see her, though. But then I hear this hubbub from the palace—I look and see Sheva and her Counselor taking Galapos to the gallows. And I watched them hang him like a criminal. They didn't know about me, so I slipped away from the crowd and rode. The Surchatain had told me to bring word back to the Commander if he met with ill."

Kam stopped to breathe as Basil and Roman grasped for some reason in all this. Then, unable to contain himself, Kam urged, "Shall we attack her, Commander? Counselor?"

Simultaneously, Basil shook his head and Roman uttered a short, bitter laugh. "With what?" Roman demanded. "Six hundred men against her fortress? We couldn't take Diamond's Head even with the number we had against Tremaine." Biting his lip and closing his eyes, he suddenly recalled, "And Colin took forty men with him to Ooster. I should have waited to send them."

"It's likely that Sheva intends to attack us now, with Galapos removed. We must ready our defenses," Basil considered. He faced Roman. "Commander, in obedience to the command of the late Surchatain Galapos, I appoint you to be Surchatain of Lystra in his stead. Surchatain—what shall we do now?" All eyes looked to their new leader.

Roman looked past those faces through the open gates to the hill country and said, "Send the women and children of the town—also my son and his nursemaid—to hiding places in the hills, and assemble every able man in the courtyard to receive arms. Then summon me from the chapel. . . . I'm going there to petition the Lord for our deliverance."

❖

Roman opened the chapel doors and shut them behind him deliberately. The hall was dim and still, with only two oil lamps burning before the rough wooden cross at the front. He approached it with heavy steps, grieving for

262

Galapos, and knelt. Firmly closing his mind to the silent accusations that he was somehow to blame, he attempted to pray. "Lord God . . ." he began, and stopped.

He tried again. "Lord God, you have rescued me so many times, and how I praise you for your mighty deliverance. Now, Lord—" His throat constricted involuntarily and he could not continue.

He forced open his throat and breathed in and out. Determined, he began again, "Lord God, you are mighty to save and to deliver. Your mercy and goodness are unending. I pray now, Lord—" His voice vanished, and once again he could not continue.

Sagging in frustration, he opened his hands to the cross and pleaded, "What am I doing wrong?" He sat back on his heels, shaking his head. "Lord, you have ordained praise, and it seems you will hear nothing but praise from me today. I don't understand why you won't permit me to ask for deliverance, but—so be it. Though those I love are dead, and we face in our weakness the threat of another invasion, still you are great and greatly to be praised. Our lives are in your hands, Father, and whether we live or die, you are the Lord. May your name be honored by all the earth. Amen."

He finished and walked from the chapel, considering how to arm tradesmen and merchants who had never held a sword before.

❖

The growing familiarity of the landscape in which the army camped that night filled Deirdre with joy. The gently rolling hills and gnarled oaks—the dry stream bed that they had crossed so many times just west of here! The following day, when the vanguard of the company caught sight of the towers of Westford, Deirdre wept profusely. "Roman, my darling, I am coming home!"

✥

Basil knocked quietly on the chamber door. "My lord?"

Roman opened it. "I'm only Surchatain, Counselor. I want no title of lord."

"Surchatain. An army has been sighted on the road from the east."

"So soon?" Roman asked, following him to the east tower.

"Apparently, right on time," answered Basil. "Kam said he had been held up almost half a day in Bresen, trying to get by some slave traders. He feared turning around and seeing Sheva's army on his heels."

As Basil said that, Kam ran up breathlessly to meet them in the tower. "Roman—Surchatain—it's Sheva, all right, leading an army. Beside her is her Counselor. I recognize him."

"From this distance?" Roman asked dubiously, peering at the flowing mass far down the road.

"When the periphery scouts spotted them, I rode out to have a look. I've got good eyes; I know who I saw," Kam replied almost angrily.

"Under the circumstances, it seems inevitable that it is Sheva," murmured Basil, squinting at the coming tide as well. "How shall we defend ourselves, Roman?"

Kam interjected, "Surchatain—I have an idea. They're approaching a bend in the road that is bordered by thick trees and high ground. It's the perfect site for an ambush. At your word, we'll hide there and attack as they round the bend. If we can just kill Sheva and her officers, her army will have nothing to fight for. We can sway them to join with you. It's perfect, my lord—and it's our only hope!"

Basil said, "It sounds reasonable." Roman considered it, silently inquiring of the Spirit within him.

Kam was tense with excitement, ready to spring for his horse. "Surchatain," he urged, "you must say quickly. They'll be at the bend soon."

"I say no," responded Roman. "If God has chosen to give us into her hand, well, so be it. But I won't return evil for evil and murder her defenseless, as she did Galapos. I alone will ride out to meet her. You will all secure yourselves within the gates, and if she slays me also, defend yourselves as best you can."

Kam stared, incredulous. "Your mind has gone soft, Roman." Basil inhaled a troubled breath.

Roman leveled an icy stare at Kam. "Are you refusing my command, then?"

Kam retreated. "No, Surchatain."

"Then I will go out alone. But I am not defenseless."

❖

As Deirdre's army rounded a bend and the road straightened to the gates of Westford, they saw suddenly appear on the road before them a solitary warrior on horseback, sword at his side. Deirdre melted in recognition of her husband. She opened her mouth but he held out his hand as a command to stop. They did, with some confusion in the rear.

He shouted, "Proceed no farther, lady, until you give an account for the death of Galapos, Surchatain of Lystra!"

Deirdre was struck dumb. Did he not know her?

"Would this be your husband?" Nihl whispered uneasily.

"I'm awaiting your answer!" Roman shouted again.

"He has mistaken you for Sheva!" exclaimed Troyce.

In agony Deirdre ripped off the fur hood to show her blonde hair and cried, "Roman!" He sat unmoved.

She flung herself from her horse and ran forward as he dismounted slowly. She fell at his feet, crying, "Roman! Don't you know me?"

He lifted her as if in a trance. In spite of her agitation she noticed new lines in his face and strands of grey hair. "Deirdre," he whispered.

"Roman, I've brought you—"

"Deirdre!" He enfolded her and kissed every part of her face.

"Roman, I've brought—"

"Deirdre—you've come back from the dead to me. I had given you up for dead. But God has returned you to me, alive and whole. . . ." This time he did not attempt to hide his tears. "But . . . who are all these?"

"Roman, I've brought you a Counselor and a Commander and an overseer and an army! There are also workers and craftsmen and even children, Roman!"

He looked distractedly on the multitude who waited eagerly nearby. Then he searched her face again. "Beloved . . . what has overtaken Galapos?"

"It was this." She drew out the bill of freedom from her belt. "He died to free me, Roman. And because of him, all these were freed, also!"

Roman shook his head slowly as he read. "I failed him. Utterly."

"No, love! He seemed to have been prepared for it. Somehow, it was necessary. . . ." Silently, he struggled to comprehend it all. Deirdre said softly, "Will you accept into service these who have come?"

He took her hand and walked to meet the company. The leaders promptly dismounted. "Husband," Deirdre said proudly, "this is Troyce, formerly Sheva's administrator. He joined with me in rebellion after her murder of Galapos." Troyce bowed low, and Roman nodded in approval.

"And this is Sevter, overseer of Sheva's palace. He took special care of me when I was newly arrived and weak." Sevter bowed, and Roman again nodded.

"And husband, this is Nihl, leader of the slaves whom Galapos freed. You will find much to commend in him," she said. Nihl bowed slightly, but his eyes hardly left Roman's face.

Roman appraised him a moment, then extended his hand. "Will you command this army you lead, my brother?"

Nihl took it. "I will, Surchatain."

For the first time, Roman smiled. He lifted Deirdre onto his horse and jumped up behind her, signaling the army forward. Cheers and whoops from behind answered him, and Roman himself led them up to the fast-closed gates of Westford.

"Open!" he shouted to the sentries hidden on the wall. Some commotion was heard, and grudgingly the gates were opened. The army entered into the midst of a silent, fearful collection of Lystrans defiantly holding on to their weapons.

Then someone exclaimed, "It's the Chataine Deirdre!"

"It is the Surchataine Deirdre," corrected Roman, lifting her down and kissing her in the sight of all.

Then the walls burst with rejoicing. It echoed off the stone up into the very hills. Deirdre was surrounded by welcoming faces. She was embraced and shaken and talked to by ten people at once. Who would have believed all these people would ever be so glad to see her? As she laughingly received them, her eyes scanned the crowd, searching.

She met Roman's eyes over their heads, for he had not stopped watching her, and her lips formed the words, "Where is our baby?"

He smiled from overflowing wellsprings of love. Reaching through the crowd, he took her hand. "Come with me. I'll show you." With the crowd milling behind them, they departed the gates and rode out to the hills.

❖

(The story continues in *Liberation of Lystra*.)

GLOSSARY

Almetta (awl MET ta)—house maid at the palace of Diamond's Head.

Artemeus (ARE ti mus)—son of Sheva and Savin; Chatain of Goerge and former suitor of Deirdre.

Arund (AIR und)—newborn baby of a slave girl who died; given to Deirdre to care for at Diamond's Head.

Asgard (AZ gard)—brother of Nihl, a Polonti.

Avelon (AV e lawn)—the holy man who worked among the villagers around Westford and converted Roman's mother to Christianity; he took the villagers to the coast when Tremaine invaded Westford.

Basil (BAY zil)—the former secretary to the overseer at Westford; because he took his servants into hiding when Tremaine invaded Lystra, he was made Counselor by Galapos.

Bay Hunter—Roman's horse, a bay gelding.

Bernal (BURN ul)—sent by Varela to remove Deirdre from Lystra.

Bettina (be TEEN a)—serving girl who befriended Deirdre at Diamond's Head.

269

Bresen (BREE zen)—trade city in Goerge which had developed a slave market; Deirdre was sold there to Lord Troyce.

Brude (brood)—a merchant of Diamond's Head who bribed Sheva for the water mill.

Calle Valley (kail)—the province due west of Lystra.

Caranoe (CARE ah no)—the overseer of the field slaves at Diamond's Head.

Chatain (sha TAN)—title given the son of the Surchatain as heir to the rulership; feminine—Chataine (sha TANE).

Cohort (CO hort)—palace guards who served under Karel, selected on the basis of appearance and family prestige; considered themselves above the standing army.

Colin (CAWL in)—son of Deirdre's uncle Corneus; younger brother of Jason.

Corneus (cor NEE us)—the Surchatain of Seir who agreed to fight with Galapos and then betrayed him, but died in the battle at Outpost One; Deirdre's uncle.

Corona (cor OH na)—capital of Seleca, where Tremaine ruled.

Deirdre (DEE dra)—the Chataine of Lystra.

Diamond's Head—capital of Goerge, where Savin and Sheva ruled; a city built on granite cliffs and considered impregnable.

drud(s)—epithet for the race of brown-skinned, black-haired people from Polontis.

DuCange (do KANJ)—the silversmith of Westford.

Eudymon (YOU di mun)—the Counselor who served under Karel and was murdered by him; father of illegitimate Roman.

Eulen (YOU len)—a renegade of Corona.

Fark—a slave trader of Corona.

Galapos (GAL a pos)—the Commander of the army under Karel, made Surchatain after the battle at Outpost One; Deirdre's natural father.

Gerd (*G* as in *go*)—renegade who dealt in slave trading.

Goerge (*G* as in *go*)—province east of Lystra, ruled by Sheva.

Goldie—alias used by Deirdre at Diamond's Head.

Gusta (GUS ta)—nursemaid of Deirdre and Roman's infant son.

Hycliff (HIGH cliff)—coastal city in Lystra where the Fair was held twice a year.

Hylas (HIGH las)—citizen of Westford who used the chapel to teach his views on God.

Jason—son of Corneus; Chatain of Seir; married Deirdre in a spurious ceremony and killed himself after the battle at Outpost One.

Josef (YO sef)—slave at Diamond's Head who taught Deirdre about God.

Kam—a soldier under Galapos whom he made a captain.

Karel (CARE ul)—Surchatain of Lystra who married Corneus's sister Regina when she was pregnant with Deirdre by Galapos; deposed immediately before Tremaine invaded Westford.

Karl and **Joel**—scouts sent by Galapos to Calle Valley to search for Deirdre.

Kevin—errand boy who served under Galapos and Roman.

Lady Grey—Deirdre's first horse, a grey mare selected for her by Roman.

Lewyn (LEW in)—a butcher at Westford.

Lystra (LIS tra)—province ruled by Karel, Galapos, then Roman, with the only navigable river emptying on the southern coast.

Marc—a soldier sent by Galapos (with Varan) to follow Roman to Corona.

Merry—the kitchen mistress at the palace of Diamond's Head.

Nanna—Deirdre's nursemaid from infancy.

Nihl (neel)—leader of the Polonti slaves at Diamond's Head whom Deirdre freed.

Olynn (AWL in)—a soldier under Galapos.

Ooster (OO ster)—capital of Seir, home of Corneus, where Deirdre was imprisoned four months during the siege of Outpost One.

Perin and **Lari**—scouts sent by Galapos to Goerge to search for Deirdre.

Polontis (po LAWN tis)—mountainous province north of Goerge, home of the Polonti (po LAWN tee).

Regina (re GEE na)—Deirdre's mother, lover of Galapos; died at the hands of her husband Karel when he discovered she had altered the laws to allow Deirdre to choose her own husband.

Rollet (rawl LET)—son of Tremaine; Chatain of Seir; rejected suitor of Deirdre.

Roman—Deirdre's guardian and then her husband; Commander of the army under Surchatain Galapos; made Surchatain of Lystra after Galapos's death; a half-blooded Polonti.

Savin (SAV in)—Surchatain of Goerge killed at the battle of Outpost One; Sheva's husband.

Seir (SEE er)—province northwest of Lystra, formerly ruled by Corneus.

Seleca (SEL e ka)—rich province north of Lystra, formerly ruled by Tremaine.

Sevter—overseer of domestic slaves at Diamond's Head.

Shekinah (sha KIGH na)—Hebrew word for the visible glory of God.

Sheva (SHE va)—Surchataine of Goerge; widow of Savin.

Surchatain (SUR cha tan)—title for the ruler of a province; feminine—Surchataine (SUR cha tane).

Tremaine (tre MANE)—powerful ruler of Seleca; died in the battle at Outpost One.

Troyce—administrator at the palace of Diamond's Head under Sheva.

Tychus (TIGH kus)—holy man who taught at the palace of Westford during Karel's rule.

Varan (VAIR an)—soldier sent by Galapos (with Marc) to follow Roman to Corona.

Varela (va REL a)—beautiful sorceress who attempted to gain power by influencing the leaders of Westford.

Wence—one of the Polonti freed by Deirdre.

Westford—capital of Lystra, home of Roman and Deirdre.